Bert and Norah

THE NICKEL DIME MURDERS

Bernard H. Burgess

Inquiries should be addressed to

Bernard Burgess
2975 Shelton Road North
Bee Branch, AR 72013

E-mail: bb2975@hotmail.com

www.facebook.com/Coywolf.publishing/

Cover designed by Kristy Kennedy-Black of Idea Creative Services
kristy@ideacreativeservices.com

Printed in the United States of America
First Printing: May 2018

Revised July 2019
Kindle Direct Publishing

ISBN 978-0-692-13412-2

DEDICATION

I dedicate this book to my loving parents, Bernard C. and Ruth L. Burgess, and to my daughter, Heidi Burgess-Myers.   Dad was a Nebraska Sandhills Cowboy Hall of Fame inductee and a rancher who also loved to write. He wrote "Images of the West" about his experiences, often humorous, growing up on a Nebraska cattle ranch.   Mom is a ranch and country woman, through and through. She falls into that class of true Nebraska Sandhills women who can do literally anything. She also loves to read. Heidi is my reason for living, and my main reason for writing. I'm proud of her and I do this in the hope that she will be proud of me. Together, they inspire me to pursue this dream.

ACKNOWLEDGMENTS

I'm very thankful to those people who played a role in the creation of this book and who helped with editing both the story and the writing, and more importantly with the encouragement to keep going. They are my mother-in-law, Clara Bass; wife, Ruth Bass-Burgess; sister-in-law, Betty Armstrong; and good friends, Tammy Bass, Frances Henderson, and DeEtta Irish. Hailey Marks of HM Photography took an excellent author picture for the back cover. Kristy Kennedy-Black of Idea Creative Services did a great job on the covers for both the e-book and the paperback.

TABLE OF CONTENTS

CHAPTER ONE: MISSY

The few remaining deciduous leaves and evergreen needles flittered in the strong breeze. It was still too early in the spring for most of the dormant vegetation to return fully to life in receding winter's grip in rural, upstate Wisconsin. The grey overcast sky and 30-degree temperature made the wind chill and wet ground feel even colder to exposed skin. Marshland and meadow had given way to a shallow hillside, dotted with a mix of spruce, cedar, ash, and tamarack trees. One could hear the wind whispering through the trees and taste the odor of the damp pine needles, wafting in the background of the senses. This gloomy day was in stark contrast to a rescue mission, which was underway. Oblivious to the rescuers, the life they would save was destined to profoundly affect their lives and the lives of others yet unknown.

It had been nearly three days since the lives of the coywolf parents had been snuffed out on the highway, a half mile away. One of the big logging rigs apparently caught the pair by surprise on the rainstorm-soaked highway. The tracking collar worn by the male had survived the hit, and the wildlife guys were sure there was a den with pups. Even with the help of two interested volunteers, it had taken almost three days of combing the surrounding woods to finally get lucky and close enough to hear the soft whimpering of a surviving pup.

Near the base of a cedar tree with low hanging branches, laden with needles brushing against his back, Albert, known to most as Bert, Lynnes laid on his stomach and reached as far as his outstretched body and right arm would go into the hole. He had to remove his coat but didn't notice the cold on his bare arm as he leveraged his reach with his feet against an ash tree. The smell of the dirt, mixed with the pungent aroma of an active den, reminded him of a cat box. "I think there's one of the little pups

9

in here," he said. "I've got hold of him and bringing him out. He's a very young one, as we figured."

As he backed out of the den with a hamster-sized, greyish-red, canine pup in his right hand, Bert presented his squirming furry find to his wife, Norah, and to the three Fish and Wildlife guys with her. "There's another puppy in the den, farther back," Bert told them, "but I think it's dead. They've been alone too long. It's a miracle this one's survived." He knew that a week-old canine baby couldn't last long without its mother.

Bert could sense immediately that Norah's mother instinct was kicking in as she took the tiny pup and tucked it inside her coat for warmth.

"Oh, wow, what a cute little thing, even if he is half starved!" she said. "But now what happens to him?" They both knew all too well that the early April weather was too cold for any abandoned baby to survive long.

Bert looked to Joe, the project leader, for an answer.

Joe hiked up his coat collar against the brisk wind and replied, "We either let nature take its course and leave him to die or see if a zoo might take him. First though, we must take DNA samples and the usual tests and measurements, so we continue to build up our database regarding the expansion of this animal into the US."

Bert could see that Norah silently agreed with him. They had been volunteers for this Coywolf Project with Joe's team for almost a month now. It had become personal with them. He turned to Joe. "How about Norah and I raise this little pup and see how adaptable they are to domestication? This one's probably not more than a week old, so it should still be prone to bonding. We can develop a lot of data and report to you on our progress. This could provide valuable information to the Coywolf Project. It would also give this pup a chance to have a good life. If it can't adapt to a domestic setting, then we realize it may have to be destroyed at some point. We live in a rural setting west of Cody, Wyoming, where the pup has room to mature outside a cage yet still under close supervision."

Bert was glad that Joe was receptive and let him make his case. He could see that the man agreed and seemed relieved. He knew Joe didn't like the other options for the pup any better than he and Norah did.

Joe eagerly responded, "I like the idea, guys. I'll run it by my boss. I'm gonna encourage her to go along with it."

The hike back took nearly 45 minutes through the mix of marshland, trees, and meadow separating their parking location from the pup's den. True to his word, Joe argued the case to his district manager as soon as they got back to their vehicles. She agreed that this could be a golden opportunity to further their study of the hybridization of the coyote and the eastern red wolf. This crossbreed, until recently mostly confined to southeast Canada and the northeast US, was ultimately destined to be in all the lower 48 states.

Their male had turned out to be female, upon closer inspection. Bert was a little embarrassed that he and three highly qualified naturalists had taken five minutes to confirm that.

"If you're gonna take someone home, it's a good idea to get

their sex right," Norah had said with a laugh.

Bert was endlessly amused by Norah's sense of humor. She could find something funny in almost anything and her teal colored eyes seemed to sparkle when she laughed. Some would call her his soul mate, seemingly tuned in to his thoughts much of the time. She had a wholesome beauty at age 48. At 5 feet and 4 inches tall, her athletic slim body was strong and sexy with great looking legs. Her round face was soft and pretty, especially topped off with her tousled, wavy, red hair. She was an intelligent, outdoorsy, woman who had traveled the globe with him and was very determined once she had a mission to pursue. Eternally curious about almost everything, Norah had many interests and loved to read and learn. One of her interests was nature, and she had jumped at the chance to volunteer for the Coywolf Project. A little dirt and discomfort didn't bother her at all if it meant doing something with wildlife. Also, he knew she loved doing anything with him. He always felt and appreciated her total respect and love.

He had found Norah by complete chance while hiking in a Minnesota state park. He had needed a break from visiting one of his uncles and decided to take a drive on that warm fall day over twenty-eight years earlier. Six miles down the trail, he paused at a scenic overlook. Two young women had also been hiking the same trail from the opposite direction and stopped for a rest break at the overlook. The wide vistas, blue sky, and October leaves were spectacular, but they were matched by the beauty of this outgoing and chatty young redhead. It was love at first sight. After more than twenty years of marriage, he knew that not even death could end his love for her. Theirs was an undying love; the kind you take to the grave.

When Norah was about thirty years old, Bert was assigned to

infantry instructor duty at Fort Sill, Oklahoma. One morning, on her usual drive to her own job, she drove past a small house along an outlying street. She had been past that same house numerous times before. That morning, though, was different. She saw flames coming from the windows and door, and a young woman dressed in a nightgown running frantically around the front of the house. A young child was in one of the windows, appearing to scream. Norah quickly took the next driveway, turned her car around, and raced back down the street to the house. She was mystified and shocked as she parked opposite the house. It sat quietly. There was no fire, no woman was running in panic, and no child was visible anywhere. In stunned silence, Norah drove on to her work. As the day progressed, she gradually forgot her unrealistic vision and chalked it up to too much television.

The next morning, as she approached the same little house, she literally slammed on her brakes and pulled over near it. Her mind was almost exploding, and her heart was racing as she stared at the smoking ashes and smoldering ruins that were all that remained of the home. An icy chill raced down her spine. She got out of her car and asked another man, an apparent neighbor, what had happened. He told her the house burned down during the night, and the divorced mother was able to get out but could not save her eight-year-old daughter.

Through her tears, Norah realized that the things she had largely ignored much of her life, her strange and often unsettling visions, must be a psychic premonition. For days afterward, she struggled with the guilt that she might have been able to do something if only she'd said something. The guilt was gradually replaced by the commitment to understand and learn how to use her gift. She could never allow such a thing to happen again without at least attempting to change that future. She finally began to embrace the apparent fact that she had psychic ability and she tried to learn how she might channel it in a positive way.

At 50 years of age, Bert had retired from twenty years in the Army and now had the time to pursue his own lifelong interests. His 5 feet and 8-inch frame was athletic strong and in great tone for a middle-aged man. His dark brown hair had shades of grey at the edges and blue-grey eyes topped off a handsome face that could always find a reason to smile and laugh. He had a talent for investigation and problem solving and soon found work with a private investigation company. Not only did he enjoy the challenge, but he was pretty good at surveillance, research and analytical thinking. His physical and mental capabilities were well suited to the rigors of investigation. He continued to work for this investigation company for the five years prior to taking a break to work on the Coywolf Project. He also had an interest in nature and wildlife. Like Norah, he wasted no time in accepting the invitation to help the wildlife guys with this project.

With the district manager's blessing, Bert and Norah packed up their newfound charge and found a local veterinarian to give the necessary shots and some milk substitute to the baby canine. Preliminary tests indicated that the pup was most likely the hybrid cross they were studying. The DNA test results, expected in a few weeks, would confirm it. Until then, with the first of many feedings in its belly, they drove the pup toward Wyoming and its new home.

On the drive home with the baby coywolf, Bert and Norah finally decided to pursue the dream they had been discussing for the past year. As they cruised westward on Interstate 94 across southern Montana, the undulating and curvy road, through the low, mountainous foothills and plains north of the Custer National Forest, stirred their creative juices. They decided to start their own P.I. business. This wasn't going to be just your run of the mill company, though, as they were going to incorporate Norah's psychic gift. This would be one more tool to be used in solving the mysteries presented by their clients. As they turned south from Billings and began the final leg along the eastern front of the Rockies into Wyoming and to their Cody home, the framework for B & N Investigations was established.

* * *

Back home in Cody, B & N Investigations and the pup's life as a human companion animal began simultaneously on Tax Day, April 15th, 2014. The business began to take shape and become viable. They started getting a few local and somewhat trivial cases, nickel dime cases as Bert called them. These were civil matters such as documenting evidence of neglect or disregard for court orders. Often, they supported divorce or child custody proceedings and usually involved a degree of discreet surveillance. Most of these cases relied primarily upon Bert's ability to hide in plain sight during surveillance and didn't require Norah's gift to a significant extent. The husband and wife couple waited patiently for that signature case which could propel them in the direction they really wanted to go. They felt that their business was uniquely qualified to find missing people and to find out what happened to them. Bert's intuitive skills, combined with Norah's common sense and psychic gift, could position them to be dominant in that area of investigation.

While the business was growing, the canine baby was growing. The little coywolf began her life with humans in one of Norah's soft, fuzzy gloves tucked inside an eight-by-ten-inch cardboard box by the wood stove at her new home outside of Cody. An eye dropper for feeding her a milk mixture started her on the road to thriving. In honor of their wonderful chocolate lab, who had died a couple years earlier, they decided to name this new addition "Mystical Missy." She would be called "Missy," like her namesake. They would raise this new Missy just like the old one, to be a close companion both in and out of their house.

Their home was a five-acre property with a one-level, two-bedroom log cabin and an attached two-vehicle garage situated along the north side of the North Fork valley west of Cody and leading to Yellowstone Park. The acreage backed up to the rough mountains on the back-north side, while the front sloped down toward the valley. A large fenced yard led a viewer's gaze from the south-facing picture window down the long sloping driveway to the Yellowstone Highway. Large dog doors allowed Missy to have generally unrestricted access to the house, garage and yard. She usually went with them wherever they travelled and became at ease in the cargo area of the Dodge SUV.

The first two years were an amazing adventure. Besides building a business, raising this young canine made their lives interesting and rewarding. Their monthly reports contributed to the database of knowledge about her hybrid species. Early research into the coyote-wolf hybrid had shown them to have the coyote's intelligence and adaptability, although with more of the wolf's size and aggressiveness. This latter trait had probably resulted in the first death of an adult human in North America, a 19-year-old woman, who was likely killed by at least two of these hybrid "coyotes" in Nova Scotia in 2009. The poor girl had encountered the coyotes while hiking alone in a park. The animals were known by other hikers who'd seen them and noticed their lack of fear of humans. Acclimated to unarmed and defenseless humans in the park, these coyotes had pursued this young woman, pinned her against a locked toilet, and killed her in the nearby foliage.

Knowing full well about this tragedy, Bert and Norah paid very close attention to the socialization of the new Missy. She rarely knew a pen or cage but was instead raised just as they had raised all their pets over the years, alongside the family. She was placed on an extensive training program and became comfortable spending time on a leash. They were pleasantly surprised to find that Missy was very trainable and eagerly and quickly accepted new tasks and commands. She was around other animals at every opportunity and adapted to their routine presence in her life. Likewise, they made a point of getting her around other people and tolerable of strangers. As she matured into her fully grown weight of about 45 pounds, her coat gradually settled into a stunning, reddish-grey reflection of her combined heritage. With her slightly shorter muzzle, broader face, and flowing tail, she was becoming a beautiful amalgamation of her coyote and wolf ancestors. Everywhere they took her she drew looks and comments.

One of the big surprises, though, was that Missy soon demonstrated an exceptional ability to track by smell. Norah discovered this by accident when playing hide and seek with one of their young granddaughters one afternoon while her family was visiting from Minnesota. Without knowing where the child had hidden, several hundred feet away and out of sight, Norah had offered the child's jacket to Missy and said, "Find her, girl, find her!" Missy paused several seconds smelling the jacket. She then proceeded to follow the almost exact path the girl took to her hiding place. The following months of purposeful training soon revealed that this young canine had a future in the business.

They realized they had one more potential tool, Missy's sense of smell. The challenge was learning how to blend together and use these capabilities in their cases.

Norah was the first to recognize Missy's potential and they both eventually understood just how truly unique their service could become. Norah told him, "This lady's not a tramp, Bert; this girl might be the difference between life and death for those people who are lost with nobody to turn to. This girl might even save one of us someday, Honey!"

Bert wondered, "Was that last statement just recognition of ability or a psychic premonition of some future event as yet unknown?"

CHAPTER TWO: BEGINNING A BUSINESS;
GROWING A REPUTATION

B and N Investigations began to flourish by latter 2015. By this time, they had learned how to effectively integrate both Norah's and Missy's abilities into many of their cases. While they considered nearly any type of case, such as divorce, child custody, fraud, and so forth, their combined abilities seemed particularly suited to those involving missing persons. Combining Bert's investigative sense with Norah's insights and Missy's nose created a unique service with a growing track record of success. The families of five children, individually lost in various state and national parks or around their home communities, could attest to the skills and abilities of this private team. Those children were located alive thanks to the psychic and tracking abilities of Norah and Missy, and to Bert's skill in interpreting and applying them.

The lost children were found by B and N Investigations, working as unpaid volunteers and merely offering their services. While these pro bono cases brought local and regional recognition to the business, the defining case had not yet materialized. It arrived in the spring of 2016 with a phone call from a desperate family in Caspar. Their teenage daughter was missing, and local law enforcement offered little or no help.

Two weeks had passed before the parents of missing seventeen-year-old Natalie became desperate enough to search online for someone to help them find her. One Wyoming company, B & N Investigations in Cody, caught their attention because of the five lost children they had found during the previous six months. Also, the father had a friend who knew Bert Lynnes and gave him a good character recommendation. Natalie's father called the company and spoke at length with Bert about his missing daughter and the failed attempts to locate her.

He told Bert how they had attempted to convince the local Sheriff of foul play in their daughter's unexplained disappearance. A deputy came to their house and did a cursory investigation; however, he and the department were very skeptical. It seems their daughter had a reputation for being a bit wild and loose with her body and the cops concluded that she had taken off willingly with one of the many young studs in the area. They were not anxious to expend resources looking for a girl who "just wanted to get laid." Bert listened to this father explain that, wild or not, this just wasn't like their daughter to vanish without a word. He described Natalie as a very sweet girl, loving to her family, with auburn hair, brown eyes, and was very nice looking. She was also a girl who had tested with above average intelligence and had an A average in high school. The father said his daughter was very popular and admitted that most boys were infatuated with her. She could be a bit spontaneous and wasn't very wise to the ways of the world, he told Bert. He said he had cautioned her many times to control her tendencies. "But you know how teenagers are, Bert. Their brains don't always keep up with their bodies," he said.

Bert agreed with that and assured the anxious parents that his company would try to find their daughter. When they had the first face-to-face meeting with the parents, he and Norah were struck by the clues which alluded to foul play. The family was generally affluent and lived in a nice upper-middle-class area on the southwest edge of Caspar. Natalie had ridden to school with one of her girlfriends two Fridays earlier and was not at the planned pickup point after school. She apparently kept her plans entirely secret even from her friends. The several kids who were interviewed by the police all claimed to have no idea where she might have gone. As was school policy, her phone had been left in her girlfriend's car. It was investigated and the texts showed an online infatuation with an unknown man. This man portrayed himself as a college student at UW and she had apparently not met him as of their last messages. His phone number was that of a cheap disposable phone from Best Buy in Atlanta. Many of the previous communications were from Laramie, home of the University of Wyoming, lending credibility to his being a recent college student. The most recent texts originated in the Caspar area, leading one to believe that he was working there somewhere. A final text confirmed that she was going to meet him after school that Friday at the local mall. The phone information ran into a dead end and the man could not be identified.

A piece of the girl's clothing augmented their small arsenal of evidence, to provide a scent for Missy. The few leads were given a glimmer of life by Norah's visions. That was because Norah kept seeing a unique stone cowboy statue in her mind and telling Bert it seemed important. There was little to go on until the fourth day in Caspar. Late on that Friday, they finally found the five-foot-tall, rock statue of a cowboy standing with his hat in his hand, on the lawn of this average looking house at the edge of town.

Early the next day, Saturday morning, B & N Investigations continued working the case which would bolster their reputation and enhance their stature among investigation companies. On that chilly but clear day, Bert sat quietly behind the wheel of his dark blue Dodge Durango, keeping an eye on his driver's side rearview mirror through the dark tinted windows. In the reverse image was the driveway and front of the house with the statue, about 200 yards behind him up the gently curving road on the outskirts of Casper. He was parked just off the two-lane road along the dirt driveway of a vacant house for sale. "How are you doing, girl?" he said as Missy slid her nose along his cheek from her berth in the cargo area, which she shared with their gear and overnight bag. She licked his cheek with a soft whimper, then nuzzled Norah's shoulder, followed by a bored yawn. Then she lay back down on her bed and resumed her nap. She was almost fully grown, just two years old, with a soft and full winter coat. She had become a trusted part of the family, not only a working canine but a family pet. The wild genes she carried were still there and respected, yet they remained subdued.

By late morning, Bert was getting stiff from the several hours on surveillance. He watched as Norah stretched and leaned back in the passenger seat, occasionally glancing in her rearview mirror while also keeping an eye on the road and traffic ahead. It was virtually devoid of vehicles. Despite the 22-degree temperature and splashes of snow, patches of open ground held promise of spring flowers to come. Wyoming winters were colder than a well digger's belt buckle, Norah liked to say. Such weather was not for the faint hearted and spring was always a welcome respite from the bitter cold.

Bert knew that Norah was also watching behind them in her side mirror. Her several days vision of this statue had led them to this house. Besides that, she'd been trying to make sense of the other recurrent visions. She had described one of the wooden doors with wrought iron hinges and locks like you might find on a Hobbit house. Another vision she depicted was of a cigar burning on a crude metal ashtray. The most disturbing of her visions showed a bloody tooth lying on a handkerchief. He knew this was a difficult mix of second sight for her to decipher.

As they sat quietly watching the house, the road, and the neighborhood in general, Norah became amused by the antics of a pair of cottontail rabbits playing in the yard next to them. She turned to Bert. "Darlin', it is even colder than we thought this morning. That one cottontail is giving the other one a jump-start, it seems."

Bert suppressed his laugh and whispered to Norah that a guy was coming out. He was getting in the pickup; it was time to get ready.

Along with Norah, he shifted his attention from the cottontails to the middle-aged, Caucasian, male climbing into his truck. As the pickup backed from the driveway and headed their direction, he hoped this man would figure their car was leaving the house for sale. The darkly tinted windows of his SUV would prevent the subject from seeing them clearly, if at all. Bert had started their vehicle and slowly pulled onto the road about ten seconds after the subject passed them from behind. He had to keep the subject in sight without tipping him off.

He followed the truck to a local food store, waited in the parking area across the street, and again picked up the subject after he departed the store with two grocery bags. The guy seemed to be heading out of town. As the road became more rural, the challenge of "hiding in plain sight," as Bert liked to say, became more difficult. He used every trick he knew to mask his vehicle from the subject. He tried to time the numerous hills to just crest a hill as the pickup was crossing the next. Then Bert sped to the top of that hill, slowed as he topped it, and coasted to keep his spacing on the subject. He used terrain, buildings, and other automobiles and trucks whenever possible to mask his car. He did not want to give the subject any reason to notice their vehicle. Norah's eyes were crucial to the mobile surveillance, helping keep the subject in sight while Bert had to occasionally focus on other traffic or road hazards.

After twenty minutes or so, the subject turned off the two-lane onto a gravel drive that appeared to go about a hundred yards to the left and ended in a small cluster of trees surrounding a rustic and somewhat junky house. Bert drove past the gravel driveway while Norah leaned his way and studied the property. He found another gravel road near a small hilltop about a quarter mile from the subject's driveway, pulled over, killed the engine, and pulled out the binoculars. Norah already had her pair focused on the subject's location.

They watched intently from a position where the subject's pickup could be seen near the distant house. After ten minutes, their subject reappeared from inside the house and then hastily went out of sight behind it. They continued to watch for nearly an hour before he returned, entered his pickup alone, and came back down the driveway. He turned back toward Casper.

"Norah, what are you sensing?" Bert asked. "Do I follow him, or see what's here?"

"I feel like she's here, Bert; just a feeling, I can't explain it more than that," Norah said. "I get the sickening feeling that she's in trouble. I feel her pulling me."

"Then we see what's here," Bert replied. "It will do no good to call the cops; we have no probable cause for a search that would stand up in court. They won't believe us. We have to do this ourselves."

For several more minutes, they observed the house, which appeared to be vacant. After about ten minutes and seeing no sign of other residents or neighbors, they drove to the gravel driveway and eased up to the house. Bert got out of the SUV, walked to the door of the house, and knocked. It was a poorly maintained but seemingly habitable house, with a few ancient pieces of farm equipment scattered randomly around the unkept and somewhat overgrown yard. The numerous evergreen trees and shrubs partially blocked the view of the place from the road. There was no answer, and nobody appeared to be there. The afternoon sun was not far from the horizon; it was going to be dark soon. They had to act, now!

Bert opened the Dodge's cargo door and called to Missy. She bounded out, literally smiling in her glee at being out of the car and ready to do something. She spun around in a circle several times, yapping and rubbing against Norah's legs, then came to Bert and followed his silent command to sit. He offered her the girl's blouse. She sniffed the shirt several times, her nose brushing against it. Then her ears shot up as she obeyed the command "Missy, find." She immediately went directly to the front door of the empty house, then worked first to the left of the door, back to the right, and bolted around to the rear of the house. Bert and Norah followed in pursuit, straining to keep her in sight.

Behind the house, Bert looked intently for Missy and, not seeing her, his eyes went to the open grassland which spread out to the rear of the house. Despite the fading light of dusk, he saw her after several nervous seconds, bounding through the tall vegetation about one-hundred-yards out. A faint footpath drifted in her direction through the dormant grasses of this livestock pasture. Bert and Norah ran after her. After nearly a minute, they lost sight of their coywolf. Her reddish-grey coat blended perfectly with the subdued tones of the pasture. Stopping, they strained to listen. Several seconds later, her excited yip pierced the cold air. They raced in the direction to which she called them.

Unexpectedly, the ground dipped down into a small ravine. At first, Missy appeared to be sitting in front of a dark cluster of Mesquite bushes. Upon second look, though, a dark wooden door, about half the size of a regular door, appeared. It had iron hinges and what looked like a homemade wrought iron lock, locked from the outside. Bert knelt with Missy, calming her excitement and praising her. Then he motioned for Norah to be quiet. They held their breath and listened. Yes, he heard what sounded like a girl's muffled sobs from within the hidden and well insulated bunker. A glance at Norah, told him that she heard it also. He asked her to stay with the girl while he went back to their vehicle for tools.

Norah knelt near the door, briefly studying the iron door hardware that had haunted her visions. The shortened and round-topped door did indeed remind her of a hobbit house door. She called out to the girl she knew was trapped inside. In just a few seconds, the girl returned her call and identified herself as Natalie. Norah explained who they were and that her parents had hired them to find her. The teenager broke into tears and wept on the other side of the door. Norah continued to talk calmly to her and assure her that she was now safe and would be going home soon. While they talked through the wooden door, Missy sat next to her alpha female, leaning against her, enjoying the stroking of Norah's hands, and occasionally licking her cheeks. She had performed her job well and she seemed to know it.

The sun was well below the horizon and darkness was tightening its grip on the day when her husband returned with a sledgehammer and pry bar. She took the LED lantern from Bert and held it so that he could study and then attack the lock on the door. Within a few seconds, his strong blows broke the latch holding a cheap padlock and allowed the steel bolt to be withdrawn. He pulled the door open. Norah followed the bright light of the lantern as it illuminated the nearly dark interior of a small underground room. A dim lantern cast an eerie light and shadows around the prison. A propane heater, apparently externally fueled and vented, provided the only heat source. A frightened, half-dressed, teenaged girl sat on a cot. She pulled a military style, olive green blanket tightly around her bare shoulders. The bruises on her forehead and her swollen lips gave testimony to the treatment she had endured. With her embrace, Norah felt Natalie's fear fade as the girl cried with the realization that she was rescued.

Through Natalie's tears and her sobbing plea to go home, Norah could see the gap from a missing front tooth. She placed her arms around the teenager, tucking a second blanket snugly around her to guard against the outside cold. As Norah led her from her prison, a cigar butt on a rusty ash tray flashed in the last beam of the lantern.

Natalie held tightly to Norah as they followed Bert back to the SUV. Missy walked close beside Norah's opposite leg, seeming to know that this young woman was as much her responsibility, now, as Norah's. As he led the way with the lantern, Norah could hear Bert dialing the phone call which would tell Natalie's anxious parents that she was safe, that she would talk with them as soon as they had her in the warm vehicle, and that he would then be calling the police.

* * *

Two weeks later, Bert called Natalie's parents again to find out how she and they were doing. They said she was doing quite well considering what she'd been through. Her father said that Natalie wanted to get on the phone for a few minutes with him. Between moments of tears, she thanked Bert, Norah, and Missy for saving her from the brutal, 40-year-old, man who had abducted her after she arranged to meet him that Friday after school. She told Bert that this man had portrayed himself online to be a 20-year-old college student. The heartthrob relationship she thought was developing was instead a complete deception. Bert could hear the remorse in the girl's voice. She told him repeatedly that she couldn't believe she'd been so naïve as to fall for the scum's lies. He reminded her that she wasn't the first teenager to be fooled with false love, and the important thing was that she was now safe.

Bert listened to her telling how the bruises were nearly gone and dental surgery had given her a bridged tooth to replace the one knocked out when she resisted her abductor. The small underground shelter where they found her had been her prison for over three weeks. Her only respite from the lonely darkness was when her abductor would return to brutalize and rape her.

Bert and Natalie's dad discussed how the low life who took her had been found within a day by the police. Bert's call and description and a review of the ownership records of the two properties were all they needed to track him down and arrest him without a fight. The assailant was still being held in the Casper jail awaiting trial. Bert told the father that he believed the man would be going away for years. He also told him that the lawsuit filed against Bert's investigation business for trespass had been summarily dismissed within 48 hours by the district judge.

The girl's father was trying to control his emotions as he spoke. "Bert, I'll be forever indebted to you and Norah and your tracker animal, Missy. I have no doubt but that you saved our daughter's life. I'm going to put a glowing endorsement on your website and tell every person I know about your business. Your team is a rare and precious gift and you're a Godsend for a family like ours. I hope that you stay the course, Sir, no matter what life throws your way. When my daughter needed you, you came through for her. People like us need you!"

Bert made a promise to him. "No matter what challenges may come our way, sir, we'll stay the course and continue using our God-given abilities to help others like yourselves."

He did not realize just how difficult it would be to keep that promise. They were going to be tested and the challenges would be severe.

B and N Investigations didn't become famous as a result of bringing Natalie home. However, their credibility and reputation were now on solid footing and their newly reworked website began to attract attention from beyond the state and region. Natalie's rescue did become the defining case that Bert and Norah were waiting for. Natalie's father and mother placed a wonderful testimonial and endorsement on the home page. The B and N Investigations business was now known for the ability to find the missing. They were leaving relative obscurity and about to come into the light of recognition. Bert and Norah knew there would be an increase in inquiries and cases and the cases would become more diverse. However, they didn't know that this exposure would now launch them on a collision course with a destiny they could not have foreseen.

CHAPTER THREE: CHANGE AND PREPARATION

The rescue of the teenage girl in Casper was the pivotal case for B & N Investigations. The recognition from that successful effort gave them more national notoriety than before. They were soon involved in more cases of lost and missing children from outside the state. A small child had wandered away from home in Idaho Falls and Bert's team joined the volunteers. With Norah's second sight and Missy's nose, the child was soon found in an old abandoned barn a half mile from her home. Another thirteen-year-old girl ran away from her home in Billings, and she was found on the second day when Missy followed her scent into the church where she was hiding. Other cases came also. A couple of them involved surveillance related to child custody matters. Another involved a divorce dispute. They were soon working one to two new cases weekly.

Then the late summer of 2016 brought a major setback! Norah had been fatigued and sleeping poorly for several months. Her usual bubbly personality became more subdued. She was eventually diagnosed with an aortic aneurism. She had to undergo several tests at a Billings hospital to determine the degree to which this might affect her. Her ultrasound and CT Scan tests and doctor visits interrupted their schedule periodically during those hot months. She was in and out of the Pulmonary Clinic four times as surgical procedures were being considered and weighed against the option of other treatments or just monitoring it.

On the 2nd of September, they again made the trip north of Cody to Billings. This modern little city sits on the plains just a short distance east of the Beartooth Mountains. The largest city in Montana, with a population of more than 100,000, Billings had a role in the early history of the region. One historical site, Pictograph Cave State Park, provides insight into the prehistoric hunters who roamed and lived in the area. Another more recent event of history is that of Colonel George Armstrong Custer's ill-fated encounter with the Sioux and Arapahoe at Little Bighorn in June of 1876. The short drive to the Little Bighorn Battlefield allows visitors to immerse themselves into the mindset of a man who woefully underestimated his adversary. His error in judgment cost his life and the lives of his soldiers and gave the Native Americans perhaps their greatest victory against the invading white man.

The Yellowstone River ran through the city. The wide, bubbling ribbon of water added to Billings' many attractions in the presence of beautiful natural vistas. Saint Vincent Healthcare hospital with its many surrounding trees and shrubs shone like a jewel in the sunlight of that early fall morning. Bert held Norah's hand tightly as they entered and registered for her latest regimen of tests and observation. This time she would be admitted for a few days while her doctor and staff attempted to determine the best course of action.

A few days later, Bert held her hand as she sat on her raised, adjustable, hospital bed, waiting for what should be the final tests and evaluation on the 5th of September. Even though the hospital did try to make their rooms homey, her room still had the underlying metallic and plastic coldness of a room for the sick. He couldn't help but notice the smell of sanitizers and cleaning agents, wafting throughout the ward. Once he had experienced this odor, he could never forget it. That odor would forever denote a hospital and sickness.

Norah was in her hospital gown, laughing and bubbly. He was happy to see her in such good spirits. She'd had several days recently when she was so tired and very lethargic. Today was a nice change from those down days. Her red hair was the center of attention with every staffer who entered the room. However, it was her cheerful and witty personality which made them return at every opportunity. She was simply fun to be around when she felt well. The fact that she was cute, Bert couldn't help but notice, had all the male nurses in the ward stopping by with any excuse to check on her.

The doctor had told them that she would be released this afternoon to go home, after this one more test was completed. As was typical of any stay in a hospital, nothing happened quickly. They had already been waiting over two hours for the last evaluation and test. Bert wondered how many people die of old age while waiting for their doctor. He concluded that it must be a rather significant number.

Bert scooted his chair closer and held both of Norah's hands. "The doctors say that you'll be released soon, sweetheart. You'll have to be less active in our business and just learn to take it slow and easy," he said to her. "We'll find the way to make your role easier, but you'll still be effective. You know that I need your help with this business and will continue to rely on you."

Norah nodded and smiled at him. "Yes, Honey, I'm feeling better, and I'll be out of this hospital in a few more hours. You know that I'll always be here for you. We'll get past this. We're going to be a better business despite this. I promised to see this through with you, and I will. This isn't going to stop me from being beside you, Bert. I want our business to be successful as much as you do."

He leaned back in the chair next to her bed, held her hand, and closed his eyes. The boredom of waiting caused a blast of sleepiness to hit him. He just had to get a few minutes of a nap.

When he woke up, he would be that much closer to taking his beloved Norah home to Cody. He drifted off to sleep. Next to her husband, Norah also lowered her head and closed her eyes. A sudden wave of fatigue had hit her, as well. She just needed to sleep for a little while.

* * *

The remainder of 2016 was a tough period. It seemed to Bert that the rest of September and October were a blur. He frequently felt the tears silently rolling down his cheeks at night. However, there was a silver lining behind the dark clouds and as the business picked up gradually, so did the personal side. He kept remembering his promise to stay the course, no matter what life threw at him. Norah kept her promise to always be there for her husband and their business.

There was a bit of a learning curve to deal with. They had to figure out how to best use Norah's gift without putting too much stress on her. Likewise, Bert had to learn to manage his own workload and stress in order to pace himself. When these challenges finally settled down with the onset of winter, their business was still going forward. They had to make some adjustments, though.

Bert now dealt entirely with clients, law enforcement, and the general public. He would have to do all the driving, so had to develop a pattern of rest stops on any longer trips. She could heap her attention and love upon Missy, but he assumed responsibility for all the care, feeding, walks, and training. Norah supported Bert in the background, dealing exclusively with her husband and not with others. This suited her psychic gift. By protecting her from other human inputs, the psychic "noise" and outside interferences were reduced. That allowed her to focus on the subject of their investigations and on making sense of her visions. She did not use a cell phone or other technologies, in part because of their possible influence upon her gift.

B and N Investigations adapted into these new roles and routine and by year's end the pace was picking up. Bert could see that the new year, 2017, held the promise of more work and greater successes for their unique business. He increasingly understood Norah's role and her psychic abilities with every case they worked, and she could more effectively interpret the feelings which would come over her. Her visions had become clearer, although it was often difficult to make immediate sense of them. Bert was learning how to relate to his psychic business partner and read her demeanor and messages when sometimes she could not.

He trained Missy every possible day to develop and hone her general obedience and tracking skills. He was thankful for all the dogs he had owned and trained over the years. They had taught him how to read a canine mind and enlist the animal's willing obedience. He used a version of reward and punishment as the foundation of her training. When she did well, he rewarded her with a tasty treat and a heap of praise. If she didn't do a command correctly, her punishment was him grasping the hair on both sides of her cheeks, looking her in the eye, and sternly scolding her. It didn't matter what he said in either case. She read the sound and quality of his voice. If she was in trouble, the inflection and volume of his voice told her so. Bert was continually amazed at the effectiveness of this style of training. One of the keys was to do it the same way, every time. Any inconsistency would produce a degree of confusion in her and result in a less-than-desired outcome.

Bert had learned that Missy was highly intelligent; thanks to the combination of genes she inherited from both her coyote and red wolf ancestors. Coyotes, especially, are known for their ingenuity and survivability. The breed thrives in virtually all environments, including urban. Even their litter size varies with the environmental influences. There was good reason for their Native American nickname, "the trickster." Her nose was equally gifted because of the same wild reasons. Her intelligence and spirit made her difficult to train, though.

The spirited puppy is always the more challenging to handle, especially for novices. He believed this was a major reason for the dumping of new puppies along the roadways and to animal shelters. Bert was angered every time he saw a dead dog along a highway. He was convinced that at least

half of those deaths was the direct result of poor or no training. Yet, the spirit which made her challenging to train, also made Missy almost flawless once she accepted the new, trained, relationship with her understanding and skilled master. His praise was her greatest reward, since she accepted him as her alpha male. Pleasing her alpha male became her driving motivation and made her into a valuable business asset, as well as a trusted and loved companion. Bert knew all too well the nightmare of having an unruly and untrustworthy animal. As a highly trained companion animal, Missy became a pleasure to be with. Bert didn't know it at the end of 2016, but they would need these business assets to hit on all cylinders, sooner than he envisioned. They were going to face a challenge unlike any they had dealt with so far. The cases they had worked would pale in comparison to the difficulty posed by those about to come. During January of 2017, somewhere miles away, a plan was being hatched which would drag B and N Investigations into the darkest side of human nature.

CHAPTER FOUR: IT BEGINS

"Ma'am, please slow down and tell me exactly what's going on and why you called us," Bert said to the obviously distraught woman on the phone. He sat down on the tree he was cutting into firewood sized blocks for splitting later. Nearby, Missy was nosing around in a pile of brush and tree limbs, exploring the scents of the vermin trails. It was a warm spring day in early May 2017, with the temperature in the low sixties. A scattering of puffy cumulus clouds drifted slowly across the blue sky of northwest Wyoming. A squirrel chattered noisily in the tree nearby, objecting to Missy rummaging around near the base of its tree. She pulled away from her brush pile and circled the tree, looking up at the loud neighbor as it peeked around the tree trunk. Squirrel could be on the menu if the little rascal got careless.

"First, where do you live Ma'am?"

Bert listened as she introduced herself as Myrtle Kennedy and said she lived in Saint Joseph, Missouri, above Kansas City a half hour or so. The strain in her voice lessened somewhat, though there was an obvious quality of panic. "My husband and I saw your website on the internet and hope you may be able to help us? Nobody else is."

"Can you tell me what the situation is, Myrtle? Nice to meet you. Just call me Bert."

She continued: "Well, Bert, in a nutshell, my parents have disappeared since about two weeks ago. We're very concerned about them. They are in their middle 70's, not the best of health though getting along okay. They live near us in a small community of Troy, which is in Kansas about a half hour west of Saint Jo."

"Why do you think they've disappeared," Bert asked. "Maybe they just decided to get away for a while?"

"That's exactly what the police said, too," Myrtle said. "We tried to tell them that this time was different. There are family matters, new baby on the way for a grandson, schools that are winding down for other kids, and so forth. They just wouldn't go anywhere without keeping in touch in some way."

Bert asked, "So, have your parents gone away for a time before this, without telling you?"

"Yes, a couple of times for a few days or maybe a week, but never for this long, and usually they contacted us within a few days. Therefore, the police have been slow to really jump on our case, though, because of that possibility." She drew a long breath, paused, and then continued. "Bert, sometimes you just know that something is wrong, you know. We know our parents and we know something is wrong. We need help and we don't know who else to turn to. Can you help us? Money is not an object; we've seen your fee schedule and know you're reasonable for what you do. The endorsements and testimonials on your website tell us you're maybe our best chance of finding them soon."

Bert pondered the woman's words and then asked, "When was the last time you saw your parents, and where?"

Myrtle's voice cracked a little as she recalled meeting them for lunch in Troy about three or four days before they seemed to vanish. "On a Friday, I think? I think they were in town for a pre-season scrimmage of a grandson's football team, or maybe it was baseball? He's in his second year of high school. They are very close to all the grandkids, but especially to him." She paused for a minute, and then added, "We tried to contact them for a visit that next Monday but couldn't find them. Since their car was gone, we at first assumed they just went out of town for the day or maybe overnight. They do like to go for country drives."

"Was there anything odd or out of place at their house?" Bert asked. "I assume you have a key and checked the house?"

"We didn't go in that day, because we just assumed, they were out for a drive and would return soon." Myrtle seemed apologetic, "It wasn't until Wednesday morning, when we still couldn't contact them, that my husband and I went through their house. There was nothing out of place, but we did notice that their toiletries and suitcases were at the house. Dad usually carried a bug-out bag in his car with essentials for an emergency, so it was possible that he could just rely on the bag for a day or two."

"You said you involved the local police, I think," Bert said. "What did they do and say to you?"

Myrtle replied, "Yes, we called the police Wednesday afternoon after we could find no clues about their location. They sent two detectives just about dark, who took notes about what I've told you. They looked all over the house and around the buildings and yard. It was dark by the time they finished, and they just shrugged their shoulders but said they'd keep looking into it. They have come back out a couple of times and searched more thoroughly during the day, but just didn't find any clue as to where my parents are." Her voice was broken over the phone as she tried to choke back tears. "This week they put out a missing persons advisement about them. So far nothing has come of it."

"Myrtle," Bert said, "I'll take your case. I live near Cody,

Wyoming, so I'll have to drive about two days getting there. We should be able to leave tomorrow by around noon. That would have us in Troy about 5 or 6 p.m., Wednesday. Can you meet us there and show us to your parents' place? We'll need to go inside the house and look around for ourselves."

With the acceptance and assurance from Myrtle, Bert packed up his wood cutting gear and led Missy back to their house. Their rather quaint log house was situated on about five acres on the north side of the valley a few miles west of Cody. They had a nice view of the valley and the road leading to Yellowstone Park. That was a drive that Roosevelt had said was the prettiest 50 miles in America, or something like that. Once his stuff was put away and he was inside, Bert fed his Coywolf Lady, as he sometimes called Missy, then he sat down near their woodstove and proceeded to fill in the new case details to Norah. She sat silently, listening to his every word, her mind working as she listened. He had always marveled at how she could focus so completely on a subject; she was an extraordinary partner. She was always eager to take on a new challenge and she had the right stuff to see it through.

There was a lot to do to get ready for a two-plus-day trip and an indefinite case, so Bert began preparing and packing the SUV. He was contemplating nicknaming their vehicle to something like "the doghouse," since he could see that he and Missy would be spending a lot of time in it. Norah thought that was cute, though she reminded him that he wouldn't spend quite so much time in it if he behaved. He laughingly agreed to behave. Thus, the doghouse was born.

Bert resumed preparations for the trip to eastern Kansas. Even though winter was giving way to spring, he always carried an emergency kit any time he traveled Wyoming and Rocky

Mountain roads. You just never knew when you might end up in a ditch because a deer suddenly ran in front of your car. At any time, the easy drive could turn into a quest for survival. It always paid to be prepared. When satisfied with that most basic precaution, he packed their gear, travel bags, and a cooler. It had to be carefully orchestrated in order to leave a decent amount of room for Missy. It was, after all, her doghouse, too. When all was ready, he headed inside to relax with Norah and Missy before going to bed early.

The next morning, Tuesday, Bert and Norah departed home for Troy, with coywolf Missy in the cargo area, which she shared uneasily with the several bags. She liked to travel but got restless easily if the drive was too long. She was too energetic to be cooped up very long. She still had most of her winter coat, and they had to keep the temperature turned down to keep her comfortable. This meant that humans had to wear coats in order to stand the cold vehicle.

They headed down highway 120 south of Cody, and about thirty minutes later dropped down into the valley north of the small cow town, Meeteetse, at one time the headquarters to both sides of the cattle and sheep wars. Later, Bert wanted a coffee so stopped briefly in Thermopolis, near the hot springs, then proceeded down through the tunnels on the Wind River Canyon Scenic Byway. This was one of his favorite drives because of its towering cliffs and stunning river views, before the last bleak miles of clay hills led into the town of Shoshoni.

He grabbed a quick sandwich at the local general store, and they headed east for the drudgery of nearly two hours of open road through sagebrush country, rolling hills, and arroyos, into Casper. From there it was mostly south on Interstate 25 through plains and ranch country. Shortly before reaching Cheyenne, they turned east to Scottsbluff, Nebraska. There, with the towering bluff of the Scottsbluff Monument in the distance, Bert hooked up with a local motel room for the night stay and some needed exercise for Missy. She was very happy to be out of the vehicle for the night.

Wednesday, they hit the road early and followed the local roads past Lake McConaughy, a massive man-made lake formed by one of the largest earthen dams in the nation, and then headed to Interstate 80. After the most boring drive in the world, in Bert's opinion, along hours of flat farmland and cornfields, they finally passed under the Interstate Museum which spanned the entire highway at Kearney. The geography here was so flat he mused, that if you looked closely on the forward horizon, you might see the rear of your vehicle.

They skipped around the south edge of the capitol city of Lincoln. An hour later they arrived in Nebraska City, home of the National Arbor Day Association, and turned south toward Kansas. After the long drive, they finally turned toward Troy, Kansas, on highway 36. Bert called Myrtle Kennedy and reported that they were within an hour of Troy. He asked if the Kennedys could meet somewhere in Troy and show Bert's team to their folks' home?

Myrtle said she and her husband were already in Troy and were very anxious to meet and lead the investigators to her parents' home. "We're very worried and hope you can help," she said. We're waiting at the BP station just off highway 36 on Locust Street."

Bert and Norah shared a desire for knowledge. They always

liked to know the places they traveled to and through and sought out some of the basic history. They had learned that the elevation and population of Troy were nearly identical, about 1000, feet above sea level and residents. The little town was named for the ancient city of Troy and was located about a half hour west of St. Joseph, Missouri. It shared a history with the larger city. Troy got its start in 1855 as a spot in the road for the wagons heading from St. Jo, to California and Oregon. Today it's the county seat for Doniphan County, Kansas. The courthouse is a very impressive red brick building, which Bert thought was too classy for such a small community.

The history lesson made the last hour pass quickly. Following quick introductions at the gas station, Bert followed Myrtle and her husband, David, north on the Mosquito Creek Road. After about 30 minutes, they turned east on a gravel one-lane road for about a quarter mile until arriving at a well maintained, one-level, ranch house on what appeared to be a small farm. They had about an hour left until sundown, so this first look needed to be efficient.

"Can you show me around the outside now, so I get a feel for the overall property?" Bert asked. He instantly liked this stocky but trim, middle-aged, brunette.

"Absolutely," answered Myrtle. She led him around the brick-sided house with its well-kept yard and trees. There were no signs of any forced entry or foul play around the outside of the house and yard. Bert's observant eyes explored every detail of the house exterior, while Norah wandered on her own a short way away, as was her custom, quietly letting her senses sniff the spiritual winds.

"Would you show me the garage and other outbuildings now?"

Bert asked.

Missy was running near them, never straying more than a couple hundred feet from Bert, and she was thoroughly enjoying the chance to stretch her legs and relieve herself. Myrtle was fascinated by this obvious coyote-like canine, since they had western coyotes all over that country. She told Bert, "She's beautiful. Is she friendly toward strangers?"

"Oh sure," Bert said. "She warms up to a stranger quickly if you act friendly and unafraid toward her. Like any animal with wild blood, she can sense fear or distrust or aggression. Just be friendly, don't act afraid, and don't push it. Give her time to come to you and choose to get to know you."

Myrtle nodded in understanding and continued familiarizing Bert with the property. The garage looked like a typical farm garage. In it was a workbench with a handful of tools on it, while most of the other tools hung in a generally neat arrangement on a front pegboard. A drill press, welder, acetylene torch, pressure tank and air hose, lawnmower obviously being repaired, and a Ford tractor occupied much of the floor space. A gas can sat on the floor near the side door, and cans of grease and oil lined the shelves. While the workspace was somewhat cluttered, as you would expect of a working garage, nothing appeared to be obviously unusual or out of place.

A quick scan of the barn, chicken house, and two sheds also showed nothing suspicious or out of the ordinary. Bert and Myrtle walked quickly back toward the house, while Missy made her last pass around the barnyard and trotted to merge with their path. Norah continued to do her own sensory investigation, following somewhat behind them at each stop, and pausing to close her eyes. She allowed her mind to feel the scene and sort through the visions competing for her attention. She didn't talk during this phase of an investigation, instead leaving that to Bert while she listened to her spiritual guides and absorbed the visionary clues.

Bert stood back as Myrtle unlocked the front door, stepped inside, and turned on the lights. She told him, "This is just the way we found it and left it when the sheriff checked it out. We can't see anything unusual except that my parents are nowhere to be found. And their car is gone."

With his trained and discerning eyes, Bert studied the rooms of the house one by one but could find nothing to catch his attention. Nothing seemed unusual, out of place, or sinister. The sun was below the horizon now, and it was getting dark. Tired, and ready to find something to eat, Bert nodded toward Norah, who was standing silently outside, lost in thought.

Myrtle looked in Norah's direction, and then turned to Bert. "Would you like to come to our house for something to eat? You could even stay with us if you like?"

"No, but thank you for the kind offer," Bert replied. "We like to eat quietly and relax; just think about the case and where to go next with it." With that, he started toward the car. "Can we meet you back at the house around 9:00 in the morning?"

"Whatever you need, we are prepared to do," said Myrtle, "just tell us what you want us to do?"

"We can meet you at your folks' house, now that we know where it is. Can you get us two items that were personal to both your parents? I need things that they touched almost daily, and which would have their scent strongly attached. Our hybrid coyote may look like any other, but she has a gift of smell that gives us a chance to find that which our eyes cannot see. Tonight, we'll reflect on the case and incorporate any psychic visions into the mix and see what we can come up with?"

"Psychic visions?" asked Myrtle.

"Yes, I started this business with my wife, Norah, who is psychic. I always call upon her spiritual support in our investigations. She often has a jumble of visions, which can relate to the case. She doesn't talk with our clients, and she prefers to keep her distance from you and rely upon the spirits to tell her things about the case. Throughout the case, we talk from time to time, especially when relaxing at night, to compare her visions with the facts that I've learned about the case. For these reasons, you'll be dealing only with me while we try to figure out what happened to your folks." With that, Bert got in his SUV, nodded to Norah who was already in the passenger seat, and prepared for the drive back to Troy.

"No problem with that," said Myrtle, "we are only interested in results, not methods. Please make sure she knows how much we appreciate her gift and her help."

After assuring Myrtle that he would pass along the message, they drove back to Troy and settled into a small Mom and Pop motel. It was one which would accommodate their rather unusual pet. Missy was still anxious to get more exercise after the long drive.

Back in the motel room after their evening walk, Bert sat in the desk chair with his bare feet resting on the bed. Norah rested against the headboard of the queen-size bed. She had her eyes closed, thinking about the case. He studied her as she sat quietly reflecting on the property they'd been inspecting. It was always a pleasure to watch her. She was very pretty with her flowing and bouncy red hair, but she also had a very fluid face. Her expressions changed based upon her thoughts. His eyes drifted from Norah to Missy where she dozed in front of the picture window. The window was always her favorite spot in any motel. She might start to sleep in other places, such as the cool floor of the bathroom. However, she invariably ended up spending the night by the window. For a minute, Bert marveled at her beautiful coat. Missy still had most of her thick winter fur, but it would be shedding in the very near future.

"This is likely to be a tough case to solve," said Bert. "I didn't see anything that I considered a clue inside the house or on the property. It's like they just disappeared into thin air."

"I'm having a tough time of it, too," said Norah. "I'm getting some very strange sensations and visions about this."

"Like what, babe?" Bert was looking out the window across the street to what appeared to be a little coffee shop and diner, making a mental note for in the morning. He loved to start his day with a good cup of coffee.

Norah continued. "Well, even though the evidence seems to say they've gone away, I have this contradictory feeling that they're there, not gone at all. Then I see glimpses of things, such as a gas can, a wrench, a blurry and shimmering figure of a person, as if you were looking at them through an old wavy window glass. Two things are really confusing to me, though. I see the numbers 42 and 35, which make no sense to me; and I see a nickel and a dime."

"A nickel and a dime?" said Bert. "What on earth could that mean?"

"I wish I knew," said Norah. "Hopefully I will pick up on more tomorrow when we have more time. Maybe Missy will add something to the solution."

With that, Bert crawled into bed and scooted down under the covers. He reached for and turned off the table lamp, and said, "Yeah, babe, let's sleep on it and see what we find out tomorrow. Lone Ranger out."

"Right, Kemosabe, Tonto going sleep." She laughed quietly as she moved closer.

Thursday dawned to a nice day in eastern Kansas. High thin clouds floated across the sky toward the east as the sun crept over the crimson horizon and cast long shadows over downtown Troy. The newly budding trees, shrubs, and grasses glistened with dew in the early morning sunlight. Another day in paradise, Bert thought, as he finished walking Missy and they prepared to resume their case. He had located a pair of vacant lots near the motel. Missy had enjoyed checking them out and looking for something to chase or munch on. It would be about a half hour drive from the motel to the property.

It was 8:00 in the morning when Bert, Norah, and Missy arrived at Myrtle's parents' place. They got there first, and, as was her custom, Norah wandered quietly around in the background, tuning in to what she could sense. Myrtle arrived a few minutes later, without her husband who had to work. Bert thought the fellow was quiet anyway and didn't add much to the case. These were, after all, Myrtle's parents, so she was the best source of information. Besides that, Bert liked this outgoing and spirited woman. He felt like she was another of his clients who could easily become a friend.

"Have you thought of anything else that might be a clue about your parents' disappearance?" Bert asked, as Myrtle opened the door to the house and followed him inside.

She shook her head.

"If I ask you about a nickel or dimes, does that ring any bells with you? Could it have something to do with your folks?"

"No, nothing comes to mind," she replied. "There was some

change left on the dresser, I think, but nothing else comes to mind."

"Can we look at that?" Bert asked. "I don't know if it means anything or not."

She led him slowly through the house so he could again look for any clues. The country kitchen was neat and clean, with just a few unwashed dishes stacked at the side of the sink. The living room was similarly very orderly, with even the few magazines fanned out for display on the large coffee table. The master bedroom suite had been made up as if for guests. The bed was made, and the bathroom towels and washcloths were all in their place. At the bedroom dresser, Bert pondered the two dimes and one nickel lying there, neatly in a row, touching each other. That didn't seem very unusual, and apparently the police didn't think so. Yet, maybe that was some clue, based upon Norah's sketchy vision.

"Twenty-five cents; two dimes and one nickel. Can you think of any significance to that?" he asked.

"No, not really," she said. "My parents were pretty neat and tidy, so they didn't normally leave much laying around, including money. But then again, it isn't all that unusual, either. The coins are laid out neatly, which I could see Mom, especially, doing."

Bert pondered that, as he moved on to another slower look around the house. Back at the front door, he asked Myrtle, "Do you have any old windows in any of the buildings, the kind that often aren't very clear and seem a little wavy? The kind that somewhat distorts whatever you're looking at through them."

She thought for a few seconds; then answered, "No, none that I can think of. Actually, I'm sure that we don't."

"What about a gas can? Any significance to that? Are there any tools missing from the shop?"

She thought for a minute, then said, "We have a gas can in the garage, and it's still there by the door. My Dad usually kept it outside near the gas tank beside the garage. His tools were mostly put in their places on the pegboard above the workbench. I haven't checked them but am not aware of anything missing. I can look at it if you like?"

"Yes, would you mind doing that? It might not be anything, but let's see if any are out of place or missing."

While Myrtle went to the shop to inventory the tools, he did a slower and more methodical walk around and inside the outbuildings again. He could see that Norah was doing similarly, ahead of him. She walked slowly around each, her head often down, thinking. She's reading the tea leaves he often thought to himself. Bert knew better than to bother her during her part of any investigation. She needed space to gain her insights into a place or case.

The gas can bugged him. The parents' can was in the garage, but she said it was normally outside by the gas tank. Was that significant? Did it mean anything at all? So far, there are no signs of foul play here. These folks and their car are simply gone. Did they just decide to get away by themselves? Not likely, he thought, because they didn't sound like the kind of people who would be gone this long without telling their daughter. No, something is wrong here. Then there was Norah's feeling that they were still here. But where? What else is around here?

Back at the garage, he asked Myrtle how the tool inventory was going?

"Well, fine I guess, but there is a wrench that I can't find. It's an open-end/box-end, one-and-a-half-inch wrench." Myrtle turned to Bert, "Have you come up with anything?"

"Nothing yet," he replied. "Can you tell me about the surrounding property here?

"We have the county road that you drove in on, to the west of us. There are good neighbors both north and south of here; one has about a twenty-acre property and does some farming. The other has around 40-some acres and raises a few cattle and a horse or two. They've been here for years and are good people. Like most people in these parts, they would help each other out if help was needed. People around here keep to themselves, though, mostly. To the east is Mosquito Creek, just a small creek that is close to the east boundary of Dad's property."

Bert asked, "Those trees out behind the house about a quarter mile, those are along the creek, then."

"Yes," she replied, "It's wet enough along the bank for a few cottonwoods and a couple of oaks to grow."

"Well, Myrtle, we haven't gotten any tangible evidence yet, but we continue to look for clues," he said. "Did you get those couple of personal items I asked for yesterday?"

"Yes," she said, "I'll run back to the house and bring them out for you. Dad's favorite neckerchief and Mom's hairbrush."

While waiting for Myrtle to return, Bert called Missy to his side, and began to talk to her and in his own way let her know that he needed her to work now. He knew from her ears and eyes when she was making the connection with him. It was hard to explain, but he often sensed the wolf in her at such times.

When Myrtle returned, he asked for her Dad's neckerchief. When she handed it to him, he held it near his hybrid's nose, gave her time to smell it to her desire, and then said, "Find, Missy, find."

Bert now had Missy on duty. She knew a treat would follow if she could find the object of her nose's search. He watched as she trotted around the barn, then the garage, stopping occasionally to sniff the ground, reversing direction several times. She was obviously picking up residual scent from the man's time around his property. She paused by the small garage door and sniffed with interest around there. Then she moved with a hastened pace behind the garage, pausing as if to confirm her findings before moving toward the east. Bert glanced at Norah, who was watching them with interest from near the barn. She nodded.

He quickly began to follow Missy through the tall pasture grass. She made her way through the mix of winter brown and spring green vegetation toward the creek. Myrtle followed closely behind Bert.

The spattering of mostly cottonwood trees along both sides of the small creek portrayed a sense of serenity at that time of late morning. The sun shined brightly as it sought to penetrate the dense canopy of leaves, casting shadows across the slow running water in the generally shallow creek. Missy paced along the creek as if attempting to regain the lost scent she was pursuing. Then she seemed to home in on a deeper section at a bend of the gently meandering creek. At last, she sat down, her signal to Bert that she had found the object of her nose.

As Bert approached his tracking animal, his first impression was that she was apparently wrong this time and confused by aging scents from the missing couple's likely hikes down to the stream. From ten feet away, he could see nothing that made him think otherwise. That is, until a brief flash of sunlight about 40 feet downstream from Missy caught his eye. Something shiny seemed to have just caught the brief beam of light upon that section of stream between the leaves as they swayed in the typical Kansas breeze. Seeing nothing by Missy, Bert walked down to where the object seemed to be and decided to get his feet wet in the shallow water, searching for the object. Then he saw the small patch of shiny metal, just visible in the silt and sand. He reached a gloved hand into the water and carefully pulled up a foot-and-a-half long wrench. It was an open-end and box-end wrench, size one-and-a-half-inch.

With the wrench in hand, Bert went to Missy and rewarded her efforts with a hug, some serious petting, and the venison treat that she loved. Then he peered into the water, which seemed dark and obscured by the shadow of the trees and a greater depth at this slight bend. He nearly fell as he was instinctively startled. From the bottom of this three-foot-deep water, the face of a man shimmered in the slowly moving water. Closer inspection disclosed the female body, almost underneath that of the man.

Norah was right. Myrtle's parents were on the property. Bert stepped back and walked out to Myrtle, who had stopped halfway to the creek. He described the scene to her and suggested she not go there. It was her decision to go. He walked to the creek with her and then called the county sheriff via 911. Now they would wait and keep watch over the scene to preserve any evidence. While comforting Myrtle, Bert briefed her that they would now follow the directions and answer the questions of the police.

Bert told the police very little about how he had obtained the clues which, in this case, led to finding the bodies. He just answered their questions and only provided what they asked for. The less they knew about his methods, the better, because most of them would not believe either him or his methods. He was concerned that their methods might become reasons to make him a suspect, or at least to raise suspicion. He just told them about being hired and that they decided to check out the stream. He suggested that Myrtle generally take the same approach. If the police wanted to know more about his service, they could go to his website, which discussed the unique and unorthodox nature of their business. Since most police departments didn't give much respect to private investigators in general and virtually no respect to psychics, Bert knew there was little likelihood of them doing that.

Before the Sheriff's team arrived about twenty minutes later, Bert had put Missy on her leash to protect her. He was pulled aside by the Sheriff to be interviewed and make a statement. The same was done with Myrtle by a Deputy. The rest of the law team went to work, looking for and documenting any evidence, both at the creek and in the house. Bert and Myrtle, once they'd made their statements, could go to their respective vehicles and wait. Eventually the bodies were removed.

It was late afternoon before the police cleared them to go. Once cleared, Bert arranged to meet Myrtle in town for a coffee and talk. He spent an hour sipping coffee and consoling Myrtle, who vacillated between calm and outbursts of sobbing. He knew that both her parents had been removed from the water after the forensics team had cleared the site. The tentative conclusions were that they had been hit in the head by an assailant using the stolen wrench, and then weighted down with rocks from the stream bank to keep them in that deeper spot. Several weeks underwater had left the bodies in very poor shape and an autopsy would be performed the next day. Myrtle promised to call Bert as soon as possible after she had any results or information. He shook her hand, hugged her to console her grief, and then walked her to her car. Norah was waiting in the doghouse with Missy, who was lying in the back. Both were eager to head back home.

Bert, Norah, and Missy spent one more night in the local motel and were on the road back to Cody before sunrise. The long drive was broken up by another stay in Scottsbluff, before making the final push to their home. The next few days would be spent cleaning vehicle and gear, writing up the report on the Troy case, and in training for Missy. They took time to rest and prepare for the next case.

A week later, Bert received an update call from Myrtle. "They found Dad and Mom's car," she said. "It was parked in a busy part of the Walmart parking area in Saint Jo. An employee there finally noticed it. The autopsy results have been briefed to me," she told him, "and the blows to the head did incapacitate both my parents. They said Mom died outright from a hit on the back of her head which punctured her skull. However, Dad was only knocked unconscious and died of drowning, probably as he was being pinned down by the rocks. The police are investigating and following all leads, but so far, they don't have anything concrete to go on. They have no idea who did this or why."

Bert thanked her for calling and again told her how sorry he was for her loss. Her uncontrolled sobbing made it impossible to talk longer and she had to get off the phone.

Bert relayed the call and autopsy information to Norah. She was visibly disturbed by it, as she had been by the way the case had concluded. Even though it was their business to investigate and make sometimes difficult discoveries, Norah was empathetic and related personally with their clients. This case was their first to find dead bodies for their clients. It hit her very hard.

She had tears in her eyes as she softly said, "So the last thing this poor man might have seen was his assailant, looking down at him through three feet of shimmering, dark water? What I thought might be old glass was actually water."

"Yes," he replied. "It was probably like looking through an old wavy pane of window glass. It could have been like your vision, sweetheart."

Bert encouraged Norah to try to put this case out of her mind and relax. He diligently began to check their email, website, and Facebook pages; answering inquiries and looking for the next case. He hoped that it would be less gruesome than the last one. He couldn't foresee that his hope would not be realized.

CHAPTER SIX: A CALL FROM COLORADO

Bert sat opposite Norah at the Honey-stained, knotty pine table which he had made some years earlier. The nice-sized country kitchen with its wood décor was a perfect setting for their early morning chat over coffee. He looked at her lovingly. She was the love of his life. She would always be the love of his life. When he uttered the words "For richer, for poorer, in sickness and in health, until death do us part," he meant every word. He adored her. She was a very pretty redhead with a nice figure, but it was more than her looks. Her personality, wit, and charm attracted him like a magnet. "This is great coffee," he said.

"I know it is," she replied. "I know that you consider coffee with cream and Honey to be the elixir of the gods." She laughed.

Bert leaned back and relaxed as he sipped his coffee and enjoyed the morning chat with his wife. The sun was up, just above the horizon, and the morning rays played across the unlighted den. From where they sat in the adjacent kitchen, Missy lay on the floor connecting both rooms. She preferred the throw rug in front of the picture window or the one in front of the fireplace, but both were trumped by her greater desire to be in view of her alpha male and female. She lay facing them, with her head on her outstretched paws. Every now and then, Bert could see one or both eyes open just long enough for her to see them still nearby. She rolled onto her side and did a big stretch, then went back to sleep.

Norah said to him, "Bert, I'm having visions lately that I can't explain. Something big is happening; I can feel it. I think we need to get ready to do some traveling. This feels like something we've never experienced before."

Bert thought about her words for several minutes. He knew that when his wife offered up a psychic feeling, a wise man would listen and take it seriously. He didn't have to understand it. In fact, he felt a chill run up his back. He started to reply, but before he could get a word out, his phone rang.

"B and N Investigations," he answered.

A man on the other end replied, "Good morning, Sir, my name is Tom Davenport. I live near a small town in eastern Colorado; Haxtun. I've been looking at your website and I'm hoping you might be able to help us?"

Bert introduced himself and the business. Then he asked Mr. Davenport what kind of issue he was calling about.

Davenport told Bert that his brother, James, and his wife, Sarah, went missing about two weeks earlier. He said there are virtually no clues for the cops to go on, and since their pickup is also gone, the assumption has been that they just went on a sabbatical, just a getaway somewhere.

"What makes you think otherwise?" Bert asked.

"Well, I guess I just know my brother," Tom said. "We haven't been close for several years, since our parents died. We did talk or visit at least a couple times every year, though. Their granddaughter called me about a week ago and asked if I knew where they were. She hadn't seen them for a couple of weeks, which was unusual. They followed her and her brother's activities closely. She is quite an athlete, so's he, and they loved to follow their sports, with summer softball and baseball going on right now. She's also an honor student. It isn't like either of them to miss the kids' activities, without telling them something."

Bert asked, "You brought in the police?"

"Yeah, sure," replied Tom, "but they couldn't find any reasons to suspect foul play. They're thinking my brother may have just decided to take a vacation for a while. The pickup is gone, so that does make sense at first glance."

This sounds very familiar, thought Bert. He wondered if there's any connection.

"Tom, are you sure enough of foul play to hire us to look into this?" Bert said. "You know that I'm about a day's drive from east Colorado."

"Bert, from what I've seen on your website, I feel like you may be the best chance of finding them. To answer your question, yes, I'm afraid that something has happened to them. Can you start right away?"

Bert replied, "It's still early this morning, so I think we can get on the road this afternoon. We should be at Haxtun around noon tomorrow, June 21st. Can you meet me there and take me to your brother's home? Does he live right there in town?"

"No, they live about ten miles south of town, in the country," Tom said. "Let's meet at the Bar Lo café on highway six and South Colorado Avenue. I'll be driving in from Sterling, where I live."

"I assume you'll be able to let us in to look around their home and property?" said Bert. "I will need to go through the home and the outbuildings, though I'm guessing the police did that as well."

"Yes, they did and for sure I can get you access. My brother and I did keep a key to each other's house, just in case," Tom said. "I will see you there tomorrow unless I hear differently. Drive safely." With that, Tom hung up.

Bert turned off the speaker on his phone, turned off the phone, and looked inquisitively at his wife. "Well, you might be right. This feels a lot like the Kansas case. What do you think?"

Norah nodded in agreement. "I have a feeling that they're connected, somehow. Maybe a call back to Myrtle in Kansas would be in order. Perhaps there's some relationship to these folks in Colorado."

Bert thought that would be a good place to start before he began to pack up the car. He picked up his phone and dialed Myrtle Kennedy.

Fifteen minutes later, he reported to Norah. "Well, Babe, if there's any connection, it isn't obvious so far. Myrtle didn't even know where Haxtun was, and was sure none of her immediate family had any associations there. Right now, we seem to have a mystery on our hands. Unless the police decide to take it seriously, I guess it's up to us to figure it out. Maybe this is just an unrelated case. Maybe these folks really are just on a quiet vacation."

By noon, Bert had their Dodge packed up, Missy's area at the ready, and had given Missy a twenty-minute run through the woods and rocky hillsides north of their house. He opened the lift gate on the rear of the vehicle and called to his coywolf to hop in. Bert climbed into the driver's seat and nodded to Norah where she was settled in the passenger seat.

"Spock is at the ready, Captain. May I suggest 50 per cent of warp speed. To a man in Wyoming, that means put the pedal to the metal, Babe, before someone runs over your ass." They both got a good laugh at her sense of humor.

They headed south to meet up with the Yellowstone Highway, and then past Cody and retracing their familiar route to the south and east. They entered Interstate 25 at Casper and proceeded south through the rolling Wyoming ranch country until reaching Wheatland, where they found a privately-owned motel. Bert took Missy out under the starlit sky for a relief walk. It was chilly with a light wind and Bert only wore a T-shirt without a jacket. He wondered if the chill on his arms and the shiver down his back was from the cold air or the case they were about to work. They returned to the motel and communed with Norah for a bit before putting in for the night.

As he turned out the light and pulled up the light covers, Bert spoke to Norah in the darkness. "Good night, my dear wife. I love you, Honey. Forever."

"Good night, Bert. You've always been my rock as well as my love," she said. "I'll always be with you as long as you're with me. I'll see you in the morning."

Next morning, they were back on the interstate well before the sun crept over the hills and valleys to the east. As they drove south, the sunlight began to light up the distant peaks of the Medicine Bow Mountain range, to the southwest. When they arrived in Cheyenne, Bert decided to go east on Interstate 80 until cutting south at Sidney, Nebraska, into eastern Colorado and on to Haxtun. This was Great Plains cattle country, so he always found the hills, valleys, plateaus, and arroyos interesting. They'd be able to glimpse Chimney Rock at times, too. It was common to see an occasional antelope, deer, coyote, or even a prairie dog town.

Haxtun was a small town of less than 1000 people, located on the high plains east of the Rockies. It covered about half a square mile and boasted an unemployment rate of less than two percent. The predominantly white population was mostly engaged in the various aspects of the agricultural industry, in which Haxtun was situated.

They pulled into Haxtun just after noon, and soon located the Bar Lo café. They had barely parked the SUV, when a tall, lanky man, with greying dark hair, looking to be in his sixties, walked quickly up to Bert's door. This distinguished, yet very country, man extended his hand. Bert shook hands and made the usual introductions. Tom Davenport asked him if they'd like to grab a burger before driving to his brother's place.

Bert thanked Tom but declined the offer to eat. He always packed a cooler for these trips, both to save time and money, and to eat how he wanted. "I'd rather just get on out to your brother's house and get started," Bert said, "Time might be of the essence here. Better to get the ball rolling."

Bert followed Tom Davenport's late model Chevy truck south out of Haxtun on south Washington Avenue. He noted the dry looking, generally flat, grassland and farmland as they drove about twelve miles out of town, then turned west on a short dirt driveway about two hundred yards to a two-story farmhouse. He got out of his vehicle, leaving Norah and Missy inside, while he strode over to talk with Tom.

"Is the place just as it was since your brother came up missing?" Bert asked as he surveyed the front door and near-side windows of the house, looking for any signs of forced entry.

"Yes," replied Tom. "Nothing has been altered and it looks just as it did when we first arrived here about a week ago. Neither the police nor I have been able to find any evidence of a forced entry or burglary. Their truck, a 2015 green Chevy Silverado, is gone, also. I think a suitcase may be missing as well, though I'm not sure about that. They could have sold or given it away."

Bert asked, "Did the police try to locate your brother's cell phones? Have you or anyone in the family heard from them?"

"No," replied Tom, "they both have cell phones, but to my knowledge nobody has been able to contact them. The police can't ping them. Their phones appear to be turned off."

"Hmmm," Bert said. "That does seem suspicious. Well, can you show me around inside the house. Would it be okay if I let my tracking animal, a very friendly female coywolf named Missy, out to roam around?"

"No problem with that as far as I know," said Tom. "I don't think there are any small animals around here now." He had no idea what a coywolf was, and he didn't care right now.

As Bert opened the back door for Missy, he softly said to Norah, "I'll be going through the house, Babe, go ahead and do your thing. I'll see you back in the car."

Norah nodded, and Bert hurried to the open door of the house. He followed Tom's lead inside and began a tour of the two-story home for familiarization. As he headed upstairs, Bert glanced at the open front door and saw Norah peering inside, and then she turned and proceeded out into the yard. He continued his tour with Tom, ever vigilant for anything that seemed to be out of order. He could see nothing that looked to be out of place, no scuff marks, footprints, or items that seemed suspect. The dining room table looked as if it was set up for a coming dinner, with two places set. A few clean looking dishes were on the counter along with a newspaper and some change. All windows and doors appeared to be secure. All in all, the house just looked normal; nothing seemed suspicious.

"Would you show me around the outside, please?" Bert asked.

Bert followed Tom through the detached two-car garage and shop. It looked like a neater-than-usual handyman's work area and garage, otherwise, there didn't seem to be anything to grab his attention. Bert did make a mental note of an empty gas can sitting on a shelf near the back corner. A four-door sedan was parked in the far side of the garage area, and an empty parking space, apparently for the missing truck, was nearer to the house. He said, "Was the garage door open, or closed, when you first came here?"

"It was closed and locked, same as the house," replied Tom. "Everything just looked as if they went out for groceries and never came back."

"Tom, do you mind if I just wander around on my own for a bit? I'd like to just take everything in, make notes, and let it sink in. Maybe something will jump out at me tonight, if not now," Bert said, as he took out his note pad.

Tom nodded approval. "Go ahead, I'm going to just sit in the house and watch TV. Maybe that will give my brain a rest for a few minutes."

Bert strolled on around the shop and met up with Norah, as Tom walked back to the house and went inside. "Anything coming through to you, Norah?" he asked.

"Amish," she said.

"Amish?" Bert asked. "What do you mean by that, Dear?"

Norah seemed bewildered. "I wish I knew. I just see a shadowy man wearing dark or black clothes and a wide, flat-brimmed hat. The way the Amish often dress. I can't see his face clearly. I think he's a white man, though."

"Hmmm," Bert muttered back to her. "What could that mean, I wonder? Anything else, sweetheart?"

"I think I'm seeing someone's hands, and they seem to be tied in some way." She closed her eyes and seemed to be looking over the distant farmland to the north. She suddenly flinched, as if stung by some insect. "Oh my God, in my mind I just heard a sharp but somewhat muffled sound. I think it was a gunshot. I smell gun powder. It's pungent."

"Do you think these folks were shot, Norah?" Bert asked.

Norah looked again to the north, as if the answers she sought were there. "I think so, Bert. I can't say for sure, though. I'm not seeing that, it's just a feeling I'm getting. I'm sensing death. I think they're dead."

"Is that all you're getting at this time?" he asked.

"Maybe," she replied. "This doesn't make sense at all, but I'm seeing flashes of a Bible. Something about money is here again. I'm seeing change."

"Would that be the nickel and dimes we saw at the Kansas house?" Bert asked.

She falteringly replied, "Yes. No. Maybe? Similar, but doesn't seem to be the same."

"How does it seem to be different?" he asked.

She thought a minute, and then added, "I don't see a nickel, only dimes."

Norah's visions seemed to taper off and she could sense nothing else right now. Bert knew she must be at a standstill. He suggested that she go back to their vehicle and relax, while he went back to the house and talked with their client a few more minutes. She agreed and moved toward the SUV while he walked to the house.

"Hi Tom," Bert said, as he entered the front door and walked toward the living room where Tom was watching the news. "I'm not finding any clues outside so far, so wanted to ask you a couple more questions before we head to a motel and sleep on all this. Can you tell me about the surrounding area?"

"Not much to tell," Tom said, "just farm and ranch land in every direction for quite a few miles. We grew up in the country and my brother always wanted a small farm like this one. He seemed to love this place and the community."

"What's to the north?" Bert asked. "Just mostly farmland? That's all I remember seeing as we drove here."

Tom answered, "Yeah, farms pretty much all the way back to Haxtun. Mostly a square mile or less, what we call sections, half sections, quarter sections, and so forth."

"This is arid country, are they mostly irrigated by wells, pivot systems, and the like," Bert asked.

"Yes, you're right. There are several private wells, and there is also a rural water district with water lines to many area farms. You may have noticed the water tower west of the road about five miles before we got here?"

Bert nodded. He had forgotten about the tower but now remembered seeing it. "Are there any mines, ditches, canyons, landfills, and stuff like that?"

"Nope," said Tom, "the only features other than the farms themselves are the dirt roads that connect to houses and wells. There are a few trees along some of these roads."

"Thanks for that info," Bert said. "On another note, did you happen to see any money left around inside the house?"

"No, I sure didn't see any," Tom replied. Then he hesitated a few seconds, and added, "On second thought, I think there were some coins left near the paper on the kitchen counter. Change left from buying the paper, I'd guess."

Bert remembered seeing the change, also, and he made his way to the kitchen, and stopped at the counter. He studied the two dimes lying together near the newspaper but close to the edge of the counter. Was it a coincidence that they were touching edge to edge? He now remembered that the dimes and nickel at the Kansas house were touching edges, also. Was this somehow what connected these two cases? That didn't make sense, and yet this coincidence seemed a bit unusual.

"Tom, I think we're going to head to a motel," Bert said. "It's been a long two days and we need to get a good sleep and think about this case. Missy needs some time to run around and get some exercise, too. Her nose is often a key resource, and it's worth the time to take care of her. I think we're going to drive around the local area in the morning and get a feel for the lay of the land. Maybe there's a clue near a road. While we're doing that, would you go to the County Seat and look over any public records pertaining to your brother and this property, please. Probably nothing to that, but it might help to check it out. Do you think we can meet up with you around three in the afternoon and compare notes?"

Tom quickly replied, "Sure, let's meet back at the same restaurant in Haxtun tomorrow. We can have a late lunch and see where we go from there."

Nodding in agreement and with a quick and firm handshake, Bert walked rapidly back to his vehicle. Once inside with Missy he explained the plan to Norah. He turned the vehicle around and proceeded east on the driveway. Tom was a bit behind him, having taken time to ensure that the house was securely locked up.

Settled into a local motel in Haxtun, Bert walked and fed Missy.

After a dinner of assorted meat and fruits from the cooler, and his homemade fruit smoothie that he had whipped up back at Cody, Bert settled back in a chair. He rested his bare feet near Norah where she leaned back on the bed. "Well, Honey, if it wasn't for your visions, we'd have almost nothing to go on here. What do you think? Any other visions since we left the house?"

Norah touched her fingers together and placed her hands thoughtfully against her chin and mouth. "I continue to glimpse the shadow figure man with the hat. I'm getting fleeting glances of an old building or house and it looks unlived in. I still have the feeling that they aren't far away, and they're dead."

"Boy, that's ominous." Bert said. "Let's review what we think we know or suspect, so far. For one, these folks appear to really be missing under foul play, and we have your visions to suspect that they're dead. Two, your visions make us think they are somewhere in the local area. Three, a man, possibly of an Amish background, seems to be involved somehow. Four, in whatever manner these folks were abducted, there was apparently no struggle and no clues were left. This guy somehow approached them without alarming them. Five, the truck is gone, and hasn't been found despite the missing person report which Tom filed several days ago. Six, there seems to be a possible connection to the Kansas case: two dimes. That is only because of your visions. Without them, this wouldn't even be noticed. This seems like a long shot and a likely unrelated weak coincidence. However, why are you seeing it?"

"You know," she said, "We should share this with the local police department."

"In a perfect world, I would agree, Sweetheart," Bert answered.

"If you think about the reality of our business, though, we just have to be careful about sharing with them. Police generally don't have a lot of respect for private investigators, often with good reason. Also, what do we really have to go on? Almost exclusively, we only have the visions and feelings of a psychic. The use of psychics is still in its infancy, where most cops are concerned. They aren't going to give it much if any credence, Babe. We have the same situation as with most of our cases we've worked. If we tell them very much, and certainly if we disclose our methods, guess who becomes a prime suspect. We do! For now, we have no choice but to keep our methods between us and our clients. Even so, the word is sure to get out eventually, and we'll either be the good guys or the suspects."

She nodded in acknowledgment. "Yes, I know," she sighed. "It's just too bad that we are on our own when we could sure use their help. I guess we should be thankful. If it was different, our clients wouldn't be coming to us. They'd be working with the police."

"Speaking of help, I need to make a quick call to Tom and ask for some article of clothing from his brother, so Missy has a scent to go on. Pictures of the brother and his wife would be good, too. We can meet at the restaurant in the morning and get these items from him before we go our separate ways." Bert picked up the phone and spoke with Tom quickly.

With that, they both yielded to the fatigue that was setting in. Bert climbed into bed near Norah and turned out the light. Missy rolled onto her side near the window, yawned, and closed her eyes. Her invisible grass bed was prepared for the night. The room was secure.

He could sense Norah's presence in the darkness. Even in sleep, it felt good to know that she was close. "Sweet dreams, my dear Sweetheart," he said.

"Good night Captain; Spock's going out." She softly chuckled in the darkness and snuggled closer to him.

CHAPTER SEVEN: MAKING SENSE OF SCENT

The next morning, Bert, Norah, and Missy pulled into the Haxtun restaurant parking lot, about 9:00. Tom was already there, an early riser apparently. He had returned from his brother's house with their favorite caps and a picture of both. The caps would provide the scent for Missy, should she be needed to find the missing couple. After a quick greeting and good-bye, they departed on their separate missions.

The sun was well above the horizon on what looked to be a clear, warm, and sunny day in eastern Colorado. A roadrunner bird raced across the highway as Bert was accelerating, stocky neck and bill stretched in front, his long tail straight behind, and his brown and white plumage flashing in the sunlight. A hawk sat on the branch of a dead tree in the nearby pasture, surveying the territory for a vermin meal.

Bert slowly drove out of town and proceeded down the road toward James and Sarah Davenport's farm. Norah sat quietly in the passenger seat, just allowing any psychic inputs to come to her. Missy had her head out the half-opened, right-side passenger window, ears laid back, mouth open, tongue out, looking for anything interesting and enjoying the wind in her face.

"I wish I was getting definite answers for us," she said. "I continue to catch fleeting glimpses of the Amish guy, but I can't make out his face and I have no idea of his connection to this case, if any. I keep seeing an old house, run down and overgrown."

"While we're slowly driving south here, I'm going to call Myrtle Kennedy and see if they've found out anything more about the case there," Bert replied.

He contacted Myrtle and asked if the police had shared any more leads in the deaths of her parents.

She replied, "Yes, they have a lead, though it's rather confusing so far. Dad's truck was located at the Walmart in St. Jo. The surveillance cameras where the truck was dumped caught a lone driver, who was dark skinned. He might be either a black man or a Hispanic, but he wore a wide-brimmed hat when he got out of the vehicle and they never did get a good look at his face. All they know is that he is well built and large, about six feet tall. Inside, the cameras show that he went into the front bathroom, but they could not pick him up after that. Kind of confusing."

"That's strange," said Bert. "Is it possible that he may have changed clothes inside the bathroom? There's usually only one way in and out, I think."

"Yes, that's what the police speculate, also," Myrtle replied. "The question is why and how would he do that?"

"We'll have to ponder that and hopefully that answer will become clear in time." With that, Bert said goodbye and asked Myrtle to keep him apprised of any other developments.

Bert shared the new information with Norah, and then they drove silently south. They passed the turn to James Davenport's house without stopping. As they surveyed both sides of the two-lane road, Norah broke the silence.

"Sweetheart, the only thing I can conclude right now, is that the killer of Myrtle's parents must be very cunning. For one thing, he was able to get inside their home, apparently, and abduct them without a ruckus. So far, at least, there's no evidence of a robbery and even the vehicle was abandoned. Wallet and purse have not been found, so some things might have been stolen from them. I'm sure that any credit cards have been flagged for activity. Since none has occurred, they must not have been used. The same with the cell phones, which are still missing and not operating."

"You're right, Honey," Bert replied. "Why was the pickup taken and later dumped miles away where it was likely to go undiscovered for a while? Was that a ruse?"

"What if that was a delaying tactic," said Norah. "Maybe that was intended to buy time so he could be miles away before any concern was raised? If so, it worked, because it was over a week later before anyone began to get suspicious and concerned about where the parents were."

"Hmmm, you are onto something, my dear," pondered Bert. "Then maybe this guy used the surveillance system at Walmart as part of his ruse, also? Did he completely change his clothing in the bathroom, or change into makeup, knowing that he was not likely to be discovered leaving the store? If so, that first set of clothes are likely in a landfill somewhere."

She thought about that for a minute. "Do you think we have the same thing going on here, Bert?"

"Norah, my dear, I wish I knew. While there are similarities, there's no hard evidence of a connection between these two. We just stumbled into two seemingly similar cases by a fluke. Both sets of relatives happened to check out our website and saw that we specialize in missing persons. That may be the only connection?"

With that, they drove silently, taking in the landscape and the area on both sides of the road as they approached County Road 54. They had seen only one old farmhouse that sat about a hundred yards off the east side of the road. No other old or seemingly abandoned houses. Norah said it just didn't feel like the one she glimpsed in her visions. They decided to pause on the old drive to that house, anyway, since Missy was whining and stirring around. She obviously needed a break.

"Out, Missy," directed Bert to his coywolf companion. She gleefully bounded out of the car and quickly found a good spot for a pee. Just for the heck of it, Bert gave her both caps to smell and ordered "Missy, find." She immediately began her usual search pattern, a rough semi-circle back and forth toward the house.

At the abandoned house, the hybrid coyote and now loyal companion sniffed her way entirely around the junk and vegetation which were invading this deteriorating building. There were no signs that she had picked up on the scent from either cap. She meandered her way back toward Bert, then came trotting to him when he called her. She sat for her meaty treat. When released, she quickly found a place to lie and chew.

They drove back north on highway 59 toward Haxtun, continuing to surveil the countryside for any old buildings. They did not find any more before reaching Haxtun. Bert decided to go east on Colorado highway 6 and just east of town he pulled onto the road to the airport and stopped at a convenient place to pull off. He let Missy out to search the various gopher mounds and grass clumps, keeping her close with his voice commands.

They continued east to Paoli, stopping a couple times to let Missy check out old abandoned houses. Nothing!

"Norah, Sweetheart, are you picking up on anything?" he asked.

"Nothing new, but I have the feeling that we're getting farther from them, Bert. There is something, maybe, though it still makes no sense to me. For just brief periods, I see the number 42 again. No idea what it means."

"Honey, you deserve a big hug. I know you're trying to get a handle on this one. You'll get it soon; I have faith in you."

She smiled and nodded. "I'd love to make love to you tonight, Captain Kirk."

He looked at her with eyes twinkling and a grin. "I'd love that as well, Mrs. Spock."

For now, though, they had work to do. He fired up his laptop, and checked several of his favorite websites, looking for abandoned or found vehicles and checking missing person reports. He found nothing relevant. He called Tom Davenport.

"Hi Tom, Bert here, have you found anything of note in the court records?"

"Nothing that seems significant, Bert," Tom answered. "How about you?"

"Nothing has yet materialized, though we are assimilating several psychic inputs," Bert replied. "We've been checking the local area and letting Missy out in a couple of possible places, but no luck. Tom, since the local police will work with you but usually not much with a private investigator, I'd like to suggest that you check with them for updates. Ask them if they've thought to check out abandoned houses in the area. My psychic is seeing such a place."

I'll call the Sheriff's department right now," said Tom.

Following the brief talk with Tom, Bert turned the vehicle around and headed back up Highway 6 toward Haxtun. They continued west on highway 6 from Haxtun to Fleming, pausing at three more abandoned farmhouses along the way. With each stop, they let Missy again smell the caps and do her search for the scent. Every time, she returned without alerting on anything. By now it was getting late and the sun was approaching the western horizon, with darkness soon to follow. "Let's go back to the motel, Sweetheart," Bert said. "It's getting late and we can do some brainstorming and make a few more calls back there. I think Missy is ready to eat, and so am I."

That evening, after another meal from the cooler and with Missy fed, watered, and given a good half hour walk, Bert leaned back in the hotel couch and made his two planned calls.

He first called Tom Davenport and they discussed and brainstormed on the case. "Tom, we've not found any concrete evidence so far to draw hard conclusions about the whereabouts of your brother and his wife. What we do have to go on are strong psychic inputs, which lead us to think that an Amish guy, or a guy dressed like the Amish, may be involved in some way. Also, we suspect that an old abandoned and overgrown house or building may be in play somehow. We have checked such buildings both north and south of your brother's place, and east and west on highway 6 from Haxtun to the adjacent towns. Our tracking animal has had no hits so far."

Bert wasn't surprised by Tom's inability to fully understand any of that.

"Can you think of any significance to the twenty cents left on the kitchen counter, or to the number 42?" Bert wanted to know.

Tom finally answered, "No, not a thing. What could either possibly have to do with my brother's disappearance?"

Bert understood Tom's bewilderment. He told Tom, "I don't know the answers yet, either, but my psychic keeps seeing two dimes and the number 42 pops up now and then. She doesn't know what to make of them, yet. They may mean nothing, what she calls psychic noise, or we will eventually find some meaning to one or both. To talk about your previous question, though, that's also complicated. This guy seems to be slicker than snot on a doorknob, as my Dad would love to say."

Bert got a kick out of Tom's reaction to that remark. Their laughter helped break the tension a little. He was both tickled and repulsed when Tom said that his brother used to delight in leaving a nostril surprise on the knob to their childhood bedroom. He had to restrain the impulse to gag as Tom described the memory. Bert laughed at Tom but kept seeing his own hand with someone else's snot on it.

"I thought that was just a sick expression. I didn't know anyone actually did that," Bert laughed. "Anyway, whoever abducted your brother and his wife did so without alarming them, at least at first. He probably escorted them from the house at gunpoint to their truck and, with their hands bound, drove them from the farm. So far, there is no evidence that this guy had any help, although it is a distinct possibility, given the logistics of abducting a couple. Especially if he acted alone, it is not likely that he would want the risk of driving a significant distance and for a lengthy period, having to keep two people under control. For that reason, I'm sorry to say that I don't think he went very far with them."

Tom let that sink in. "What are you saying, Bert?"

"My psychic has seen visions that make us fear for their lives. We're working on finding them but brace yourself for the possibility that they may not be alive, Tom."

Bert wasn't surprised when Tom replied that he had already accepted that possibility. Tom said that he could read the signs and asked what he could do to help with finding them?

"I need you to stay in close contact with the Sheriff's department, Tom. Let me know of anything they find out so we can operate with any and all possible information and cooperate where appropriate. In the meantime, I'm going to continue turning over all possible stones in trying to figure this out and find your brother. I think this guy set up this abduction in such a way as to create doubt and to delay any serious investigation. By taking them from the house, apparently unharmed, he minimized the chance of leaving evidence. By taking the truck with them, he made it look like they just left for a private getaway, creating doubt and delay in looking for them. Since there is no sign of robbery or break-in, and no sign of the truck still, this leads to further doubt about whether there is even a crime here."

He could see Tom thinking about that for a minute as he looked away toward the western horizon and shifted his feet. When Tom looked back at Bert, he agreed with the assessment. He admitted that both he and the sheriff's people were thrown off for several days. Tom felt that the police still weren't sure if there's a crime committed here.

"So, how's he hiding the truck then, Bert?" said Tom.

Bert was slow to reply. He stated that he thought there must be two people involved. It would be difficult for just one to take and hide the truck. His guess was that he or they left it in a large parking area somewhere, so it would blend in and not be noticed for several days. This would also lead to more delay in really investigating this case. A major question yet to be answered was motive. Was this purely random? Or, was there some reason that Tom's brother and wife were targeted? Bert told Tom that the plan for tomorrow was to begin to interview some of the neighbors and any friends that they could find and see if anyone could shed light on a possible motive or suspect.

With that, Bert said good-bye to Tom after again assuring him that they would do everything possible to find his brother.

Bert turned to his wife. "Norah," he said lovingly, "I don't know what I'd do without you. It's your gift that gives us the edge in finding these poor missing souls. I dearly love you and I'd hug you all day long if I could. I'm so sorry that you got sick and couldn't be as involved in our business as you wanted to be. Yet, Sweetheart, your involvement now may be even more critical than ever before."

Tears welled up in her eyes. "Bert, you've always been the love of my life. Sick or not, I will always be here for you as best I can. I hope you know that. You're my Captain."

Tears trickled down both his cheeks. "Norah, my love, I do know that. I also know that you are more special and important to me than you've ever been. I would be absolutely lost without you, Mrs. Spock!"

Bert suppressed a sob, cleared his throat, and picked up the phone to dial Myrtle Kennedy back in Kansas.

"Hello, Myrtle, Bert Lynnes here; just wanting to know if there have been any more developments with your parents' case?"

Myrtle answered in a frustrated voice, "No, not a damn thing. The police don't seem to have the slightest idea who may have killed them. No leads. I think you may be the only real hope we have of finding that out, Bert. I want you to know that we appreciate you very much."

"Thanks; I'm sure sorry about all that, Myrtle," he said, "but we'll just continue to do our best and work to bring something to light soon. It's too early to know, but the case I'm currently working on feels connected somehow. We don't yet know if so or how. Let's just keep in touch and see what develops. Please feel free to call me anytime if you feel the need. Take care of yourself, Myrtle. Say hello to your husband for me."

Bert put his phone down and turned back toward Norah, "Dear, you said you saw the numbers 35 and 42 in a vision during the Kansas case, right?"

She thought a few seconds, then answered, "Yes, Bert, it was during that case. I never could make anything of them, though. Still can't make anything of them."

"Didn't you tell me that you saw the number 42 in a quick vision shortly after we started working on this Colorado case?" he asked.

"Oh, yes, you're right, Sweetheart," she replied. "That's possibly a clue that these cases are related in some way. Maybe the same guy is involved in both? But why, though? What could be his motive?"

"I wish I knew," he answered her. "Another possible clue is the coins. While different, you saw coins in a vision at both locations and there were in fact coins at both. We could never make a court case with either of these, yet your number and coin visions seem to be tying these cases together. Tomorrow, I think we should start with interviews of next-door neighbors and follow leads to other friends. See what comes out of that."

"I agree with that," replied Norah. "I continue to sense that this couple are not far from here, and I keep seeing the Amish guy and an old dilapidated house. Yesterday and again today I heard what sounded like a muffled gunshot. Today I noticed a sharp pain in my throat and the taste of blood in my mouth. I could smell gunpowder. I'm afraid they're dead, Honey."

Bert turned out the light and leaned back into his pillow. In the darkness, he felt sorry that his wife had to endure such seemingly tragic visions, so incomplete that she had a hard time making sense of them. It must take quite an emotional toll on her, he thought. He wished things were different right now. He would love to make love with her. He reached toward her and drifted off to sleep.

* * *

The next day was sunny and warm. It was nearly 80 degrees when they left the motel around 8:00 and headed south to hopefully hook up with the neighbors.

The neighboring farm to the north appeared to be small, maybe even a hobby type operation. However, the middle-aged couple were friendly. They invited Bert into their house and seemed very willing to help. He politely declined the invitation, and they talked in the shade of a large tree in the well-manicured yard. It was soon obvious that they knew the Davenports but didn't have a close relationship with them, just a casual neighborly one. They had not seen anything that aroused their suspicion and couldn't shed any light on the disappearance. Bert had asked their permission to let Missy roam around while they talked. They didn't see him present the victims' caps to her and order her to "Find", before she jumped out of the vehicle. As far as they knew, she was just wandering around their place. Missy returned without a find and ready for a treat. Bert thanked them and headed on down the road to the next neighbor.

"Nothing there of value," he said to Norah. "Hopefully this next one will be more fruitful."

Norah was quiet as they drove up to the farmhouse to the south of the Davenports' place. She didn't talk much when she was reading the tea leaves, as her husband loved to say. She observed the larger and more productive farm than the previous one. It didn't feel sinister to her.

Bert walked to the door of the house but was intercepted by the call of a man coming from the shop. He turned and walked out to greet this seemingly friendly but inquisitive fellow, an older man but very athletic looking. After introductions, Bert again asked if he could let his "dog" out of the SUV for a stroll. It only took one look for this country man to see that this was no ordinary dog. For the next ten minutes, Bert told him the history of Missy and how she came to be with him. All the while, Missy conducted her search of the place, around the outbuildings and house, oblivious to the owner but under the watchful eye of Bert. He could tell she wasn't finding anything.

"Can I ask when you last saw the Davenports?" Bert inquired.

"Oh, my gosh," the neighbor replied. "I think it was around two weeks ago that I saw their truck leaving one evening just about supper time. I was just going inside to eat and saw the truck leaving."

"Did you see anyone else?" Bert asked. "Or notice anything out of the ordinary?"

"No, I didn't see anyone else or anything that would make me feel suspicious," the man said. "I just assumed they were going to town to eat."

Bert had another thought. "Do you know what day of the week this was?"

The neighbor thought for almost a minute before finally replying. "I think it was early in the week, maybe a Monday or Tuesday. I wouldn't normally be coming inside at that time on a weekend."

After inquiring about any friends, the Davenports may have, Bert thanked the old fellow and called Missy back to the car for her working treat. As they headed back north toward Haxtun and the first name the old farmer had given him, Bert had a question suddenly hit him.

"Norah, do you remember when you first were telling me about your visions and sensations around the Davenports' place. Do you remember where you were mostly looking, what direction, and do you know why?"

She thought for a while about that. "Well, I do remember a sense of being drawn in a certain direction, north, I think. I don't really know why, but I felt a pull almost."

"That's what I just remembered now, too. I asked you a couple of questions about any visions you might be having, and each time you seemed to sort of look toward the north as if you were reflectively thinking in that direction. Babe let me ask you something. If you wanted to hide a body where it wouldn't likely be found for a while, would you hide it near their home area, or would you take it farther away where fewer people are likely to know the person?"

She didn't hesitate. "I would take it farther away where they are probably less well known."

"As I study the map," Bert went on, "I see a main road leading north out of Haxtun on the opposite side from down here. It is also a way to get up to the Interstate highways, if the perp was hoping to get far away quickly. I'm thinking we should look north of Haxtun. What do you think?"

Norah pondered this for just a few seconds. "Yes, I think that makes sense. Bert, it feels to me as if the dead may be reaching out to me; trying to pull me toward them. Maybe their spirits are calling out to anyone who can hear them to find them."

As they arrived in Haxtun, they used GPS to locate the residence of a friend reported by the second neighboring farmer. The friend was at work, but his wife, appearing to be around 60 years old, met him at the door and said she also knew the Davenports.

"Ma'am, can I ask when you last saw James and Sarah Davenport?" Bert said.

She replied quickly, "Oh, for sure. We saw them at the opening game of the Haxtun town baseball team several weeks back; on a Friday evening. They have a grandson who is out of high school and just started playing for the town team. Sports are big around here. Almost everyone follows the local teams. We sat next to the Davenports and had a couple hot dogs with them. There was nothing out of the ordinary, though."

Bert thanked her, once he was sure there was no additional information to be gained, and they got back on the road to the far side of Haxtun. He located Colorado highway 59 and they proceeded north.

This stretch of two-lane road proceeded through open farm country to the north, jogging east then back north a couple of times. They noticed several old rundown houses, reminiscent of someone's past broken dreams. Bert stopped at each and let Missy out with her search instructions. At the first two, she returned with nothing except the pleased look of a canine happy to be out of the vehicle and run around a bit until receiving a treat. When they turned to the north at the second jog in the highway, though, something was different.

He saw that Norah was the first to react. She sat forward and closed her eyes, intently looking within for that which might be without. "Bert, I'm getting a blast of sensations when we drove up here. It's like everything I told you last night is hitting me at once. In addition, I hear a woman crying. This is close to them, Honey."

Missy was acting nervously in the back of the SUV, too, whining, turning around, and pacing between the open windows on both sides of the vehicle. It was as if she knew something was coming. An old farmhouse came into view to the west of the road.

Bert pulled into the rundown and grassed-over driveway leading to this deteriorating and collapsing farmstead. He quickly opened the back and ordered Missy on her search. She bounded out excitedly, and then ran back and forth near their car, going up the driveway a few feet, and then returning. He could tell she was picking up something, but was it the victims' scent? She seemed to have no interest in the rundown house. Puzzled and perplexed, he reluctantly called her back into the car and closed the lift gate. He surveyed the location. Another, obviously occupied, farmhouse was about a quarter mile away. This old building was literally about to fall, and much of it had already collapsed. Did the perp pull up here with the victims, and then decide against it? If so, was there another better choice up the road?

"Norah, what do you think? Do we continue up the road, or do we go somewhere else? What are your senses and spirit guides telling you?"

"Sweetheart," she replied, "I feel that we're on the right track and should keep going north. My sensations are still coming in bits and pieces, but I have the growing feeling that we're close to James and Sarah."

They proceeded up the highway to the north, in the direction of two interstate highways. After about five miles, Norah again leaned forward. Her expression let Bert know that she was feeling and seeing more now. She had her eyes closed as she spoke to him. "We're close, Bert, I can feel it. I can feel their last moments. I'm feeling their fear. I feel a knife at her throat." Tears flowed down her cheeks.

To the east, about two hundred yards, emerged a tree line and next to it a seldom-used dirt road leading to another abandoned but standing house. What was probably once a pretty yard was now overgrown with wild roses, mixed-growth cottonwoods, and tall grasses. The farms seemed larger here and the closest farmhouse looked to be about half a mile away to the northwest. He pulled a hundred feet up the old driveway, avoiding the ruts, and stopped.

Missy was anxiously awaiting the opening of the lift gate, and he had to order her to stay until he could again present her with the caps and direct her to find. She bounded out of the back compartment and hit the ground with her nose down, sniffing determinedly as she meandered at a trot back and forth across the driveway. She seemed to be picking up a very old and faint scent that drew her closer and closer to the house. Bert reached into his Sneaky Pete holster and pulled out his 40-caliber Ruger semi-auto, put his thumb above the safety, and held it to his right side as he cautiously approached the structure. He felt his breathing quickening and a chill went down his spine. He forced himself to breath slowly and deeply.

When Missy was about 50 feet from the house, her head came up, she stopped and sniffed at the air, and then she bolted straight to the right side of the house and around behind it. Bert heard her excited bark, which told him instantly that she found something. He motioned for Norah to remain near their vehicle. He instinctively knew she didn't need to see what he knew he was going to find.

Missy sat on her haunches behind the old house, her tongue panting from excitement, looking at the two deteriorating bodies lying near the back wall. "James and Sarah, we've finally found you," Bert sadly whispered.

* * *

Three hours later, they were still sitting in the driveway. Bert was talking in a low tone with Tom Davenport in Tom's truck. Three police cars and an ambulance sat around them with lights flashing. Bert had given a statement to the police. He just said that he stopped to let his dog out to take a pee break, and the animal went to the back of the house, where he found the victims. Bert knew from the numerous questions that the cops were not one hundred per cent convinced how he came to be there. After talking with Tom and getting all contact information, though, they were satisfied enough to let them leave. Norah had remained in their SUV, watching everything through the dark tinted windows. She was drained emotionally and just wanted Bert to deal with the police. Channeling the last moments of the dead was stressful for her. She wasn't just an observer. She was stepping into the shoes of the victim.

Bert turned to Tom. "Please keep in touch and tell me if you hear of any information about the killer. This case will not be complete until the person responsible for this is facing judgment. So far, we have no motive. We suspect but don't yet know if this guy has an accomplice, and we don't know if he is done or just getting started. The police will be trying to determine all this also. So, if you stay in touch with them and keep me updated; it might help me to be of some help, too. I will tell you, Tom, that there is a lot of similarity with a Kansas case we worked recently. I don't know if that's just a coincidence, or if the same killers are involved in both. The answer to that will become clear in time."

With that, Bert said good-bye, got back in his SUV after putting Missy in the back, and they drove on north toward Interstates 70 and 80. It would be a long drive home to Cody.

Norah looked at her husband as he drove, his mind obviously churning away on the case. "Bert, while I'm sorry for the Davenport family about their loss, yet I'm proud and glad that we were able to give them some closure by finding the bodies of their loved ones. If not for us, it very well could have been days, weeks, or even months before they might have been found. Now, if only there was some way for us to help bring the killer or killers to justice."

They drove along in silence for a long time. The rolling hills and pastures of cattle passed them without notice. Both were pondering this last question. Neither could see any way for that to happen. It would take highly unusual circumstances for them to be further involved in the hunt for this cold-blooded killer.

What they could not know then, was that there were highly unusual circumstances involved.

CHAPTER EIGHT: WORD OF MOUTH

Back at home outside of Cody, with the car unpacked, everything cleaned and put away, and Missy well run around their property, Bert relaxed in the living room of their cabin. Norah stood near the front picture window, staring across the North Fork Valley, leading to Yellowstone Park. They both loved this location, their home, and everything about the old-time cow town turned tourist town. This was a peaceful and serene place to live in the winter months when Yellowstone was inaccessible from the east. It was equally exciting and bustling during the summer tourist season. The throngs visiting Yellowstone were similarly enthralled with the Cody Night Rodeo, The Buffalo Bill Historical Center, the historic Irma Hotel, the Buffalo Bill Dam, and the myriad of western bars, saloons, guest houses, restaurants, and scenic drives.

Bert felt relaxed and peaceful for the first time in days. He leaned back in his easy chair and enjoyed the warm July sun streaming through the window, illuminating his beloved Norah. Nearly three weeks ago they had celebrated Independence Day, a big event in Cody. American flags adorned every street, corner, store, and truck around the town. He loved the values of this small country town, now doubled in size by the onslaught of tourists. Main street became a symphony of activity and street sounds as everything from travel buses, towed campers, sedans, and pickup trucks graced the ribbon of concrete and asphalt. Dogs, of all sizes and breeds, jumped excitedly from side to side in the boxes of many of the pickups. Their presence was not lost on Missy.

Missy enjoyed the walks around town, he knew, even though she didn't particularly like being on a leash. It was necessary, though, to her development within their business. Shortly, he would do their usual training regimen, also necessary to keep her sharp and obedient. Right now, he was sleepy. He was jolted awake from a brief nap by his ringing phone.

His greeting was answered by Myrtle Kennedy, calling from Kansas. He was pleasantly surprised to hear from her. He asked how she was holding up and if there were any new developments.

"No," she replied. "Nothing new here. They don't seem to be any closer to identifying that bastard than they were two weeks ago. I'm calling about something else, though. I'm active on Facebook and I've shared the story of my parents with my Facebook friends. I've mentioned your business and how you helped find Dad and Mom. Well, last night I got a call from one of those friends' friend from northern South Dakota; a small town called Selby. This lady's sister and husband have been missing for a couple of weeks now, and it sounds a lot like my parents' situation. They said they've hired a local private investigator from Aberdeen, quite a distance away, after the local police have drawn a blank. That investigator has not come up with anything and doesn't think he should keep the case. An honest guy, apparently. Anyway, this sister relayed by way of her friends an inquiry to me and wanted to know about you. So, I've answered her questions and she wanted me to ask if you'd call her if you think you could take her case?"

Bert didn't hesitate, "Sure, Myrtle, anything for you. If you think I should call her then I'll call her. What's her name and number?" He wrote both down in his journal.

Following a few more minutes of chat about how her family was doing, Bert hung up, briefed Norah on the circumstances of this new development as best he knew them and dialed the number. With Norah listening on the speaker with him, the phone rang three times.

A woman picked up after the third ring of her cell phone, "Hello, Toni Lamont here, may I help you?"

"Hello, Missus Lamont, this is Bert Lynnes of B and N investigations in Cody, Wyoming. Myrtle Kennedy relayed that you would like to speak to me about a situation you have up there."

She answered quickly, "Glad to meet you Mister Lynnes. I'm Toni. Yes, I heard about your handling of the case in Kansas, and I would like to have you help us with a missing person case here. My sister, Lizzie, and her husband, Jake Lofelle, are missing with virtually no clues. Three weeks now."

Bert could tell that she was struggling to keep her composure. Her voice sounded stressed and cracked at times. "Please just call me Bert, Toni. I'm glad to meet you. Can you tell me the situation and specifics?"

Toni drew a deep breath before answering. "About three weeks ago, we became concerned that we hadn't heard anything from my sister, Lizzie, or her husband, Jake. Lizzie and I talk at least a couple times a week, so when I couldn't reach her after nearly a week of trying, we went to their home and couldn't find any sign of either of them. Their car, a Honda SUV, was gone, but there were no indications of where they might be. We got the police involved right away, but they have literally nothing to go on except they're gone. Because the car is gone, they aren't convinced that these guys didn't just go on a private vacation. After a week of getting nowhere, I hired a PI out of Aberdeen to see what he could find. He became so perplexed after a week that he told me he wasn't sure he had the resources to continue the case unless more leads developed. That's when a friend told me she heard of you through Facebook connections."

"How old is your sister, Toni?" Bert asked.

Toni answered, "She's 54, two years older than me. Her birthday is next month. Jake is a couple years older than her. Their two kids are grown, married, and live out of state."

Bert then asked. "Have you been through their house? Anything that seemed questionable? Money lying around, signs of forced entry, et cetera?"

"We didn't see anything at all that was suspicious or unusual." She replied. "Their phones were gone also. Nobody has been in contact with them, though. It's as if they're turned off. The police are monitoring their credit cards, and nothing on those. Bert, we live in a rural farm and ranch community. Things like this just don't happen around here."

Bert looked at Norah, saw her nod of approval, and came back to Toni. "Toni, we'll take your case. This is our specialty, so hopefully we can help. It's Monday now. We can leave in the morning and be there by night. Can you and your husband, I didn't catch his name, meet us in Selby about 8:00 Wednesday morning and lead us to their home? Do they live right there in town?"

"They have a small farm about eight miles north of Selby," she answered. "My husband is Troy."

This was beginning to sound familiar. "Then we'll meet you at 8:00 Wednesday morning in Selby. I'll call you Tuesday evening to arrange the meeting place. In the meantime, please think about anything which might be even remotely significant. Also bring a personal item of both Lizzie and Jake; something they used regularly so my tracking canine has a scent to follow. Please don't disturb anything around their property. Leave it as close as possible to how you found it. Take care of yourselves. We'll work together and try to find them."

Toni was crying as she managed a thank you and hung up.

Bert looked across the table at his wife. "Norah, this is sounding too familiar and it seems to have a similar M.O. with Kansas and Colorado, yet there's no hard evidence that they're connected. All we have is circumstantial and could just be coincidence. Even if we take this theory to the police up there, I'm afraid they'll see us as the only commonality between these three cases. For some reason, we're getting drawn into what feels like a serial killing spree, without the hard evidence to back it up. I think we just must treat this as a separate case and see what develops. Are you getting any inputs about this?"

"I do agree with you about not going to the police," she said. "I'm sensing that there's a connection between the previous deaths and now this missing couple, though. The one concrete thing I'm seeing is a nickel and dime. Other than that, the unexplained 35 and 42 flashed across my mind as you were talking with Toni. I wish I had some inkling what any of these things mean."

He pondered her words. "Well, then I guess it's time to get packed up and ready to go early in the morning. You seem to be right; we're going to be doing a lot of traveling!"

Tuesday morning, July 25th, 2017, dawned with a windy chill, typical of even a summer morning in this part of Wyoming. It would get into the 80 to 90-degree range later in the day; also, typical. With Missy packed up excitedly in the cargo area and Norah comfortably in the passenger seat, they headed south to connect again with the Yellowstone Highway and on to Cody and points east.

Entering Cody, they soon passed the world-renowned Buffalo Bill Historical Center, one of the main attractions. Bert remembered the Native American pow wow that he and Norah attended a couple years earlier at the center. It was fantastic and fit in nicely with his interest in the American Indian cultures. While there were numerous world class exhibits inside, his favorite, even over the firearms museum, was that of the Plains Indian. With its interactive light and audio productions, it was a realistic look back in time to a culture and people whom Bert had the utmost respect for. He was anxious to make another visit to the BBHC as soon as their schedules allowed.

Having passed through Cody and headed toward the Bighorns to the east, Bert called Tom Davenport, knowing he might not have cell phone reception at times. "Tom, this is Bert Lynnes again. I hope you're doing okay. I'm leaving on another case but wanted to check in with you and see if there were any more developments regarding your brother?"

Bert could tell that Tom was happy to get the call. Tom told him that he was intending to call a little later and that Norah really must be psychic. He had just found out that his brother's Chevy truck was found in the parking lot of the Regional Medical Center in Sterling. That parking area often had numerous visitors and overnight guests, so it wasn't noticed for quite a while. The police had taken the truck and were looking for evidence now. Bert was told that a Sheriff in a neighboring town confided to Tom that his brother was shot in the abdomen at close range with a small caliber gun, likely a 22-caliber handgun, probably with a silencer. Then his brother and wife had their throats cut almost from ear to ear. It appeared that they died instantly

"Oh, that's awful, Tom! I'm sorry for you and your family's loss. That's incomprehensible! Whatever I can do to help get this guy, I'll do. Thanks for providing those details; I know that's tough on you. Maybe it'll help to eventually get the killer where he belongs. Take care of yourself. Give yourself time to heal. Death is never easy to deal with, especially unexpected death of a loved one. I've experienced it myself, and it lives with you forever. You just have to find a way to live with it. Some say the dead never really leave you, so listen for the still small voice that may be your brother's. I'll talk with you again soon, Tom. Call me anytime." With that, Bert soon ended the call to allow Tom to deal with his unbearable sense of grief.

It was still early in the morning as they crossed the beautiful Bighorn Mountains in north central Wyoming. This was one of their favorite places on earth and this morning reinforced their belief again. The mix of open meadows, forested hills, and occasionally snow-capped mountain vistas was geographic eye-candy. In the early spring, one could see an absolute explosion of wildflowers on the high mountain meadows. This morning they saw no less than half a dozen moose and several herds of elk, grazing on the lush grasses of these high valleys.

At Sheridan, they proceeded east on Interstate 90 toward Spearfish, South Dakota. Near the small community of Sundance, they continually glanced toward the north, hoping for the distant glimpses of Devils Tower. That ancient volcanic plug, Native American sacred site, and National Monument rose hundreds of feet above the forested hills. It was a fascinating addition to any vacation itinerary, and a favorite spot for rock climbers. Those who took the relatively easy half-mile hike around the base of the Tower could literally sense the Native American reverence which permeated the area. With the Tower behind them, they proceeded to Spearfish and then headed north and east on state roads until reaching the small rural community of Selby, South Dakota. It was approaching darkness by the time they found a small Mom and Pop motel which would accommodate Missy. They broke out their usual cooler meal, entertained Missy with a nice walk around town and on a dirt road at the outskirts; and then readied for bed.

Missy often made them laugh. In addition to her antics at one of their stops, trying to catch a field mouse, bounding excitedly and poking her nose everywhere she thought the little vermin might be trying to hide, she could be a hoot in a motel room. She had to investigate every nook and cranny before she would settle down, poking her coyote nose under every piece of furniture. Once satisfied about the security of the place, she sought out a perfect spot to pitch her bed. Often, she would bed down in front of the window, but she usually tried several places before arriving there. Once satisfied that she'd found her spot, she would sniff all around it, and then turn in sometimes as many as a dozen tight circles. Her wild genetics directed her to crush the invisible grasses down into a suitable nest for the night. While they totally understood it, Bert and Norah always delighted in quietly watching this ritual canine behavior.

"Good night, Sweetheart," Bert said softly, "I love you, Norah!

I would be nothing without you."

Her smile told him she felt the same, as he drifted off to a much-needed sleep. "Likewise, Captain. Your ship really would be lost without me, Captain Kirk."

* * *

The jacket felt good at 8:00 the next morning as Bert completed his walk with Missy. The mostly clear sky was interrupted by only a few scattered high cumulus clouds, dotting the blue background like so many marshmallows tossed about. Just like Wyoming, this far north often presented you with a morning chill, even in the summer. Bert tugged the zipper of his jacket to near his chin to keep out the light breeze.

He surveyed the town while waiting for his clients to arrive. Selby was obviously an agricultural community. Northern Plains Co-op, the largest inland fertilizer plant in the upper Midwest, was one of the largest businesses. The railroad played an important role in the distribution of grain from the region to the rest of the globe. Selby boasted the only father-son governors in the state's history, the Mickelson's. At about 1900 feet elevation, the rich farmlands were equally beneficial for wildlife. The area was known for its upland game and waterfowl hunting and fishing.

Bert met up with Troy and Toni Lamont outside his motel. After brief introductions and handshakes, he arranged to follow them to Toni's sister's home. He assured them that his team would do their best to find their missing loved ones.

Troy was a well-built man, about six feet tall, trim, and with slightly greying dark hair. He had a friendly demeanor, a broad smile, and a strong handshake. Bert found him to be instantly likeable. Toni was an equivalent woman, though much shorter but also with dark, shoulder-length hair, and a friendly and warm personality. Bert liked them both immediately. He could tell that Norah did also.

He followed silently behind Troy and Toni as they went mostly straight north from Selby about eight miles, before turning into a farm driveway and pulling up to a one-level house sitting alone at this stretch of road. This modest looking brick home sat amidst a plethora or shrubs, flower beds, and trees in a well-manicured yard. The owners obviously took pride in how they lived. The closest neighboring farm looked to be about a half mile away.

Bert got out of his vehicle and closed his door, leaving Missy and Norah inside. Norah would get out a few minutes later and stroll around the property as she always did, while Bert surveyed the house with their clients. She felt uneasy around other people and needed quiet in order to communicate with the spirits surrounding the site.

Bert walked up to Troy. "Would there be any problem if I let my Coywolf tracker, Missy, out to stretch her legs and sniff around the place?" he asked. "She's a partner in every sense of the word and needs to do her brand of investigating, too."

"No problem at all," replied Troy. "You'll have to tell me all about her later. I've heard of the Coywolf but so far none have been identified out this way. I'm curious to hear about her. We have the standard coyote all around this country, so very familiar with her relatives."

They unlocked and entered the well-kept house and proceeded

to give Bert a slow tour of each room, pausing frequently while he quietly studied every detail. In the master bedroom, something caught his eye instantly. Lying on top of a long dresser were two coins, just touching each other. One nickel and one dime lay in the middle of the dresser.

He turned to his clients, "Do you guys know anything about the change lying there? Was it there when you first entered the house?"

Toni was quick to reply. "Yes, it was there. We have not touched nor moved a thing since we first became suspicious. It was there when the Sheriff and the first private eye were here, too. None of us thought anything about it, but didn't want to disturb anything at all, just in case this house becomes a crime scene."

"That's good," answered Bert. "We hope it isn't a crime scene, but it's better to be safe than sorry until we know for sure."

Bert continued to survey the rest of the house with the same intense scrutiny. Despite his training and knowledge, he could not see any evidence that something sinister had taken place here. "Would you show me around the outside and outbuildings, please?"

As they exited the house, Bert knew that his wife was probably behind the darkly tinted windows of his PI vehicle, still reading the tea leaves after meandering around outside. The two hours he was inside the house likely gave her all the time she needed outside. Missy returned from her foray near the shop to join them as they walked the yard, front and back.

Bert strolled slowly and methodically around the property, led primarily by Toni. Troy seemed to be adopting an investigator approach, himself, and he was scrutinizing the outside just as intently as was Bert.

"This is where they normally parked their Honda," Troy told Bert, as he pointed toward the cement pad in front of the detached garage door. "It was gone from the moment we first came to check this out. Hasn't been seen since."

They continued to walk around the outbuildings. Bert kept a watchful eye on Missy, reading her body language as she sniffed and explored the territory. He always marveled at her typically coyote gait, and the way she froze instantly when something caught her attention. Often, she would freeze with one paw held in mid-air. Once all her senses had identified the source of her curiosity, she would relax back into her hunt.

When the outside walk was finished, Bert had nothing. He could find no evidence of foul play anywhere. This was becoming uncomfortably familiar, he thought. "How about we sit at that backyard patio and review everything that we know so far about this situation?" he said to Toni and Troy.

They talked for nearly an hour, reviewing and discussing every detail that Toni and Troy could think of. They were pretty sure that the missing couple was last seen by family at the June 30th baseball game between the Selby town team and Onida's. Several of their good friends played for Selby. Based upon that, the couple may have been missing for almost a month now.

"An apparent crime without evidence of a crime," he said to Norah as he entered and closed the door to their SUV. "I hope your spirits have given you something for us to go on, Honey."

Norah gave a very slow nod of her head. He knew that this meant she was picking up on something but was still processing it and trying to understand it.

They slowly drove the various small county roads around the missing couple's property, taking in the area while they talked. If this was linked somehow to the earlier cases, as the nickel and dime suggested, then chances are the victims were not far away from their home.

As they drove the farm countryside, Norah began to piece together the visions and impressions as they came from within. "I have the strong feeling that we're dealing in some way with the same killer. It feels the same, though I have no idea how he's connected or why these people. It's perplexing to me to try to make sense of that."

Bert sure agreed with her frustration. "I know what you mean, Sweetheart. Once again, you seem to be our best hope now. Are you getting any visions that might help us?"

She seemed to be searching for her words. "I'm not seeing an Amish guy this time; instead I'm seeing a profile, like the bust of a policeman. Can't see his face clearly."

"What makes you think it's a cop?" Bert asked.

She thought a couple seconds, and then said, "It's his cap. He has a police type of cap on, with emblems."

"Hmm," Bert replied. "That's interesting. Could a cop be involved in this?"

"I don't know," she replied. "I'm seeing nickels and dimes still, and they seem to be relevant to this case, somehow. And a bat; I think it may be a baseball or softball bat."

"Seriously? Were these folks attacked with a bat? Are they lying somewhere, bludgeoned?" Bert knew his rhetorical questions required no answer right now.

"I purposely didn't mention it to you to see if you still picked up on it, Norah. There was a nickel and a dime lying in the middle of their dresser. Do you have any idea what that could mean?"

She slowly shook her head. "No, Honey, I sure don't. There must be some connection with that, though. Otherwise, why do I keep seeing those coins?"

He asked the hardest question of all. "Are these folks still alive, Norah?"

She answered in a hushed tone. "No, Sweetheart, they're dead. That much I can clearly sense. I feel a sense of fear and dread, smell gun smoke, hear a gunshot. I have the taste of blood in my mouth, Bert. They've been killed. I think they were shot."

Bert was quiet for a while as they continued to drive, look, and think. He knew this was hard for her. Among other things, she was a sensitive, psychically. She felt the pain and fears of others. The tears in her eyes told him to leave the questions alone for a while. He reflected on what he knew or theorized.

Missy's whines reminded him that she hadn't been out in a good while. He found the first dirt road that seemed to just go into a pasture to the windmill. He pulled over and turned off the car. Norah strolled a few hundred feet or so down the road, lost in her thoughts. Missy paced up and down the fence line and then proceeded ahead of Norah down the dirt road. She knew this was her time. Besides taking a much-needed pee, she was actively looking for vermin to snack on. You can take the coyote out of the wilderness, but you can't take the wilderness out of the coyote, Bert mused.

Bert pulled the cooler to the back of his open vehicle. It was as good a time for lunch as any, he thought. He watched as a dirty pickup was slowing down and came to a stop on the highway next to them. A middle-aged man was driving, and a woman sat next to him, both wearing well-worn straw hats.

The man leaned out his driver's window. "Hey, you having car problems?"

"No, thank you for asking, though," Bert replied. "Just stopped for a picnic lunch and to let my canine out for a minute."

"I was going to ask you about that coyote. Is that animal with you? She seems tame, but you know, a lot of us around here will shoot a coyote if we get the chance." The man seemed matter of fact with that bit of information.

Bert laughed at that, partly to disarm the fellow. "Yes, she's tame. I raised her as a puppy. Barely had her eyes open when I pulled her from her nest. Her parents were killed, and she would've died otherwise. She's now a trained tracking dog, or coyote. She's a great companion, too."

The guy surveyed Missy intently. "Well, she is a beautiful animal. Just be sure to keep her close to you so nobody mistakes her for one of the calf-killers we occasionally have to deal with."

"Can I ask you a question?" Bert said. "You folks seem to be from around here. Do you know Lizzie and Jake Lofelle?"

The woman spoke up. "We sure do. We've known Jake since he was a little boy. See them every now and then. We hear that something might have happened to them. Nobody has seen them in a while. How do you know them?"

Bert calmly presented his PI license to the man, and then said, "We've been hired by Lizzie's sister to look into their disappearance. My coyote there is a tracking animal and she's found several people in past cases. We specialize in cases of missing persons. Do you folks know of any reason or of any person who might harm them? Or any other people here who might shed some light on their absence?"

Again, the wife chimed in first. "Oh no, they were a very nice couple; just good country people. I don't think anyone around these parts would have any kind of grudge with them. They were pretty good friends with the people next door to the south. The Bouchards."

Bert thought a minute, then asked, "Have you seen any Amish guys or maybe a cop around here lately, especially about the first part of the month?"

The driver beat his wife to the answer. "Nope, sure haven't. Other than the bunch of Sheriff's deputies that were out shortly after the Lofelles were noticed missing. No Amish around here at all to my knowledge. The closest ones are in the eastern part of the state."

Bert shook the fellow's hand, thanked them both, and as they drove away, he returned to his cooler and a sandwich. Norah and Missy were almost back to their car, and Missy was excitedly turning around Norah's legs, sure that a snack was coming to her, as well.

"Gotta keep you in close around here, girl," Bert cautioned Missy. "Don't want you getting shot for looking like one of your bad relatives."

They ate their snacks and Bert followed Missy's lead, sneaking in a quick pee beside the old road. Norah quipped as he got back in their vehicle, "You can take the boy out of the country, but you can't take the country out of the boy. You and Missy make a good pair." She laughed. Then they proceeded back toward the Lofelle home and the next-door neighbors.

The farm neighbor to the north offered no worthwhile information. Missy didn't alert on anything around their place, either. They continued to the neighbor to the south.

The place was obviously a work of love for the owners. An attractive tri-level frame house, white with green trim, was nestled in a large and well-manicured yard. The grass was like a green carpet, with flowers everywhere, and tall mature trees were scattered randomly about. Spruce trees lined the perimeter of the yard. Bert could see that these folks took a lot of pride in their property. Even the shop, barn, and other outbuildings were equally maintained. He couldn't see anything resembling junk anywhere.

They pulled up to the Bouchard farmhouse, killed the engine, and Bert went to the door. Before he could knock, an older man, with the tan, leathery skin of a farmer, opened the door and greeted him warmly. Bert introduced himself, told them why he was there, and asked if he or his wife could remember anything from around the time the Lofelles went missing.

Mr. Bouchard walked out and closed his door. "Let's sit at my picnic table over here. Nice out here." He motioned toward a polished oak table that nestled in the shade of two large trees. He obviously loved showing off his handiwork. They sat down.

"My wife went to town for a few groceries today," Mr. Bouchard confessed, "otherwise I'd have her bring us out some snacks. She's a great cook and loves having visitors."

"Sir," Bert asked. "Would you mind if I let my pet coyote out for a little bit? She's very tame, well trained, and is my tracking animal. She's an essential part of my PI business."

Mr. Bouchard had no issues with that and seemed interested in seeing Missy. Unseen by the old gentleman, Bert gave her his usual search order, and let her out of the vehicle. He knew the first ten minutes were going to be spent answering this man's questions about their unusual hybrid animal.

Back at the table, after the expected discussion about Missy and how she came to be part of the team, Bert wanted to get down to business. He asked if they had noticed anything at all out of the ordinary earlier in the month, when the Lofelles probably disappeared.

"No, nothing has been unusual around here in months," Mr. Bouchard laughingly replied. "Well, wait. This isn't very unusual, but I did notice a pickup, sort of darker colored, extended cab, driving unusually slowly one day a while back. I had to pass it, and it had an out-of-state plate, I think one of those eastern states. Don't know which now. We don't get many out-of-staters out here, so I did notice that."

"Did you see the person driving it?" Bert asked.

Bouchard thought for a bit. "You know, I couldn't really see anybody inside. It had some of them dark windows, kinda like you have."

Bert was watching Missy with occasional glances and noticed that she was very interested in the area around the picnic table. She finally sat down in her alert position right next to him.

"Mr. Bouchard, have the Lofelles been here to visit you recently?"

The old man gazed across his yard toward the meadow and seemed to be lost in thought. After a few seconds, he said, "Yes, they were here the weekend before the fourth of July. We sat right here and had lunch and a good talk. Come to think of it, it was that morning on my way back home from town that I saw that outa-state pickup."

Bert realized he might have just gotten some key bits of evidence. While Mr. Bouchard tried to be very helpful, he didn't come up with any other information that seemed valuable. Bert thanked his host and said good-bye. A pat on the head and another treat greeted Missy as she hopped in the back of the SUV. Bert waved out his window as he drove back toward the road. He was very impressed with this old gentleman's warmth, hospitality, and eagerness to help. It was easy to see why the neighbors would like them and want to be around them.

"We might have a lead and another bit of information," he said to Norah as they drove toward Selby and a motel. "Mr. Bouchard saw a dark out-of-state pickup near here the weekend before the Fourth. It was driving so slowly that he passed it a little way from here. He was on the way home to have lunch that day with the Lofelles that afternoon. My guess is that they are the last people to see the Lofelles alive."

"Did he see the driver or any passengers?" she asked.

"No, it had darker tinted windows like we do," he replied. "It was an extended cab pickup, so would easily have room for up to four passengers, too. Did you get anything while waiting for me back there?"

"Maybe," Norah said slowly. "I'm seeing a number 83 on some kind of a plaque. Also, a bridge, I think. I sense something ominous there. A feeling of fear. I hear her sobbing. I feel a sense of death. I'm feeling a pull to the west from here, Bert, just as I was drawn north back in Colorado. I think they're west of here."

Bert was taking mental notes of what she was saying, as he always did. "Let's get to the motel, get settled, and check with Toni to see if anything has developed with her. Then we'll recap and see what sense we can make of all this."

Two hours later, they were in a small motel near the outskirts of Selby, had eaten, walked Missy, and then checked in with Toni and Troy.

Toni answered the phone. Her voice sounded strained and broken. "I was about to call you," she said. "Lizzie and Jake's car has been located in an industrial parking lot near the airport at Mobridge. The plant operates around-the-clock. It blended in and nobody gave it a thought all this time until they were going to repaint the parking lines and couldn't figure out who owned it. They called the cops then, and we just got the call from the Sheriff. The Sheriff is finally taking this serious now. Have you got anything?"

Bert pondered this new development. "That might be an apparent deception to keep the police at bay for a while. The neighbors, Bouchards, saw an out-of-state pickup with tinted windows just before the Fourth of July and before they had lunch with your sister and Jake. He didn't know if it was significant or not. I think it might be. Perhaps as significantly, my psychic has gotten some inputs that may be helpful. I won't go into those yet, but we'll be checking those out and see if they might lead us anywhere. I can tell you that she thinks we need to focus to the west of here. Take care of yourselves. This is a tough thing to go through. I'll talk with you again tomorrow."

Norah had been listening to the conversation. "This continues to sound eerily like the previous two cases, my love. While you were talking with Toni, I started to see something about Indians. American Indians, I mean. It's kind of fuzzy and I don't know what it means."

"Hmm, what could that mean I wonder?" Bert pondered. "What do you think about everything, dear?"

She took a minute to answer. "Bert, I think these three cases are somehow related. It feels like the same person or persons are involved, but other than a few coins I have nothing to substantiate that. And, the coins don't really make much sense. What could twenty-five, twenty, and fifteen cents mean? So far, I'm seeing two possible men, one who seems to be Amish, and the other a cop. That seems like an unlikely pair. I keep seeing numbers that make no sense. What could 35, 42, and 83 have to do with this?"

He thought about that for a minute. "Sweetheart, let's take it one thing at a time. If in fact the same people are doing this, and I think there must be at least two, then the coins must mean something, and these cases are related. There's a reason you're seeing them. If that's true, then what's next? What if we're looking at a serial killing spree and they aren't done yet? What if the coins are purposely left as a kind of taunt or a calling card? Maybe just to see if the police are smart enough to pick up on it."

"What if they're a countdown to some final or grand event?" Norah replied. "If so, then there will be another with one dime. If that happens, then we'll know for sure. And how will we know anyway? We've been drawn into this by pure chance, not once but now three times, maybe. What's the chance that we'll be hired to any future cases?"

"Good questions," he said. "If we assume that these cases are connected in some way, then the coins are also, because your visions connect them. If that's all true, then are they counting down to something? Does the countdown end at a nickel, or at zero?"

"How are these victims then related?" Norah asked. "We haven't been able to find a single thing that ties them together. Are they chosen purely randomly?"

Bert had another thought. "These people are all in small rural communities and they, so far, all live in the country. Is that by coincidence, or by design? A commonality could be that country and small-town people have a greater sense of security and safety than a lot of other bigger city people. That might make them an easier mark."

Norah replied to that. "Yet, there must be some way the victims are chosen, individually. The killers are far too efficient to just pluck these folks out of the air."

"You're right, Sweetheart," Bert continued that thought. "These guys, or women possibly, seem to be cunning and have this well planned out. Somehow, they can enter the homes without causing a stir and without leaving evidence, other than the coins. Each time they have taken the victims from their homes and killed them some distance away, apparently for pure sport. The only things that are verifiably stolen are the wallets, purses, and phones, and those seem to just vanish. Nothing is used that might be traced. A vehicle is taken from the home, along with the victims. We don't know their methods of doing that, but it is effective, whatever it is. The vehicles seem to be part of a deception to throw these small-town Sheriffs off the trail for a while. It creates a degree of doubt whether a crime has been committed at all. The location where the victims' vehicles are dropped off seems to be carefully thought out. Each has been in a busy parking area and placed to blend in for a while."

Norah chimed in. "That's right, and even the one surveillance video from that first Walmart might have been purposely used for deception. The driver could not be identified and could not be detected leaving the store. Somehow, he seems to have known about the cameras and used them to further throw off any investigation."

"While it seems improbable, based upon typical serial killings, that two killers are working together, I don't see how these methods are done without an accomplice," Bert said. "This very well may be an exception to the norm wherein two like-minded killers are working together."

Bert shifted the focus to the present case. "Norah, I've been thinking about the number 83 that you saw in a vision today. It seems like it may be specific to this South Dakota case. Let's look over the map and see if there are any roads or highways around here with that number."

They pulled up the area map on Bert's laptop, and began to methodically scan the local area. It didn't take long. A state highway 83 jumped out at them both at the same time.

"Bert, that highway is only a short distance to the west of where the victims live, and northwest of Selby. I also saw a bridge," she added. "Let's see if there are any bridges near there?"

Bert was first to speak. "Norah, the only thing I see is what looks like an earthen bridge which seems to split Renz Lake, going north and south."

"That's very close to what I've been seeing." Norah responded. "The grass covered sides could explain why my vision of this as a bridge seemed fuzzy at the edges."

Bert looked at his phone. It was nearly 10 PM, too late to go out there tonight. He called Toni and Troy back and asked them to meet up in Selby at 7:00 in the morning. He felt that they should be along; which was an exception to how he normally would work such a situation.

He smiled as he watched Missy. She had gotten up from her spot inside the bathroom; probably chosen to get as far away as possible from the phone chatter. Now that it seemed to be quieting down, she wanted to stand guard closer to them. She was going through her spin in front of the window, readying the invisible grasses for her night's sleep. Norah was watching and smiling, also. They loved that animal.

Just as he was about to get into bed, the phone rang again. It was Troy Lamont.

"Bert, this is Troy again. Bad news! We just got a call from the Sheriff. They found Lizzie; she's been killed. Toni is having a real breakdown right now, and her best friend is on the way over to be with her, too. I feel that it's important to go with you tomorrow morning, so it will only be me. I need to get back here by noon, though."

"Troy, I am so sorry! Please tell Toni that, also. If you can go in the morning, I think it would be good, but I'll understand if you can't. Did they tell you where they found Lizzie?"

Troy replied, "Yes, it was west of Mobridge a few miles; south of highway 12. There is a scenic byway which goes off to the south and west. It's an unpopulated area for the most part. She was about a hundred yards off that road, in a hollow with a lot of vegetation. A couple of kids happened upon her when their parents stopped to let them run around. She's been dead for several weeks, they said."

Bert again gave his condolences and said good night. He turned his laptop back on and pulled up his mapping program. His eyes followed state highway 12 as it passed through Mobridge, crossed the Missouri River, and continued west. He found the byway in just a few miles.

"Norah, you were right about there being a connection to our American Indians. The byway where Lizzie Lofelle was killed is the Native American Scenic Byway."

* * *

It was just before seven the next morning, when Bert, Norah, and Missy met up with Troy Lamont at the Dairy Queen. Under a blue sky, the light breeze was chilly. It would likely warm up into the upper eighties by afternoon. Bert and Troy both wore light jackets for this quick morning briefing on Norah's psychic visions. He took the lead with Troy following as their vehicles traveled up highway 83 to the north. The road followed a nearly straight path along the level geography of farmland pastures and meadows, interrupted only by driveways to the few farms on both sides.

When they reached the south end of the earthen dam and bridge segment which split Renz Lake, Bert pulled off the road, followed by Troy. He exited the doghouse and let Missy out the side passenger door. Bert gave Missy the command to sit and presented her with the male victim's gloves, provided by Toni the day before. He directed her, "Missy, find!"

Missy seemed more excited than usual as she sniffed and searched to the right side of the road, ranging in a couple hundred feet semicircle. Not picking up anything, she crossed the road and searched to the west side and the south side of the west lake. Again, finding nothing, Bert ordered her to follow them as he slowly drove the length of the dam and pulled off at the north end.

Just as he pulled off the right side of the road, Missy began to excitedly sniff the area on the opposite side of the road, pacing north and south with her nose to the ground. She gave a short yap as she seemed to almost bolt down the bank and along the north edge of the water. By the time Bert got out of his SUV and crossed the road, she was yapping briefly in a small wooded area just to the north of the lake and about two hundred feet from the road. As soon as he was running her direction, she sat down with her face looking intently into the heavily grassed spot around several small trees. Bert didn't draw his pistol this time. He knew that what he was going to find was not a threat. He was thankful that Norah was safely in their car. This was bound to upset her, as did the news last night.

Bert stopped near Missy and observed and photographed the scene with his phone's camera. He cautioned Troy to stay at least ten feet away as the distraught man dropped to his knees upon seeing the body barely visible in the thick grass. Bert knew it was Troy's brother-in-law, despite the decay of several weeks in this unseen location. Troy's sobs caused Bert to slowly walk back toward the vehicles, trying to fight back his own tears. He would never get used to this. No matter how professional he became, his natural sensitivity to others made such a scene very emotional for him. Gathering his composure, he again unholstered his cell phone and dialed 911, asking for the County Sheriff.

* * *

Bert leaned against his vehicle as the Sheriff's vehicles and ambulance arrived. Two of the deputies, one seasoned and swarthy, the other looking to be new to the job, took down his statement. Troy was doing the same with another deputy by his pickup.

Bert observed the older Deputy standing in front of him, legs apart and arms crossed. This Sheriff looked at Bert with the air of one who was superior and totally in charge. He listened to the Deputy's words carefully. "So, Mr. Lynnes, you were hired by the Lamonts to try to find Toni's sister and husband. You say that you came to this spot because of the visions of a psychic and once here your wolfdog found the body by scent. Is that correct?"

Bert knew this fellow didn't believe him and was trying to catch him in any inconsistency. He expected, feared, and respected this any time he had to get too involved with the cops. "Partly yes, Sir, I do consult with a psychic on virtually all my cases and she's uncannily accurate. We wouldn't have found this location without her psychic inputs. My animal is a coywolf, a coyote-red wolf hybrid found mostly in Canada and the northeastern US. She's nearly as good a tracker as a bloodhound."

The expected grilling and trick questions continued. Bert listened intently as the man said, "This psychic. Who is he?" He knew that the Deputy heard him say, "she."

Bert chose his words carefully and made sure to sound respectful. "She's my wife, Deputy Miller, I always consult with her. She does her own spiritual investigation of our cases. I do the legwork and deal with our clients and others.

Deputy Miller knew that a wife could not be compelled to testify against her husband, so for now, he figured she didn't matter. Besides, she was supposedly psychic, so she could say anything and claim she saw it in a vision. Useless as a witness, he thought to himself. He walked down to where the other statement had also been completed, from Mr. Lamont, leaving the younger Deputy to keep an eye on Bert.

After several minutes' discussion with Troy's handler, Deputy Miller and the other officer returned to Bert, ordered him to stay put, and summoned the younger deputy to come aside for a pow wow.

As the three officers huddled together away from Bert and Troy, Deputy Miller stated his position. "I've got to tell you; I don't buy this crap about a psychic. In my opinion, Lynnes had to know more than he's admitting about where this body was found. If it was up to me, I'd slap him in the slammer until he came clean."

The officer who interviewed Troy, responded to Miller. "Sir, I'm kinda with you on that. However, Troy Lamont was adamant that this is exactly how it happened. He said he would testify in court on behalf of Mr. Lynnes. So, unless Lamont changes, I think we'd get nowhere to charge Lynnes for anything, at least right now."

Miller didn't bother to ask his younger apprentice for an opinion, considering his inexperience to be unworthy of listening to. They returned to Bert.

Bert received the tentative verdict from His Highness. He listened as Deputy Miller said, "Mr. Lynnes, you're free to go. However, don't think we're done here. I don't believe in this psychic nonsense, and if we get anything that leads to you, we'll be back in touch." With that, Deputy Miller spun on his heel and stomped back toward the others and the forensics guy. Bert had to constrain a chuckle at the man's pomposity and self-aggrandizement. Miller was confirming why Bert avoided dealing with most law enforcement guys.

Bert noted that the younger fellow, Deputy Haskins, did not move away. The young Deputy was slightly shorter than Bert, trim and well built, and had a full head of thick dark hair. He looked like he might have some Native American ancestry with his darker skin tone and higher cheek bones. Bill said in a hushed tone meant only for Bert, "Mr. Lynnes, not all of us are as old school as my boss here. I do believe there is something to the metaphysical, and I don't personally discount your psychic. In fact, I'm more than intrigued by what you do. I'd like to call you, soon, and talk about that more, just personal between you and me. Not official. Is that okay with you?"

Bert knew he could use an ally, but also saw the opportunity to educate someone in law enforcement about his company's unusual methods. "You bet, Deputy Haskins, please give me a call. I'd love to visit with you about this. It's what makes our business unique, and very effective." The young Deputy Sheriff nodded, and quickly walked back to the rest of his unit.

Bert then said his good-bye to Troy, and again offered his condolences. "I know how deeply a loss, such as this, hurts, Troy. I've been there. Please assure your wife that although she will never completely get over this, you just eventually learn to live with it. Suggest that she take comfort in the belief that her sister will never really leave her. If she will just close her eyes and open her mind, she might yet hear her sister. Give Toni my best wishes. I'll keep in touch with you guys. Please let me know if there are further developments."

Bert drove away with a large sigh of relief. He turned to Norah.

"Dear, this is a prime example of why I hate to deal with law enforcement. There is always someone who doesn't understand our business and doesn't care to try. At least that younger fellow is open-minded. He might even call sometime to discuss it. You know, Honey, it's late afternoon, we're tired, and we don't like to travel at night. Let's just go over to Mobridge and stay the night. I'd like to see that Native American Scenic road tomorrow morning, anyway. Then we can work our way back home; maybe stay a night or two in the Bighorns for some scenery and relaxation." He knew that her nod of approval was all that was needed to confirm the route back home. It would be good to take their time getting home after three difficult and emotionally draining cases.

As Bert drove west on Highway 12 toward the city of Mobridge, they said little. The relatively level countryside with low hills and farm valleys led them in the direction of the setting sun, with a welcomed calmness. The stress of these cases had taken its toll. They didn't want to talk about much of anything for a while. He donned his sunglasses and lowered the driver's visor against the late afternoon sun. The reddening horizon hinted of another coming day of good weather.

CHAPTER NINE: AN ALLY

After settling into a small motel near the edge of Mobridge, Bert took his Coywolf companion on a long walk to the outskirts of town and down a dirt road. Once out of town, he released her from the leash. She gleefully ran at full speed a couple hundred feet one direction, and then reversed direction and went full speed the other direction. Her full grey-red tail streamed behind her. She came to a sudden stop, ears straight up, her sharp nose and eyes fixed on a clump of grass, and her right paw raised and poised in mid-air. She turned her head slowly from side to side, listening to the tiny movement in the grass, undetectable by a human ear. In an instant, she pounced, her nose buried in the grass. Bert couldn't help but laugh as she came up with a mouse and gulped it down in one move. She wouldn't require so much food tonight, he thought. In his mind he could hear Norah saying, "You can take the coyote out of the country, but you can't take the country out of the coyote."

Back at the motel, he broke out the cooler for the usual evening meal. He leaned back in the chair, talking to Norah as she sat on the bed. They were enjoying a discussion about their dreams and plans for their Cody property. The ring of Bert's phone startled both.

The man's voice on the phone asked, "Mister Lynnes, is this you?"

Bert was a little puzzled. "Yes, this is Bert Lynnes. May I ask who you are?" The voice was familiar, but he couldn't place it.

"Hi, Mister Lynnes. This is Sheriff Deputy Bill Haskins. We met at the crime scene today on highway 83. Please call me Bill; I'm not very formal. I'm a country guy. You said you might be willing to discuss your investigation methods and your use of psychic inputs. Are you still okay with that?"

He doesn't mess around, thought Bert. "Sure Deputy, I mean Bill, I'd be happy to talk about our methods with you. Is there anything in particular you want to know about?"

Bill got right to his point. "Bert, I understand how your psychic is able to draw clues and visions from the environment surrounding a crime that has occurred. Well, I don't really understand it, but I know generally that she's pulling in the energy from a tragic event. I've seen your results, so I know it's real and is an investigative asset. What I'd like to know is, can she see into the future? Can she sense what the bad guys are going to do, as well as what they've done?"

Bert pondered that for a bit, glancing at Norah. "Well, Bill, she's able to gain some future insight sometimes, but not as clearly as from a past event. Since we specialize in finding missing people, we generally deal in what's happened, rather than what can happen in the future. Is there a reason for your interest?"

Bill responded slowly. "Yeah, there is a motive behind that question, Bert. As a Deputy Sheriff, I must be careful about what I'm going to tell you. So, this is Bill Haskins talking now. I can sense that you're an honest and reliable guy, Bert. Can I trust you to keep this conversation in confidence, between you and me?"

Bert replied without hesitation. "Yes, absolutely, Bill. I'll maintain our talk in confidence. I'm sensing you have something rather significant you want to tell me."

"Good," Bill said, somewhat relaxing, "I want you to look into another case up in Montana. I have a relative, an uncle, who lives in Brockway, Montana, a small town in the east part of the state. He told me yesterday about a couple who were just reported missing a couple days ago near him; a neighboring town of Circle. The missing people are ranchers about twenty miles west of both communities. This couple hasn't been gone more than about four days now, so the scent is much fresher than the case you just worked. They missed a major family event yesterday, and the warning flags went up quickly. Otherwise, the details seem very similar to the Lofelle case, as well as the previous two you just worked."

"Oh, so you know about our recent work, then. You've done some homework it would seem?"

Haskins was unapologetic, "Yes, I checked you out right after I got off duty today. I'm very interested in your line of work and your methods. In addition, I know my uncle is friends with the missing ranchers, and I'd like to help him. I think your skills may be what they need. I'm sure he would hire you, even if the kids don't, if I recommend you."

"They have kids. How old are the missing people?" Bert said.

"I think they're in their forties," Bill replied, "they have a daughter who works in Miles City, a twenty-something son in college in Missoula, and a son who lives with them and is in high school in Circle."

Bert did the math and said, "I guess we'll be working for your uncle. Is there something else, Bill?"

Bill was slow to reply, as if weighing his own logic. "Yeah, there is, Bert. As a Deputy Sheriff, I was able to access the reports on the previous two cases you worked. My gut tells me we may be looking at serial killers. The problem is that there doesn't at first glance seem to be anything other than speculation to connect them. The M.O. is very similar in all three. Because this abduction, if that's in fact what it is, just occurred, you may be able to get ahead of them if they plan to continue. I have no jurisdiction in Montana, and they'd probably laugh me out of the state if I approached their Sheriff about using a psychic private investigator to help. So, I can help you behind the scenes and off the record, to the extent possible, if you will use your methods to try to catch up to those bastards? I know you're a retired Army officer and you know how to use a weapon to defend yourself, or I wouldn't be advocating this."

Bert understood and asked, "Bill, does the present report on the missing Montana couple say anything about what was found in the house? I'm curious if they found any change left out, such as nickels, dimes, and the like? Also, is a vehicle gone as well? What are the missing persons' names?"

Bill was quiet as he seemed to be rifling through papers or using his computer. After about three minutes, he returned to the phone. "Sorry about that. My uncle's friends are Duke and Terry Williams. The 2016 Ford pickup, red, is gone. I can't find any mention of coins, though. I'll see what I can find out tomorrow."

"Bill, tell your uncle that we'll meet him at a place of his choosing tomorrow afternoon or evening. I think we can get to the area in a day's drive. Would you just text me his name and phone number when you have the chance?"

"Bert, before you go, I'm curious. Why did you ask about coins?"

Bert knew this was only circumstantial. "My psychic has had visions of nickels and dimes at all three of these cases. They are not in the same denomination but seem to be counting down by a nickel. At the first, we found two dimes and one nickel. There were two dimes at the Colorado house. We found a dime and a nickel in the Lofelles' home. Bill, so far this is the only real link which seems to connect these murders. Because it's corroborated by sixth sense, it's basically circumstantial and wouldn't stand up in court. If this is a real link, then there will be a lone dime left in a prominent location in the home of another victim."

Bill thought for a few seconds before replying. "Well, I have to hope that there is no dime at the home of my uncle's friends."

With that, they said their good-byes and hung up. Bert turned to Norah, "Well, Sweetheart, the run continues, just as you sensed it would. Only now we have an ally in law enforcement. And, we have the chance to gain ground on the killers, in terms of time and hopefully location. If this is our killers at work in Montana, we may be only four or five days behind them now, instead of the month for the previous cases. We may be able to catch up to them?"

He knelt beside Missy, curled up in her favorite spot in front of the window, and stroked her head and back. She didn't open her eyes. She just sighed and stretched out on her side. She was one very content coywolf. Bert said good-night to Norah and whispered, "I love you, Norah. I don't know what I'd do without you."

"Why, Darlin', you'd be nothing without me." They both laughed in the darkness.

* * *

They were on the road early the next morning. Just west of Mobridge on highway 12, they came to the turnoff for the Native American Scenic Byway. Bert noticed the tears welling up in Norah's eyes and he knew she was sensing Lizzie's death. "We don't have to go down there," he said.

"Just stop here a minute," she said. "I want to get past this. I can feel her fear; she's trying to cry but she can't. She has something, maybe tape, over her mouth. She can't see her hands. I think they are tied behind her back. They're pulling her, she's trying to get free but they're too strong. I see the barrel of a gun; it's getting larger and larger. Fire. No, a flash. I can taste blood. Then nothing."

Norah turned away. It was time to go on. She quietly sobbed with her face to the window. Bert fought back his own tears, partly for Lizzie, and partly for his beloved wife who also endured Lizzie's rape and murder. Norah didn't just see such an event, she experienced it. She felt it.

They drove up highway 12 for hours, passing through miles of low hills and valleys. By early afternoon, they arrived in Glendive, Montana. Bert called Bill Haskins' uncle, a Montana cowboy it seems, and arranged to meet him in Circle outside the Wooden Nickel restaurant. Bert knew that Norah would not want to go inside. He would grab a couple of burgers to go, while she stretched her legs outside the car. She didn't like to be around many people, especially crowds. She picked up on too many unrelated sensory messages.

Bert got out of his vehicle and closed the door. "Hello, I'm Bert Lynnes," he said to the tall, rangy, middle-aged man who approached him.

Bill's uncle confidently offered a handshake. "Hi Bert. I'm Bob Madison. Glad to meet you. Looks like you're going to be helping me for a while."

Bert liked the fellow instantly and shook his hand warmly. Madison was fit and trim, like his nephew and looked to have Native American heritage. His dark, weathered skin, coal black hair, and piercing eyes gave testimony to a bloodline which Bert had always admired. He had the feeling that you could trust this man with your life. "You bet, Bob; glad to try to help. I would love to talk more, but I think time is of the essence here. Can you lead us to their ranch so we can get started and try to find your friends? You can fill me in on the details as we look around. My psychic wife isn't unfriendly, but she just likes to keep to herself during an investigation so that she doesn't get a lot of psychic interference from anyone. I have a tracking animal that I know you'll be fascinated with. She's a Coywolf that we adopted as a puppy. She's friendly, as well as an asset to our investigative capabilities. I understand they have three kids, and the youngest one is in high school and has been living at home. Will he be there, Bob?"

"I think the youngest son is staying in town tonight with friends, Bert. He's very worried but is a shortstop on the high school baseball team. They have another game this afternoon. We thought it would be best for him to play and try to take his mind off this situation for a while. They follow all his games and would want him to keep playing, if possible. They beat a big rival last week here, and that puts them in the driver's seat for winning their league."

"Sounds good," said Bert. "Probably best if he isn't here right now, unless he knows something that might be helpful? I assume he doesn't, or you'd be telling me?"

Bob agreed. "You're right about that. Just follow me. We'll go to the northwest on Horse Creek road for close to twenty miles. Their ranch headquarters and house are just off the road on the left about a quarter mile."

The afternoon sun was low enough that it was starting to glare and require sunglasses, as they drove in a westerly direction. Bert loved the serenity of this mostly ranch land as the rolling hills and fields passed on both sides. An occasional antelope grazed, seemingly unconcerned as they passed within a hundred yards of them. The 84-degree temperature was keeping everything at a slower pace.

He followed Bob's dusty pickup as he turned south on a gravel driveway leading to a one-level, brick, ranch house. He parked next to the pickup and met Bob outside. Together they studied the house. Like the other homes they'd investigated, this one also was well maintained, attractive, and showed pride-of-ownership. The yard hadn't been mowed in about a week, but otherwise the mix of green grass, flowers, shrubs, and evergreen trees gave a warm and friendly persona to the property.

Bob spoke first. "I came up here just as soon as the son called me two days ago. They missed his ball game that day, which is unheard of for them. They were just at the one before; Monday, I think it was. That was five days ago. The boy saw them Wednesday morning before leaving to meet up for lunch with his team. He called me next morning, and I called the local Sheriff and my nephew down in South Dakota. Bill is a heck of a good kid, and

I wanted to get his advice."

"What's the Sheriff have to say?" asked Bert.

"Just what my nephew said he'd say," Bob growled. "There's no evidence of a crime. Their pickup is gone, and they might just be on a second Honeymoon. They do find it strange that they didn't make the game or tell their son, though. So, they aren't blowing it off; they just don't really know where to start other than searching for reports of abandoned vehicles. Cell phones seem to be turned off, so they can't ping them for a location. That's why Bill suggested that we get hold of you."

Bert weighed the information. "Bob, do you think we should try to get involved with your Sheriff? If we can work together with him, it might increase our odds of success."

Bob wasted no time in replying. "Absolutely not, Bert! I know this guy well. He's a good guy and takes his job seriously, but he's very old-school and closed-minded as hell. Soon as this half-blood Sioux mentions your psychic, he'd probably have us both escorted out of the county."

Bert knew that attitude all too well. "Then let's look inside and around the house. See if we can pick up on anything they may have missed. Have you been inside? I presume the young boy has. Do you know if he moved anything around or found anything unusual?"

"He and I talked for a good while when he called," Bob went on. "The boy said he didn't see anything out of place. I told him not to move or remove anything, just in case it came down to an investigation. I know the lad well. After doing the chores he heads right for the barn and his horse and either practices his roping or goes for a ride until dark and bedtime. He lives and breathes baseball and horses. He may be part Indian but he's all cowboy. He's a mix of Billy Mills, Crazy Horse, and Tim Bagnell."

Bert digested that analogy for a minute as they walked around the house, looking for anything suspicious. He realized that Bob thought very highly of this teenager.

Bob opened the door to the house, and they began Bert's slow, methodical exploration of every room. There were no signs of a forced entry anywhere, or of a struggle. Bert stopped abruptly when they got to the kitchen and combined dining room. He let out a low breath, undetected by Bob. In the middle of the large wood, seemingly homemade, dining table was a lone dime. He documented it from several angles and zoom with his phone camera.

Bob found this odd. "What's with that table and dime?" he asked.

Bert pondered whether he should share his suspicions with this man. He decided he owed it to him. "This is the fourth case I've worked like this in the last couple of months, Bob. Each one has had a strange combination of nickels and dimes in the houses. This lone dime may mean nothing at all, or it may mean that this relates to those other three and involves the same guys. I just don't know." This last statement was a stretch of the truth. Bert already knew that this was very likely the work of the same guys.

Bob was silent for a long time before he asked, "What happened to the people in those other cases?"

Now it was Bert's turn to pause. Finally, he knew he had to tell Bob the facts. "They were all murdered, Bob. The perpetrators are still on the loose. That's why your nephew wanted us to come here. He thinks our unusual investigative team may be able to get ahead of these guys and stop them."

Bob was silent. He led Bert around the remaining parts of the house without a word. Finally, as he reached the front door, he opened it, and spoke as Bert walked out. "Bert, let me know of anything I can do to help catch those sons-a-bitches. Let your coyote out so he can get a run in while I show you the rest of the place."

Bert let Missy out for a run and pee, while Bob escorted him around the barn, sheds, bunkhouse, and shops. As they entered the barn, Bert looked back in time to see his wife almost back to their car. She had apparently finished doing her own walk around the property, as she usually did. He hoped like heck that she was getting something.

As they completed their survey of the property, without finding anything suspicious, something caught Bert's attention as they walked back toward the vehicles. A new looking plastic gas container, a three-gallon one he thought, was near the driveway close to the garage. He hadn't really noticed it before, though he saw it. There was a small piece of cloth wrapped around the handle. He touched it with his toe. It was empty. Did that mean anything? Norah saw a gas can in a vision back in Kansas. He left it alone without touching it.

"Any neighbors around here?" Bert asked. He didn't see another house in any direction from where he stood near his SUV.

Bob pointed to the west. "There's a ranch about a mile west of here, and another nearly three miles to the northeast. They're the closest ones. I doubt they saw anything."

They discussed the case for a few more minutes. Bert told Bob that this was another case where he was probably going to lean very heavily on his psychic wife's connection to the spirit world. It was also likely that Missy's nose would play a part as well. Her nose usually cut hours down to minutes when it came to finding someone.

"Well, tell your wife that I really appreciate her and would love to meet her. Is she here?" Bob asked.

Bert replied, "She's in the car, Bob, but she's very much a loner when it comes to working these cases. As a psychic, she must keep her mind free to sense only those thoughts and senses directly related to the case. Anything else is clutter and gets in the way of her effectiveness. We hope you understand, and I'll tell her that you appreciate her. She'll like to hear that."

Bert promised to keep Bob informed of any developments and to check in with him each day. He asked Bob to check in any way appropriate and try to come up with any reason for someone to have a grudge against his friends. With that, Bob headed back to Circle, intending to meet up with his friends' son. Bert, Norah, and Missy headed for the ranch neighbor to the west.

The west rancher was a friend of the Williams, but they could not shed any light on the disappearance. They were certain, though, that it had to be the result of foul play. They were adamant that those folks would never miss their son's baseball game.

The ranchers to the northeast offered nothing but the same sentiments. No further clues.

Bert headed toward Circle. As he drove, he turned to Norah who had been very quiet and introspective. "Sweetheart, I know you've been reading the tea leaves. What have you come up with, Honey?"

She responded in a low voice. "Because we got here very soon after this crime occurred, relative to the others, my visions and sensations are much stronger, Darling. I see the shadowy figure of a man wearing a hat, a western hat I think, kind of like those outback hats. He isn't a black guy, but his skin seems sort of dark, like maybe he's tanned or maybe Hispanic. Out here, I guess he could be Native American. He's holding some kind of container, plastic and not real big. It might be one of those gas containers. His face isn't clear to me, fuzzy like, you know. I also see the coins again, though it goes from both nickels and dimes to only a dime, sometimes. He's connected to the earlier crimes; I can feel it."

Norah paused, drew a deep breath, and slowly continued. "The man is dead, Bert. I mean Mr. Williams. He can't speak, I feel like his mouth is probably taped shut, and he can't move his hands. I can feel his fear, his anguish, and the feel of earth under his knees. Then he dies. It feels like he was shot in the back of the head. He was executed. Not very far from here, either."

Bert pulled into the local McDonalds restaurant in Circle and parked. He didn't say anything for a while, internalizing what his wife was telling him. "What about Mrs. Williams, Terry?"

Her reaction was his answer. She looked away and he knew she was suppressing a sob and grappling for composure. "It was worse, Honey. She was taken to a different place, raped, and then executed. I feel what she felt, vividly. It was awful, brutal, and inhuman. These guys are animals, Bert. No, that's a disservice to most animals." She couldn't go on. She didn't need to. Her shoulders were shaking with the sobs and a sense of great loss. A sense of great fear. She could feel the hands of strangers on her body and the brutality of sexual assault. She was consumed by the sense of doom, the knowledge that she would be killed. The knowledge that Terry was raped and killed.

Bert felt a crush of helplessness. He could do nothing to take away the pain his wife was feeling as she channeled the victim. Her pain and fears were palpable and all he really could do was understand what she was going through and give her the room and support to deal with it. His heart broke every time she went through such torment.

This time, he decided to give her some space. He also knew she always had preferred eating out of the cooler. He went inside the restaurant. It was obvious that this was a sports-minded community. A large banner heralded the baseball team. Ads all over the place offered game day specials, and posters displayed the scores of the games like medals on a soldier's chest. He walked up to the pretty young woman at the cash register. "I'll just have a burger and milk. You guys must be having a heck of a year in baseball."

She was friendly and eager to engage. "Oh my, yes, this is maybe the best team we've ever had here. Fourteen and one, right now. You're from out of town?"

He welcomed her bubbly demeanor. "Yes, I'm from down under, in your neighboring state of Wyoming. How do you know that?"

"Just a guess and noticing the little difference in your clothing compared to the boots and blue jeans that you see from the locals here. We don't get many strangers here in Circle. You're the second in a week, so there must be mass migration taking place." She laughed.

Bert digested that for a few seconds. "You have a great personality and must talk with everyone. Where was the other stranger from?"

"Oh, there were two of them. They stopped in here maybe a week or so ago. It must have been a day or two before the earlier ball game, because they also asked about it. Seemed like fans of the game. Talked like they might go to it."

Bert asked, "I might have bumped into them a ways back. Was one of them a black guy?"

"Nah, they were both white guys, I think. One either had a good tan or maybe some Hispanic blood. Almost had me fooled because they looked like they were from around here until they opened their mouths."

"What do you mean?" asked Bert.

She happily responded. "They were dressed just like most guys in these parts, but they had an eastern accent. You know, kinda like they were from New York or Boston."

"Hmm, maybe they weren't who I was thinking of. Did they drive a red sports car?" Bert made that up hoping to get a different response.

"Hahaha, don't I wish! I'd have asked them out. No, they drove a grey pickup, extended cab with back seat." She saw some humor in that.

Bert was surprised by that detail. "There are pickups everywhere around here. How did you happen to notice theirs?"

She was happy to tell him. "The cashier here sees nearly everyone who drives up through that picture window. There are very few cars that have dark tinted glass, like yours does. However, there are 'NO' trucks around here with dark windows. So, theirs stood out like a sore thumb."

Bert received his order and thanked this young woman. "Miss, you're a great cashier. With your personality and attention to details, I bet you account for at least 20 per cent of the business here. Thanks for chatting with me. Oh, one other question if you don't mind. Did those lads say where they were going from here?"

She was again quick to reply. "Thank you, sir. They did mention Wyoming and asked me what the best route was to get to Cheyenne."

"What did you suggest? I'm heading to Wyoming myself soon."

She didn't hesitate. "Oh, I told them I'd go southeast to Glendive and pick up Interstate 94. But if they wanted a more scenic route, go southwest to Brockway and west. You're awfully curious, are they wanted or something?"

'Bert didn't want to alarm her. "No, I'm just curious about anyone from the east coast. Thanks again, young lady, you're a gem." With that, he went back to his car and to Norah and Missy.

"Norah, if you're up to it now, maybe we should go back to the Williams' driveway and sit for a while. Perhaps you can focus on where their bodies might be? What do you think? Keeping up with these guys is important and you are the key."

Norah leaned back and drew a deep breath, regaining her composure. "I think that's a good idea, dear. I know that Duke is relatively close, but I think she's farther away. We have to call on their spirits to tell us where."

They drove back out to the victims' ranch, eased a couple hundred feet into the driveway, and stopped. They got out and sat on the back of the open cargo compartment, while Missy meandered nearby. Norah leaned back with her eyes closed.

Finally, she stood up. "Bert, Duke is not far from here. They wanted to get rid of him quickly, because she was the object. I'm drawn down the road to the west. I'm seeing Duke's feet as if I'm looking through his eyes. He's being led off the road and down a bank into what looks like a shallow ravine or dry stream bed. He doesn't go far, maybe less than a hundred yards from the road. There's a stand of low shrubs and grasses. He is forced to kneel. I see the vegetation near his face. Then an explosion of light and darkness. I can taste blood. He's shot and died instantly. He's somewhat close to here, Bert."

Bert decided they needed to have a witness, and they worked for Bob. He called him. He explained to Bob that they were sitting in the ranch driveway right now and reviewed the visions that were pulling them to the west. He asked him to come and go with them on a quest to find Duke.

"I'll be right there. Leaving Circle now. I'll leave the boy here. I don't think he needs to see this." Bob was resolute.

Bert called Deputy Bill Haskins while waiting for Bob and brought him up to date on all that was happening. He told Bill about finding the lone dime, and what that likely meant. Bill offered the latest news from Selby that the victims had both been shot at close range with a medium caliber handgun. Tentatively, forensics thought it was a 38 or 40 caliber, or possibly a 9-millimeter. They discussed how this was a different weapon and caliber than at the previous murders. They both wondered if there were different murderers, or did the murderers have several different handguns? Was this another ploy to hide the fact that the same killers were involved in all three crimes?

Bob drove up about fifteen minutes later. He had driven fast. Bert met him at his driver's window briefly. "Thanks for coming, Bob. We need you along, though this might take a while. Can you take the rest of the day, if needed? I think we need to take both vehicles in case one needs to stand guard while the other might have to do something else, just in case."

Bob nodded affirmatively. "Lead on, sir. I will follow.

Bert drove slowly west on Horse Creek Road, searching the sides for a grassy ravine-like topography. A possible candidate came into view in a couple miles. Bert pulled over and stopped. Now it was Missy's turn.

Missy's ears stood erect as she waited on the opened cargo area of the SUV. Her eyes were alert as she waited for Bert to present her the old work gloves worn by Duke. His favorite leather gloves, according to Bob. He carried them in his hip pocket even if he wasn't wearing them. She jumped out and Bert closed the lift gate.

This Coywolf canine was now on the hunt. She trotted in the pace of her coyote cousins, ears forward and nose near the ground, searching for the scent of her subject. She surveyed the several hundred feet on the more pronounced south side of the road, and then the north. It was obvious that she didn't pick up the scent. She got her treat from Bert anyway, after jumping back in the vehicle. Bert closed the door and they again drove slowly west.

Twice more they stopped and checked sites that seemed to fit Norah's vision. Each time, Missy returned without alerting on anything. They drove another two miles toward the sun, now a third of the way down toward the horizon. Another deeper ravine came into view, primarily on the south side of the road. The closest ranch was about a mile to the east. The terrain was more rolling hills here. Bert noticed that Norah was sitting forward and looking more intently. She's feeling a pull to this place, he thought. This is it.

Missy was acting more alert and nervous here, too. She bounded out quickly as soon as Bert opened the door. She sniffed about halfway across the road to the north, and then reversed and made her way down the bank to the south. She had her nose almost to the ground as she loped near the bottom of the depression as it meandered and curved in a southerly direction. She was about four hundred feet from the road when she slowed, and then stopped. Bert saw her sit down and look back at him to see his acknowledgment as he trotted toward her, Bob in close pursuit. She turned her head back to the object of her search, in the thick brushy spot in front of her. The body of Duke Williams lay face down with his hands behind him, bound by a large zip tie. The caked, black blood covering his head and back left no doubt about his death.

Bert looked at Bob, who pulled out his cell phone. Bert's nod was all the acknowledgement Bob needed to know. He dialed 911 and passed the details for the County Sheriff. Then Bert and he sat down on a low grassy bank and guarded Duke's body while beginning the long wait for the authorities to arrive.

By late that afternoon, the Sheriff, two of his deputies, and an ambulance had passed through the fence and were parked at the side of the ravine near the victim. Bert's SUV and Bob's truck were still parked on the side of the road. The sun was low in the western sky, hanging just above the low hills on the horizon. The hottest part of the day was now behind them and the temperature was just beginning to recede toward the cooler evening.

A couple of neighboring ranchers had stopped to see what was going on, and then proceeded on toward Circle. Norah and Missy remained in their SUV, content to stay out of the proceedings behind the tinted windows. Norah was leaning back with her eyes shut, tuning in to the murder of Terry Williams. Missy vacillated between lying on her side, snoozing, and pacing the cargo area. She was tuned in to the goings-on outside.

Bert and Bob had made their statements to two of the deputies, and now the Sheriff approached them. He was a large man, stocky and a little heavy, but otherwise looked like he could wrestle bears for a living. He shook Bert's hand again, nodded to Bob, and then focused on Bert. "So, you used the visions of a psychic to locate this place for the body. Bob here tells me that you're legit, or I'd feel compelled to arrest you as a prime suspect. So, Mister

Lynnes, I'm going to give you the benefit of the doubt and believe you. Your wife cannot be compelled to testify against you, so no use to harass her. As horrific as this crime is, I don't want to leave any stone unturned to get our hands on the bastards who did this. What can you tell me about this?"

Bert noticed Bob's surprise at the seeming openness of this Sheriff. It wasn't in character with the man Bob had described. Was the Sheriff sincere or just hoping to set Bert up?

Bert was in a quandary, but felt he had to trust in this man as much as possible, though. "Sir, a series of unlikely circumstances, referrals, and so forth has resulted in our working now four of these cases. Cases that appear to be the work of serial killers; very vicious men. The M.O. is virtually the same in all cases. There are no signs of a struggle, telling us that these guys are somehow approaching the victims in a very disarming manner and catching them off guard. Then they have evolved into binding them with zip ties, duck taping their mouths, and removing them from the property along with one of the victim's vehicles. All the victims have been brutally murdered. My psychic believes this woman has been raped. She was very upset by the graphic vision of that rape. The bodies are being hidden in different rural locations, and the vehicles have all been hidden in plain sight in larger parking lots where they are not likely to be discovered for a while. The victims have all been rural people in small communities, which is apparently not by accident. We cannot get a good fix on the faces of the perps, but it's looking like they are mastering the art of blending in. Their crimes seem to be escalating, if my psychic is right, with rape now on the agenda. It's like they're evolving, learning how to master their evil craft as they go. There is a strange calling card, apparently. At every crime scene there has been a combination of nickels and dimes, apparently left intentionally. This would not even be noticed, except that my psychic has seen these coins in her visions at every crime scene. They appear to be counting down to some final act. If so, there is only one or maybe two to go. We may have two clues, Sheriff. Two white guys with east coast accents have been connected to a grey extended cab pickup with dark tinted windows. They may or may not be the suspects. The killers are not done, Sheriff. There will be other deaths unless we can stop them. I'm sorry, but I still don't know your name sir?"

The Sheriff thought about everything Bert had said, including the last question. He had often wondered what in the hell his ancestors were thinking. He had the most improbable name for a Sheriff in history, he figured. The only time he appreciated it even a little was during an election, because nobody could forget him. Finally, he admitted, "My name is Sheriff Jim Darling, but you can call me Sheriff and if you call me Darling, I might still have you arrested." He was sort of laughing halfheartedly.

Bert fought back a chuckle, having to literally bite his tongue. The more he tried to suppress the laugh, the harder it tried to come out. Finally, it was either turn blue or just cut loose. He started to laugh, and it became so uncontrollable that both Bob and then the Sheriff chimed in and before long all three were laughing hysterically. When they finally got the humor out of their system, Bert patted the Sheriff on the back, offered his hand, and said, "Well, Sheriff, I am very glad to meet you and just Sheriff is fine with me. We need a Sheriff to catch these bastards and I don't care what your name is as long as you help do that."

With the tension broken and Bert a couple steps closer to being partners with these three men, he looked toward the last rays of the setting sun. The Sheriff nodded in acknowledgment and pronounced that they had done all they could do at the murder scene. He said they should all call it a night and get a fresh start in the morning. He told Bert that if his psychic wife thought Mrs. Williams was around here, then he was good with following her lead, wherever that took them.

The entire caravan pulled out, with the Sheriff in the lead followed by the ambulance. They all headed back to Circle. Bert knew that he and Norah needed to talk and try to determine whatever was possible about Terry's location. Norah sat quietly all the way back and turned to face the Williams' ranch driveway as they passed it. Bert knew to keep quiet and let the lost souls talk with her.

Back at the motel and with everyone fed, watered, and walked, Bert leaned back in the chair with his feet propped on the bed, talking with Norah. She sat at the head of the bed with her knees pulled up, watching Missy sleeping in front of the window. Norah broke the silence. "Honey, I've been trying to channel Terry since we left out there. I'm getting a rush of glimpses as if a high-speed shutter through her eyes. Almost all a bit of a blur, like she's looking out a window at hills, valleys, fields, fences, and ditches all flying by at high speed. Now and then I see the numbers 35, 22, and 42 pass at various points through my mind. I get a fuzzy and fleeting vision of a sign with Copenhagen, I think. It's all blended together. Then it seems to slow down, and I see low brown hills with a mix of greener vegetation. I see the grasses more clearly, as if she's on foot. I see her feet sometimes, and they seem to be tripping or maybe she's being dragged. Then she's being forced to her knees and raped. They both do it. I hear her crying; I can taste her tears. I can close my eyes and hear the gunshot and feel the bullet shattering her brain." Once again Norah looked out the window, with tears streaming down her cheeks.

Bert thought about this, trying to make some sense out of it. "Well, we can be sure they drove her out to some desolate place not too far away, where they felt they were unlikely to be seen. That's their M.O., so far. Maybe we can eliminate some variables. You've seen the numbers 35 and 42 several times during the previous cases, so the new 22 must relate to this case. In South Dakota, the number you saw turned out to be a state road sign. Maybe 22 is a road sign and she was so restrained that she could barely see it or maybe envision where she was being taken." He had the map out and began looking for any roads with the number 22.

"Is there a Copenhagen, Montana, anywhere?" Norah asked. "I've not been able to find it. If it's on a sign it's going by so fast, it's just a blur. Copenhagen is the capital of Denmark. This couldn't have something to do with Denmark, either the country or the word, could it?"

Bert's voice was slightly higher and faster, as he exclaimed, "Honey, I've found a Montana highway 22, not too far south of here. It runs in a northwest and southeast direction. I Googled, but there doesn't seem to be a Copenhagen in Montana. However, Babe, there is a small town of Cohagen, and it's on highway 22. Probably about an hour's drive from here."

Norah followed his logic. "That's probably it, Bert, it was such a fleeting glimpse that it could have been Cohagen, rather than Copenhagen."

Bert contemplated something. "Sweetheart, several times, without you realizing it I think, you have been drawn in a certain direction. In Colorado, it was to the north. The bodies were to the north. You felt that Duke was west of Circle and west of the ranch, and he was. It's as if the victims have sent out a directional signal which you are somehow picking up. I've noticed you looking toward the southwest of Circle several times today, including now. From where you're sitting, you're looking out the window to the southwest."

Norah thought about that, and then nodded in agreement. "You know, you're right, Bert. I don't always realize when I'm being drawn to a certain direction, at least not right away. It's like an invisible and undetectable pull that causes you to glance or look in a particular direction."

"Dear, if I draw a rough line from Circle to the southwest, it goes in the vicinity of Cohagen. I think the spirit of Terry Williams is drawing us to look for her around Cohagen."

Norah nodded in agreement. She could sense a feeling of understanding coming over her. Terry's spirit was calling to her. Her mind was answering.

Bert made a conference call to Bob and the Sheriff, telling them what they had concluded. "Gentlemen, I think we need to get all the deputies you can spare and search up and down highway 22 both ways from Cohagen. We need everyone to scour the topography on both sides of the road, identifying every place along that road for at least twenty miles in each direction, where a rape and murder might occur. The ideal spots will be relatively close to the road, out of sight of the road, and not likely to be seen by anyone. If a small and seldom used road leads to such a spot off the main highway; then it would be more ideal. They could get their vehicle out of sight, too."

Sheriff Jim Darling didn't hesitate nor question Bert's thoughts. "Let's do it! Let's meet at the Wooden Nickel at 7:00 in the morning, and we'll decide. Then everyone can cover their territory."

Bert added, "We'll be there, Sheriff. If you can have each searcher get the word to me when they find a likely place, I'll bring my Coywolf to that spot and let her verify if it's a go or not. That will save a lot of time. I feel that we're going to find this poor woman tomorrow."

There was an air of solemn excitement and enthusiasm when they said their good-byes. Bert was keyed up, but he knew they needed to get some sleep, if possible. Tomorrow could be a long day, but also the day they help bring Terry home. He could already feel the bittersweet emotions that were to come. There would be the enthusiasm that comes with finding someone, but it would be crushed under the weight of sadness that comes with rubbing shoulders with death, and with evil.

"Good night, Norah," he said, "kisses to you all night long. My love for you knows no bounds, Sweetheart."

"Kisses to you too, Darling," he heard in the darkness. As he lay back and closed his eyes, in his mind came the haunting melody of a favorite singer, Sarah McLachlan. As he drifted toward sleep, he whispered, "I need some distraction from this, Norah".

In the darkness, he heard her answer. "I pray that you find some peace tonight, Honey. That you find peace in the arms of an angel."

* * *

Sunday morning dawned bright and clear. It was 50 degrees with a chilly breeze. Bert and company were the second to arrive at the Wooden Nickel restaurant, about ten till seven. Within a few minutes, Bob, Sheriff Jim, and two deputies had assembled and determined which section of highway each would search. They headed out in single file toward the little town of Cohagen.

Bert, Norah, and Missy arrived in Cohagen, third in line. He parked near the intersection with Highway 22. Cohagen wasn't a little town, he thought. It was a spot on the road. However, they would wait at that spot for the calls that were sure to summon them. The others paired up and headed both directions on Highway 22. Missy seemed to know that it would be her turn now. She paced from one side of the SUV to the other, peering out the partially lowered windows and sniffing the air.

Within ten minutes the first call came. It was Bob, telling him that the older deputy had a likely looking place about seven miles southeast of town. A small dirt road led to nowhere into some low hills on the right side of the road.

B and N investigations, the entire team, soon arrived where the deputy was parked. Bert let Missy search the area for a good ten minutes. She picked up on nothing. Bert, however, did pick up on something. He noticed that Norah kept looking in the rearview mirror, in the opposite direction from which they had come. He asked her, "Norah, are we going the wrong way? Is Terry back that way?"

The question seemed to startle her, but she replied, "Yes, Bert, the pull is back the other way, the other side of Cohagen. I feel her calling me."

Bert told Bob about Norah's sensations, and said he now felt the fastest way to search was for him to drive his team to the northwest from town. Between Norah's commune with the dead woman, and Missy's nose, that seemed to have the best chance of a quick resolution. Bob understood and agreed. However, he said that he and the older deputy would search about five miles farther since they were already down here.

Bert drove to Cohagen, didn't blink so he wouldn't miss the town, and continued northwest on highway 22. He already had a couple of calls about places up here to investigate. He stopped at the first two, and let Missy confirm that they were not the right spots. He met up with and discussed his current strategy with Sheriff Jim.

As they slowly continued to drive northwest of Cohagen, Bert kept an eye on Norah, watching her demeanor and expressions. "We're getting closer, aren't we?"

She didn't hesitate. "Yes, dear, we're going toward her. I feel her pull; I feel the agony and despair of her final moments. Her spirit is getting stronger the farther we go."

The Sheriff called him. He was about five minutes ahead of them now. "Bert, I have a good candidate here on the south side of the road, on your left. Let's check it out. You'll see my car just off the road on a dirt road. More of a dirt trail, actually. It doesn't look to go to any ranch that I can see."

As they turned left off the highway and parked behind the Sheriff's car, Bert agreed with his choice of location. This was indeed the kind of place he would expect these killers to choose. There were a series of low, choppy hills, and the dirt road curved in and around them, quickly disappearing from anyone driving on the highway. It looked to be an ideal hiding spot.

He knew that Jim seemed to trust him, but he was still a Sheriff. Bert felt it best to call Missy up to the Sheriff's car and show her the woman's boot which Bob had provided. With the Sheriff watching, he ordered, "Find, Missy."

Missy immediately started her search pattern, doing a couple of short semi-circles near the right side of the faded road. She was not interested in the left side at all. She seemed to be struggling to locate the scent, as she slowly made her way down the grassed over trail. Because of the grass, it was not likely to reveal a tire track. "If she was still in the vehicle as they drove down here, her scent would be very faint," Bert said to the Sheriff as they followed Missy on foot.

They followed Missy for over two hundred yards, as the road curved right and left around low, choppy hills, knolls really. They could no longer see the highway behind the rises, and there were no neighboring ranches in view in any direction. Missy stopped, her ears pointed forward, eyes alert. Then she turned off the trail to the right and began a slow trot around a low knoll, and then back to the left behind it. She continued weaving around two more similar knolls until she reached a depression which looked like it held water at times during heavier rains. The grass was heavier and greener here, with two to three-foot-tall shrubbery surrounding the low area.

Bert and Sheriff Darling caught up with her, panting hard from the exertion of their run to keep her in sight. She was sitting down at the edge of the low area where grass met shrubbery, looking into the dense scrubby vegetation. She was the first guardian to watch over the lifeless and partially nude body of Terry Williams, where she had been dragged into the more-dense brush from the low grasses of the dry pond.

Bert called Missy aside, praised her, and gave her a well-deserved treat, while the Sheriff called for his deputies and instructed them to call an ambulance and coroner. He carefully surveyed and began to document the crime scene. There was little doubt in his mind what had happened here: rape, followed by a gunshot to the back of her head. Her wrists remained bound by a half-inch wide zip tie, and the duct tape still clung to her mouth. He continued his slow search of the area, while waiting for the more detailed crime scene investigator on his force of five officers. Then he focused on a tiny flash of white about twenty feet to the side of the victim. As he approached it, he could see what appeared to be a white handkerchief, stuck in the rigid base of a small mesquite bush. Did these guys finally make a mistake?

Bert discussed the wadded handkerchief with Jim while waiting for the others to get there.

"In all likelihood," said the Sheriff, "this belonged to one of the killers. We will not know that unless we can extract some DNA other than the victims from it." He knew Terry and was finding it difficult to refer to her as the victim, but he had to try to distance himself in order to think clearly. It also helped to suppress the rage he felt, welling up inside him like a volcano about to blow. "At best, it will take a week or longer to confirm what, if any, DNA may be on this. Same for prints, and there's almost zero chance of getting a print off that piece of cloth. That's one more week for these scumbags to be farther away and closer to doing this again. If that's their handkerchief, do you have any suggestions how to confirm it now?"

Bert thought for a few seconds. "There might be a possible long shot," he replied to the Sheriff. "If I can get Missy to take in the scent, and command her to search for it, her actions may give us that answer."

"Do it, Bert," commanded the man and not the Sheriff. The Sheriff knew he might be putting his career in jeopardy. "We need a break to catch these sorry SOB's."

Bert called Missy to the wadded handkerchief where it remained as evidence, stuck among the mesquite thorns. After she took a long sniff of the cloth, he gave the command, "Find, Missy."

They both stood back and watched this domesticated wild animal, now among their best hopes to apprehend those whom they reviled with pure hatred. Missy showed great interest all around the small grassy depression, especially near Mrs. Williams. Then, as if she knew her subject wasn't there, she began to follow the unseen scent markers out of the depression and back along the path they had all come in on from the trail. Bert and Sheriff Jim followed her at a trot, once again getting more exercise than their aging bodies were intending. They watched as she arrived back at the trail, stopped, then walked around with her nose to the ground. As if the tiny molecules of scent were imbedded in the grass on the downwind side of the trail, she began to slowly meander around in what looked like a circle about fifty feet in diameter. Then she began slowly to follow the same meandering walk, with nose to the ground, back toward the highway.

When the Sheriff reached the trail, he paused where the canine had made the curious circle. Almost imperceptible to the eye, the bent grass was nearly back upright. As he followed it with his eyes, he could barely make out the path where a vehicle had turned around.

Bert saw the Sheriff wave off any further pursuit of the killers' scent. He called Missy back and they hastily returned to the crime scene. The ambulance and other vehicles would be arriving shortly. As they approached the cold body of this woman whom Bert felt he knew, the Sheriff turned to him.

"Bert, if I let that handkerchief go into evidence, there is not much chance it will be of value. However, if you have even a part of it, do you think Missy can continue to pick up the scent of the murderer who lost it?"

Bert replied quickly, "Yes, Sheriff, if I keep it bagged and as it is, she should be able to follow that scent for quite some time."

The Sheriff pulled out his pocketknife. He used it to pull the handkerchief from its hiding place. With a gloved hand, he carefully stretched out what looked to be a new handkerchief, looking for manufacturer, laundry, or other markers. Not finding any distinguishing marks on it, he gave the knife to Bert, pulled it tight, and instructed Bert to cut it at the top. Once it was cut about an inch, the Sheriff tore it in two pieces. They placed one piece in a plastic bag, which Bert always had on hand. It went into his pocket. The other piece was returned to the mesquite bush. This done, they waited the two more minutes until three deputies arrived, escorting the ambulance and coroner.

The Sheriff oversaw the crime scene investigation and the removal of the body, while one of his deputies took a statement from Bert. The deputy said the Sheriff wanted to speak with him before he left.

About an hour later, with the sun beginning its plunge toward the western horizon, the ambulance and law enforcement teams began to leave. Sheriff Darling said he would walk with Bert back to the highway. He paused to look Bert squarely in the eyes. "Bert, I trust you. Three days ago, I would have thought your methods were a hoax, but now I know without a doubt that you're legit. I'm doing what I can to keep you on the trail of the son-of-a-bitches who killed these people. I could call for the FBI, but I don't believe they have any better chance than you do of bringing those guys to justice. I know the feds would at the very least ridicule and blow you off, and there's a good chance they'd spend their time trying to make you the prime suspect. They wouldn't pay one damn bit of attention to a county sheriff in Montana. I'm sure you know that, while I didn't destroy evidence, I tampered with evidence, and I'd be in a hell of a bunch of trouble if that comes out. I also trust that you know I did that because I believe the scent on that piece of cloth could lead your Coywolf to the killers, hopefully before they can kill again. Sooner than the FBI could put it all together. If they can put it all together. The truth is that if these killings all happened in Boston, New York, Philly, or any other major city, the feds would be all over it as a serial killing spree. But because these have happened in rural states to farmers and ranchers, those Ivy League boys could really care less. They are still more than content to treat these as unrelated murders and leave it to the county sheriffs to figure it out. That's if these have come to their attention at all."

They arrived back at the highway. Bert turned to this man who was now more of a friend than a sheriff. "Sheriff, your secret's safe with me. You also have my pledge that, to the extent that fate will allow, we'll do our best to keep after and get ahead of those heartless scumbags. If I need your help, I won't hesitate to ask for it. Bob has offered his help, as well. Let's keep in touch and see if together we can nail the scum."

Bert listened as the Sheriff recapped their situation. "So, what we've got to this point is four murders of rural couples in four agricultural states. The M.O. seems to be very similar in all four cases, otherwise they are so far not connected in any way other than by your psychic and by some pocket change. Is that how you see it?" he asked Bert.

Bert nodded. "Yes, Sheriff, the one common thread, unprovable in court, is an odd countdown of nickels and dimes, which have been seen in the mind of our psychic in each case. We don't know where the countdown ends. Is it with a nickel or with zero? That means there may be one more murder planned, or two, depending on that answer. Our best circumstantial guess is that these two guys are going to Wyoming, our home state, next. I think we have the chance to catch up to them and hopefully get ahead of them there. It's worth a shot and we want to get these murderers before they kill again."

Bert accepted the Sheriff's extended hand as he said good-bye and good luck. He told Bert that he'd be ready to help any way he could, and to just call if needed. He handed Bert his business card, something he apparently rarely did. Bert took it without laughing at the name, Sheriff Jim Darling.

After returning to his vehicle, loading Missy, and starting the engine, Bert handed another treat to Missy over his shoulder. He looked at Norah, who was waiting patiently for him to bring her up to speed. She knew they had found Terry. "Honey," he said, "we're headed for Wyoming. We're no longer investigators, we're now hunters and we have allies in the hunt. We have others eager to help us."

"Good," she replied. "I want to get these men and put them away for a very long time. An eternity would be nice, as long as they go to the right place."

CHAPTER TEN: THE COWBOY STATE

August 1, 2017 dawned with a typical Wyoming "breeze," a 30-mph wind. It made the 60-degree temperature at Burgess Junction, in the Bighorn Mountains, seem considerably cooler than the thermometer indicated. Bert and Norah had decided to take this scenic detour on the way into their home state. The Bighorns were one of their favorite places on earth. A jacket would feel good as they exited the little rustic cabin they'd rented for the night and took a brisk walk with Missy around this beautiful high mountain valley. In the morning light, the surrounding mountains and forests took on an even greater beauty as the early rays of sunlight pierced into the woods and cast long shadows from the lone trees around the campground. There was no chance of seeing one of the area's many moose here, though they were likely grazing near the roads in the many small mountain meadows. There was no better place to see moose, elk, Sandhill cranes, and mountain wildflowers than in the Bighorn Mountains. "A best kept secret," Bert muttered. Despite being on a retractable leash, Missy obviously agreed.

"I'm glad we stopped here overnight, Bert," Norah said enthusiastically. "This is one of those special places that calms and soothes the soul. I needed this beautiful detour for my mind. Too many things to feel sad about, lately. The chance to inhale fresh air, feel sunshine, and be lost in mountain beauty is like manna from heaven. Spending precious time with you and Missy is icing on an already great cake."

They completed their walk, and soon left the junction of the main roads traversing this mountain paradise, and headed west, deciding to stop and do the mile hike to the mysterious Medicine Wheel. This ancient and Stonehenge-like wheel, laid out in stones on a high mountain plateau overlooking the steep western drop-off to the arid valley below the Bighorns, was a baffling mystery to the experts to this day. A 360 degree turn to view the surrounding peaks, forests, valleys, and the expansive openness to the west, made it easy to imagine the special allure and aura of this place during an ancient ceremony. To further imagine it at night under the stars, brilliant in the night sky at this elevation, with small fires burning at the points of the circle, was mesmerizing. There were many theories about the origin and purpose of this sacred Native American site. Bert hoped it would also be an inspiration to Norah and himself in their quest to find the killers. At the least, it proved to be another interlude from the stresses to come, and an inspiration and tonic for the soul.

After leaving Medicine Wheel, they pulled over at the last scenic overlook before descending the steep and winding road the hundreds of feet down the western slope. From this vantage point, one could be absorbed into the arid, undulating, grey and brown hills stretching out toward Cody. In the distance, the Rockies were a panoramic backdrop to the visual vastness.

Bert pulled out the plastic bag containing his piece of the white handkerchief, found at Terry Williams' murder scene. He laid it on the dash in front of Norah. "Sweetheart, I know you have so much pressure on your shoulders, but it seems like you're still the key to finding these guys before they kill again. What can you sense from this cloth? It's our only physical connection to them."

Norah leaned forward, with her face only inches from the cloth; her eyes were closed. She seemed to be clearing her mind of every thought and distraction, attempting to draw the tiny bit of energy left on this cloth by a stone-cold killer. This was a new direction for her psychic gift. So far, she had been pulled by living or dead people to find them. Now she had to change her focus to a living person to see what he was going to do, rather than what he had done. She didn't know if she was psychically up to that task. She knew she had to try.

After several minutes, she leaned back; her eyes still closed. She focused on the world inside her mind, closing off the world outside. "He's not done killing. There is an ultimate objective he's striving for, and it will be devastating to someone. Many people. The killings are not random; there is a method and a purpose. It's as if they are practicing for the final act of a play. I glimpsed a missile. It just seemed to appear and then disappear. It seemed like it was somehow standing guard over something. I see a buffalo high on a ridge, just standing there. Then it was gone. This guy is looking for something. I think it's their next victim. They're searching. I feel like they're here in Wyoming."

Bert thought about her words for several minutes before speaking. "So, if we can determine both their method and their purpose, we might be able to find their next victim before they do?"

"Yes, Honey," Norah replied, "I can feel him planning and thinking about how to reach his goal. I just can't get a sense of what that goal is. I have the strong feeling that he or they are here in Wyoming, though. It feels like Wyoming is a steppingstone on their path. It doesn't feel like it will end here."

Bert reflected on her revelations. "Well, there are a couple of missiles at the entrance to F. E. Warren Air Force Base, in Cheyenne. You drive right by them on the Interstate. They would have undoubtedly noticed them if they passed through Cheyenne. The Terry Bison Ranch is just off I-25 right before it enters Colorado. There's a metal statue of a bison on top of the ridge there. If they went that far, they would have seen it, also. They could have seen live buffalo in the pastures, as well. If they are staying in Wyoming, they might have even stayed in the campground at the Terry headquarters. It has guest facilities, old time stores, winery, campground, and cabins. As you know, it's quite a tourist attraction as well as a large working buffalo ranch. Do you think you could be seeing those places?"

She was slow to reply. "Yes, I think it's possible, Bert. When I try to see what this man is seeing, the visions are clouded by his interpretations of reality, not reality alone. If he's looking at a buffalo but thinking it's a cow, then what I sense is mixed up. I'm also getting visions of a crowd, mulling around at an event. At times, they seem to be standing in a line for food, maybe; or to get into something. This killer seems interested in them, though, because I see people passing in all directions. He's watching them. I can't tell if this is a past or a future vision. Maybe it's both?"

"Anything else?" Bert asked.

Norah's eyes were still closed, peering into the ether of her brain. "I catch fleeting glances of a nickel, Honey. There's a thought-out meaning behind those coins. Also, glimpses of the number 42, again. It's very faint and fleeting, as if on a billboard or something, and then gone. I still don't know what it could mean."

Bert had no idea what that number could mean. He reflected on her words. "From what you're sensing, it seems like they have driven the length of Wyoming and are searching for their next victim. How do they select them, though? You feel that it's a process or a method. But what is it? You continue to see coins, now a nickel. Does that mean they are planning one last killing; or is zero the last? What do you say to a night in Cheyenne? Maybe a night in rodeo town will bring more clarity."

She didn't reply for a minute. "Bert, Honey, I'm tired of being on the road. I get the feeling that they're going to be planning the next move for a little while. I think we may have time to go home for a respite. We're only about three hours away from up here by Medicine Wheel. I will try to channel this guy from home. Right now, I'm not picking up on anything else. It's as if he's dropped off the channel."

Bert shifted into gear, pulled out of the overlook, and began the slow descent off the mountain toward Cody on US Highway 14A. He told his wife, "I understand, sweetheart, this has been a tough period for us, you especially. We'll go home where we can rest and try to figure out this guy and his buddy. Missy could use the down time as well."

For the next two days, they stayed at home near Cody, relaxing, changing out and cleaning gear, getting ready to pack up the cooler again, and giving Missy a lot of outdoor time. Two or three times a day, Norah focused on the piece of torn handkerchief, her eyes closed, clearing her mind, and trying to channel the last person to touch the cloth, a vicious murderer. Nothing! Had she lost him? Was it temporary? Was it permanent?

Friday, the fourth of August was chilly and breezy in the early morning as Bert walked Missy through the woods and mountainsides north of his home. She always loved being outside, and Bert constantly marveled at what a beautiful animal she had become. With her reddish-grey coat, long bushy tail, and the sharp ears and nose of her coyote ancestors, she looked every bit the wild creature she descended from. There was just one difference. Missy was comfortable being with these humans.

Norah remained at home, taking an easy stroll around the

yard, and relaxing in front of the picture window. She knew her husband would be several hours walking in their beloved mountains with Missy. After an hour of relaxation, she moved to the kitchen table, sat in front of the now familiar bag of white cloth, and closed her eyes. She hadn't seen her husband return early, enter the back door, and then stand silently, watching her.

Bert slid quietly to the floor and sat against the wall, watching his pretty wife. He could see the relaxation in her face slowly change to stress. He knew she was finally picking up something from their prey.

In her mind, Norah saw a fuzzy panorama unfold at varying speeds. She saw roads, grasses, fences, occasional trees, and livestock whizzing by. They seemed to be doing a lot of driving now. She couldn't tell where they were, only that they had been moving. The number 20 came flitting through her mind, and again 35 and 42. She saw what looked like a grave monument. Then the visions became cloudy and fuzzy; they were fading away. Gone! She finally opened her eyes. It was then that she saw Bert, sitting on the floor by the back door, watching her, lovingly.

He got up from the floor and came to the table, sitting down across from her. "I could tell you were getting something this time." He had learned to recognize the subtle changes in her expression and demeanor when she was able to channel a spirit or soul.

"Yes, Darling, I saw a mix of things as if looking through his eyes. It was a jumble, often fuzzy, and not easy to make sense of. They are driving, it seems like a lot. I saw a panorama film almost, of scenes from the roads of Wyoming."

He interrupted her. "What kind of country did you see?"

She replayed her memory of the mix of visions. "It was mostly farm and ranch land, I only saw a few or no trees."

This confirmed Bert's thought process. "Then it sounds like they are concentrating on the east half of the state. At least they must not be spending much time in the forests or mountains. That narrows our search a little." Not much, though, he thought to himself. We've eliminated about one-third of the state, maybe.

"The previous numbers 35 and 42 showed again, fleetingly. Also, the number 20. It seems to be on a sign; maybe a road sign. I'm not sure."

"Hmm, I still don't know what the first two numbers mean," he said. "In the previous case, the number 22 was a state road. I wonder if that might be the case, here." He pulled out his laptop and opened the map function. A search of the state of Wyoming revealed what he already knew. US highway 20 ran essentially east and west from Cody to west Nebraska. A long way to cover, if that was the 20. It covered mostly farm and ranch land, too, all the way.

She added, "The gravestone is really puzzling. There are probably thousands of cemeteries and hundreds of thousands of graves in the state. What kind of sign is that? Is it a sign, or is it just something they happened to see?"

"Boy, Sweetheart, I haven't got a clue on that one. Maybe you'll pull in more clarity as time goes on. Anyway, you've given us a few clues to go on, so I thank you again, Honey. I could not do this without you."

Bert decided to make some update calls. He first called his clients from the previous cases. Although law enforcement at each was soliciting the general public for any information or tips, none were working out. Sheriff Jim in Montana reported that the victims there appeared to have been shot with a 22-caliber handgun. Judging by the damage, it was probably a 22-magnum, he said. Bert discussed with the Sheriff the apparent fact that different caliber guns were used at each killing, along with a knife once. Were there different killers, or were they clever enough to throw one more question into the equation?

Bert received another bit of information from the Sheriff. The Williams' red pickup had been found. It had been parked in a busy, non-monitored parking area of an all-night grocery store in Miles City. There was a new wrinkle in the killers' MO. They had traded the victims' license plate for another, outdated, Montana plate. This may have been removed from an abandoned vehicle a few towns away. It did serve to add another day or two to the time required to find and identify the vehicle.

When Bert talked with Bill Haskins in South Dakota, Bill pointed out that without Norah's psychic inputs, the murder victims would probably not have been found for weeks or months. The tactics the killers were using seemed designed to delay and misdirect any investigations. Likewise, Missy's nose had likely saved hours if not days or weeks that would otherwise have been required to find the exact location of the victims.

After the calls, Bert discussed the strategy with Norah to try to home in on these guys. "Norah, I'm thinking it might be prudent to spend some time on the road and see if you or Missy can pick up their scent. They seem to be lying low right now, or just taking their time. If they're going to pick another victim, they must be doing a lot of planning. What do you think about spending a couple days on the road and see what the two of you might detect?"

Norah finally replied, "Yes, I think that might be a good idea, dear. I'm pretty sure I can channel at least the guy who used this handkerchief, my only concern is whether I can really pick up on where he and they are going. I see clues about what they are seeing, where they've been, and maybe even where they may be going and their future intentions, perhaps. The problem I'm feeling is trying to determine which is which. Am I seeing something he is seeing right now, something he saw a while ago, or am I seeing into the future and what he will be seeing? Maybe it doesn't matter which is which, if the result is that we can determine where they are or where they will be. I think we should do this. I'm getting antsy being here at home and knowing there are killers in our state who are probably preparing to kill again. Knowing we may be able to stop them."

"Good, it's settled then. We need to proactively get caught up to these guys. We were very close in Montana and came away with a greater insight into their plans. If we had been two weeks behind them there, we might not have bumped into that little cashier who remembered them. She even remembered where they said they were heading. So, this time, we're in the same state with them, before they kill. We have a chance to get to them, I think."

They decided to take the weekend to get ready to go, train with Missy some more, and parlay again with Sheriff Jim, Deputy Bill Haskins, and Bob. Monday morning, August 7th, they drove from their home and shortly began to follow one possible clue from Norah's visions. That possible clue was US highway 20, which departed Cody and headed in an easterly direction toward Nebraska.

Initially, they drove the desolate miles through the grey and brown terrain of sagebrush and antelope country to the small community of Greybull. There, Norah sat with her eyes closed, before the bag containing the torn handkerchief, attempting to channel the killer. Meanwhile, Bert offered the open bag to Missy for her to sniff and then he let her loose in a few places around town, searching for the scent. Her nose tried, but it found nothing. Norah, on the other hand, was getting some contact with her subject.

When Bert and Missy returned from their last nose search, she turned to him as he slid behind the wheel. "They're still driving and looking, Honey. I see Wyoming ranch scenery passing by as if from a vehicle on the interstate. It's impossible to say where they are, though. I'm picking up on a new fear, because the word "prostitute" flew by in one vision. Are they now looking for prostitutes as their new victims? Or, are they just wanting a good time?"

"Prostitute?" Bert questioned. Did you see a woman or just the word?"

She replied quickly, "I only saw the word, Sweetheart. And there was another thing. For some reason I see one red cow, like a white-faced Hereford. She seems to be floating, as if she's hovering in the air."

"Good grief!" Bert was baffled by that. "What in the heck can one cow mean? I mean, this is Wyoming. It's full of cattle. That's more far-fetched than a prostitute."

With more questions than answers, they backed out of parking and proceeded on highway 20, in the easterly direction which they hoped held some answers. Over the next three days, they would slowly drive from Cody all the way across Wyoming and even to Harrison, Nebraska.

East was at first south, as they passed through the small towns of Basin, Manderson, Worland, and Kirby, en route to Thermopolis. At each place, they stopped and repeated the psychic and scent searches, as before. The results were the same, until the downtown square in Thermopolis. In this town, whose name sprung from the thermal hot springs and bathhouses, Missy seemed to pick up the scent, and then lost it in about ten seconds. They must have gone into the little main street coffee shop, and then departed in their vehicle. She led Bert into this quaint little bookstore turned coffee bistro. It did claim to be pet friendly. He decided to get one of their exotic coffees and made it his excuse to chat with the woman behind the counter.

"Great coffee", he said to her, "are you getting many out-of-towners through here?"

She leaned against the counter in front of him, anxious to have a stranger to talk to. "We're still getting a few now and then. You know that Yellowstone drives the tourist industry around here. When the Park is open, tourists are like flies, when it's closed, we turn into a locals-only cow town, again. Are you one of the flies, or a cowboy?"

Bert had to laugh at that, "Well, I'm neither one. I live outside of Cody, but I'm going through here doing some investigative work. Do you mind if I ask you a question or two?"

"On one condition," she said. "First tell me what on earth you're doing with a coyote on a leash in my store?"

Bert knew she was dying of curiosity about Missy, but he purposely wasn't saying anything after he saw the "Pets Welcome" sign on the door. "She's my working companion. She has a great nose and I've learned how to adapt to her skills in my line of work."

The woman laughed, "So she trained you to use her nose? Is that pretty much it?"

Now he laughed. "Well said, that about sums it up. The reason we came in here just now is that her nose tells me the couple of guys we're looking for came in here, probably in the past few days. Have you noticed one or two guys in here lately, probably with east coast accents?"

She thought about that for a bit as she gathered up some dirty glasses and cups. Finally, she came back to him. "Well, it's still on the tail end of tourist season, so we get all kinds in here. Even guys with coyotes come in from time to time." She laughed again. "I do remember several guys that might fit that billing, though. A couple of black guys, obviously from the east somewhere, were in here yesterday. Several days ago, maybe, there were a couple of white guys; actually, two or three groups, I think, who seemed to be with a busload of gawkers."

"Gawkers," he asked. She had a great sense of humor, he was thinking.

"Yeah, you know, they have their heads out the windows, gawking this way and then gawking that way."

Bert couldn't help but laugh at this woman's weird humor. "So, the couple of white guys, what do you remember about them?"

"I remember that they looked like the rest of us around here, but they definitely weren't from this area originally with their accents." She became very serious. "I also remember that one of those guys gave me the absolute chills. One of the men from that tourist bus accidentally bumped his arm and spilled some of his coffee. The look he gave that guy could have frozen gasoline. That's all I really remember about them. That was enough."

The humor was no longer in the conversation, so Bert thanked her, and he and Missy returned to Norah where she sat on a bench in front of their vehicle. It was rare for her to venture out of their car around strangers. As he walked up to her, a voice called out behind him.

"Hey, Mister, you forgot your wallet. You might need it to buy some coyote food later." The young lady had gotten her humor back. "Good luck to you and that tracker; I hope you find your guys."

After retrieving his wallet, Bert and Norah settled back in their SUV, and he asked her if she picked up anything more.

Norah leaned back against the seat. "I have the sense that they were here, and I'm seeing what looks like these streets and others flitting by, as if from their car. Or truck. I sensed a frustration, too, as if they didn't find what they were looking for here. I heard the rumble of tires on the road and the wind around the front of their moving vehicle. They left here. I can't get a sense of where they went, though."

With a few more clues, perhaps meaningless ones, they left Thermopolis and continued south on this segment of highway 20. Soon they would pass through one of the most breathtaking places in Wyoming, the Wind River Canyon Scenic Byway. With its massive towering cliffs, trapping the road against the fast-moving river, it was an awe-inspiring drive. Ironically, Bert always thought, this natural wonder was quickly followed by some of the ugliest country in Wyoming, as they arrived at the town of Shoshoni and turned east toward Casper.

There were no indications that their subjects had stopped in Shoshoni and they drove on toward Casper. Their only stop was at the infamous "Hell's Half Acre", where, to their surprise, Missy did seem to catch the scent of her human prey for a couple minutes. This odd geological scarp of heavily eroded caves, ravines, and rock formations was a frequent stopping spot for travelers headed for Yellowstone. Norah saw only the word "prostitute" fly by her mind and nothing more.

Casper was too big. It would be a crap shoot if they happened upon any scent, so they stayed overnight there. The next day they continued down highway 20 as it was piggy backed by Interstate 25. Then they continued east through several smaller towns, stopping in each to search the internal and external winds with Norah and Missy. Missy picked up the scent for just a brief time at a stop in Pawnee. As they approached the border with Nebraska, Norah again began to connect with her subject, although all she could really put her finger on was a fleeting vision of the mysterious grave marker and a number 85, which flew in and out of her consciousness in the blink of an eye.

As they were driving back west on highway 20 from Nebraska, Norah began to get stronger sensations that the killers were close, and she felt an almost imperceptible pull toward the south. They reached the high-plains town of Lusk, with a population of about 1500 and an elevation just over 5000 feet. They turned south on the two-lane highway toward Torrington. It was not lost on them that this was highway 85.

"They've been on this highway, Bert, I can feel it," she said. "They're still looking for their next victim."

They continued down highway 85, continuing to stop at all likely places. A couple of times, Missy appeared to catch the scent briefly, seemingly confirming that the suspects indeed had been on the road. They spent two nights at a motel in Torrington, a city of about 6500 population which sat along the North Platte River. Rich in early western history, this town arose near the Oregon Trail, Fort Laramie, and was a stop on the Pony Express. If Bert and Norah had any slack time, he wanted to spend a couple of hours at the Homesteaders Museum.

Mostly they were trying to catch glimpses into the killers' minds by way of Norah's psychic connections. Once again, her visions seemed to slow down. She did catch another glimpse of the cow, still as baffling as it was mysterious. Likewise, she sensed something about a prostitute, again, but this also remained puzzling. For the most part, she could perceive little else to go on.

Bert pondered all that they had. He concluded that the only thing they felt confident about is that the killers seemed to be in the state of Wyoming, somewhere. It also appeared that they were looking for their next target. He looked at Norah and confided in something that was beginning to weigh on him.

"Norah, we've tried everything we can think of to find these guys, but we're just going in circles to some extent," he said. "We know they're around but we're having a hard time zeroing in on them or their next victims. Honey, this is the first case we've ever done entirely at our own expense. Nobody has hired us on this one, and we don't even have a case yet. I'm afraid that we're going to have to go back home and assess your visions from there, because of the costs."

"I know, dear," she replied. "Trying to look into the present and the future is proving more difficult than I thought. I'm trying to communicate with the future dead, rather than the past dead. The ones in the future don't know yet that they're going to die unless we can get ahead of their killers, somehow. I understand the money concerns; I've been feeling that, too. We aren't made of money. This is really our first pro bono case. And our clients don't know yet that we're working for them; working to save their lives. So, let's do this from home, dear."

After giving Missy a much-desired run on a rural road outside of Torrington, they headed back west to meet up with Interstate 25. They could only hope that the peace and serenity of their Cody home would allow Norah to tap into the cold, heartless mind of a murderer. And somehow close the distance between them and him.

CHAPTER ELEVEN: CLOSING IN

The drive north on I-25 was uneventful for a while, with both Bert and Norah saying little. They were lost in their own thoughts. Norah had been staring out the passenger window, relaxing her mind as the Glendo Reservoir passed by to the east of the Interstate. Suddenly the number 18 flashed before her unfocused eyes. She sat forward, startled. Without saying anything to Bert, she tried to fathom what this possible sign was trying to say to her. Then she saw it.

As they approached the next exit, the road signs heralded the options. They had been on the one a few days before. Heading to the east was US highway 20, which they first traveled. What she now noticed, though, was the collocated US highway 18. It and 20 ran together to the town of Lusk and beyond that 18 went into South Dakota. Was this the 18 she just saw? "Bert, Honey, please take this exit. I have the feeling it may be significant."

He quickly made the move to the exit without sideswiping anybody. "What are you sensing, sweetheart?"

Bert eased onto the side of highway 20 and 18, eastbound, stopped the car, and turned toward his wife, waiting for her response.

"I just had the number 18 flash across my consciousness right before we got to this exit. I have this strong feeling that it means something about these guys."

He thought about that for a bit. "You know don't you, that this section of road is part of US 20 that we came down a couple days ago? You were here then, and we knew from your visions that they'd been here at some time ahead of us."

Norah quickly replied, "Yes, dear, I know we've been on this road before, but it was highway 20 to us then. Now, it's just become highway 18, in my mind. I feel that means something to us. I just don't know what it means, other than they've driven on this part of it."

"Hmmm! Boy, I sure wish we knew. Since we've been down much of this section of road, though, and we know they have also, maybe it's still best for us to just go on home and see how many pieces we can bring together into cohesive logic?" He didn't really want to go back on a road they'd already covered.

"That's okay, Honey." She knew he was anxious to go on home and work from there. "Let's work on putting the pieces together while I try to keep the channels open to this brutal SOB so I can get into his mind."

Bert sensed a change in her. Her whole demeanor seemed to shift from a woman who had been following tracks in the snow, to a hunter now trying to think like her prey and figure out where the next tracks would be.

On the drive back to Cody, they stopped periodically to let Missy roam around a little and stretch her legs. These were also opportunities to discuss the various tidbits they thought they knew or suspected about these killers. They both agreed that the coins were a countdown for these guys to some event they considered to be their ultimate goal. They still didn't know if a nickel or zero was the end game. They shifted to the next open question. How did these two manage to take all the victims without a struggle?

Bert suggested a process to try to answer that burning question. "How about we try to piece together everything, the hints and clues, we have about these two and see if we can get a picture of their MO with regard to taking the victims?"

Norah agreed. "We for sure know that they are capable of seeming like nice, everyday guys. Yet, at the same time there is a dark and evil side hiding behind that mask. They seem to be very cunning and apparently highly intelligent. The very first time they dropped off a victim's vehicle, in St. Joseph, it almost seems like they purposely tried to use a surveillance camera to deceive the law. The guy on the camera film looked to be maybe black or Latino, yet everything since then points to white guys. Did that guy use makeup?"

"You're right, Norah," Bert said. "And what about the two times you saw gas containers in your visions and there were gasoline containers at the crime scenes? I can only come up with one possible and plausible explanation for that. Almost every farmer and rancher have a gas barrel for filling up tractors and such. They approached the front door, carrying an empty gas can and asked for gas, saying they were nearly empty. Once inside, they could more easily get the jump on those unsuspecting people."

She concurred. "Then maybe the Amish guy I thought I was seeing wasn't Amish at all, but part of a well-thought-out disguise. It isn't uncommon for Mormons to float around these communities, dressed somewhat like that and with hats, proselytizing for their religion, and even carrying a bible. If one or two of these people were at your door, you'd have little apprehension about opening the door and even letting them in. The fact that these killers are targeting rural farm and ranch families tells us that they know these are usually very unsuspecting and trusting people. Besides that, a rural setting is much easier to pull off a crime without being seen. Bert, these victims were all intentionally targeted because they were salt of the earth country folk. They shared the false and fatal belief that they lived where things like this just don't happen."

He felt tears welling up in his eyes as he thought about her words. "I think you're right about all that. From what we've heard, it seems like these guys have developed the knack for blending in. They seem to study the local clothing and adapt quickly to look like everyone else."

"And we know what kind of vehicle they evidently drive. That grey truck with extended cab and tinted windows seems to be a common thread," Norah added. "We also know that a common MO is to take one of the victims' vehicles, maybe to transport them in. Then they use a tactic of hiding it in plain sight someplace where it isn't likely to be discovered for a few days. At least once, they even switched the license plates. This seems to be purposely done to delay the start of any serious search for the victims and to temporarily mask the fact that a crime has occurred. It buys them time to be far away when someone becomes suspicious."

"Again, that all makes perfect sense and seems to be a common thread among all these crimes. One thought keeps nagging at me, though," he said.

"What's that," Norah asked.

"We are almost certain that there are two guys working together. How can we be sure that there aren't two vehicles? Maybe they both drive separate vehicles." He leaned back and sighed. "To complicate this even more, these guys are smart enough to feel the pressure of someone getting closer to them. That means they are also smart enough to know that noticeable grey truck might be a liability. They could trade it for another vehicle."

That question hung in the air like a bad smell the rest of the drive to their home outside Cody. They were both inside their heads, reliving each case and asking themselves the other burning questions that required an answer if they were to be successful.

Back at home, they alternated their time between home responsibilities and the case ahead of them. Norah relaxed and enjoyed her setting much of the time, but also spent time before the piece of handkerchief and trying to see through its energy to the mind of a killer. Bert spent time outdoors, walking and training with Missy, tuning up her tracking instincts and skills with increasingly difficult challenges. Over the weekend, he went squirrel hunting with his trusted Ruger .22 rifle. He purposely left Missy behind. He returned with three squirrels, cut the tail off one, and walked several miles into the hills and mountains behind his house. There, he hid all three squirrels in various places, separated by at least a quarter of a mile. It took all afternoon.

The next day, after a night in the cool fall air, he brought Missy outside, offered her the tail from the one squirrel, and ordered her to "Find, Missy." At first, he thought he may have confused her a little too well. She meandered around where he had brought in all three of the varmints. However, she began to pick up the fresher scent of his most recent trip into the mountains. Slowly, she began the methodical search farther and farther into the mountains. She paused at the first place where he cut off the path to hide one of the squirrels. After a few seconds, though, she continued along the path, until also passing up the hiding trail of the second squirrel. It only took her about fifteen more minutes until she was sitting in front of the tail-less squirrel, looking at Bert as he came huffing and puffing up the last two hundred feet of rocky hillside. He had no hesitation in offering her a couple of her favorite treats, after this display. No problem with her, he thought! Too bad that Norah couldn't see the performance.

Other than the daily walks and training, there was little happening with the case until Wednesday, August 16th. That afternoon, Norah was again trying to channel the mind of the murderers, when she was suddenly hit with the clearer picture of a fenced graveyard and a lone gravestone. What was it about this one grave that seemed to have impressed her prey? The vision slowly faded away after about 30 seconds. After that, there was again nothing.

Thursday, in the late morning, Norah was standing at the picture window, enjoying the views and thinking about the future. Just as suddenly as the day before, another vision slowly came into her mind. This picture was not perfectly clear, but she saw again the same cow she'd seen a couple times before. This time, though, the cow seemed to be standing on some writing. She couldn't quite make out the words, but it now seemed as if this was a sign of some kind. Where in the world was a sign like that? It faded away, and then was followed by a sense of two children playing. At first, Norah smiled as she watched a small boy, about five years old, playing with a little girl, appearing to be a couple of years younger. After twenty or thirty seconds, this vision, too, slowly faded from Norah's mind. Her smile disappeared, as she suddenly sensed that these two children were going to die. They were going to be victims of these heartless men. This was not the future that she wanted to see.

The rest of Thursday was melancholy for both Bert and Norah. She had shared her latest visions with him, and they now had a newfound sense of urgency coupled with desperation. They just didn't know enough to get ahead of these guys, yet they could sense that time was running out. It was very frustrating. As he said good night to Norah, Bert repeated what he often said, "Sweetheart, I do not know what I would do without you. I know you're trying so hard to find these guys and I believe you'll do it. You know I love you, always!"

Friday, August 18th, dawned clear and chilly. This was a typical fall morning for this part of Wyoming. Beautiful, but you needed a jacket. It would have been a great morning to sit on the front porch and sip coffee, but the cloud of an impending doom hung in the air. Norah couldn't enjoy the morning, either. She stared out the picture window, the piece of cloth on the side of the couch, and her mind reaching out through an undetermined space. She had to get inside the mind of this man before he killed again. There was something else nagging at her, too, but she just couldn't get her mind wrapped around it. "What the hell is it," she wondered.

Norah sat and stood in front of the picture window all morning, as if it was somehow a portal to the world beyond and hopefully inside a man's mind. The bagged, partial handkerchief lay on the arm of the couch. Bert left her alone to her thoughts and busied himself on the myriad of things he had to do around his property. There was never a shortage of things to do there. He knew, as he told Norah often, that in this case, he truly was nothing without her.

About one in the afternoon, Bert came back inside, sweating from chopping and splitting wood. "How's it going, Sweetheart," he asked.

She turned toward him. "Bert, do you remember a book we

looked at before you retired from the military and we moved here? It was a book about Wyoming. If I remember right, there was a chapter on brothels, whorehouses, and the like. Something from that is eating at me, but I just can't put my finger on it. Do you remember anything?"

"Uh-oh, is this a setup?" He laughed at that. "Why would I remember a chapter on whorehouses, my love?" He laughed again, and then became serious. "Well, I vaguely remember reading that book. I remember looking at the pictures mostly. There were beautiful pictures of beautiful places. That's one of the reasons we came here. Why are you asking?"

Her answer came quickly. "I just can't place what it is that's bugging me, but I know it might be important. Bert, we must get ahead of this and very soon. I feel that those guys are ready to strike again. Yet, we don't even know where to look."

He pulled off his work boots and sat down near her. "Okay, let's think about this logically as well as psychically. Where'd we first start picking up the trail of these two, thanks to Missy's nose? Highway 20, right?"

"Right!" She replied. "And, the second road was highway 85. We also concluded that highway 16, I mean 18, was on their path as well. So, what do these three roads have in common?" She saw where this might be going.

Bert excitedly opened his laptop and pulled up the map of Wyoming. For the first time in two weeks, he felt like they might be onto something. "Norah, there's a common point where all three of these roads come together. Lusk, Wyoming! We were through there a week ago."

She stood up with an air of optimism for the first time in days. "Lusk, yes, and there was something about Lusk in that book. I remember the name. Something about a prostitute."

Now Bert jumped up, too keyed up to sit with the laptop, and sat it on the table. He began to Google for prostitutes in Lusk, Wyoming. "Oh my God, Norah, that's the reason you've been seeing prostitute so much. The most famous prostitute in Wyoming lived a short while near Lusk back in the late 1800's. She was murdered by her partner, a bad dude named 'Dangerous Dick', of all the names you could have." He had to laugh at that. "She was nicknamed 'Mother Feather-legs' because of her favorite frilly undies. She's buried ten miles or so south of Lusk. Her lone grave sits in a small fenced graveyard. This may be the only monument to a prostitute in the United States. Lusk is where these guys are planning to get their next victims, Norah."

She was literally floating with enthusiasm. "Bert, we have to get ready and go. We're the only ones standing between killers and their future victims. Nobody else can stop them. It's on our shoulders."

He checked the time. It was two-o-clock on a Friday afternoon, and it was five hours drive to Lusk. It would take them about two hours to get ready to leave. "Norah, if we hurry, we can be in Lusk by nine tonight. We have to figure out how to find either them or their victims before we get there, if possible." He quickly began gathering their bags and packing the car.

By four-o-clock, they were passing through Cody, heading for Lusk on US 20. They both knew that the hardest part was yet to come. Who was the target, and how do they stop the killers? Bert felt for his pistol and the extra magazine pouch on his belt. He instinctively knew he might need them this time.

As they drove, Bert brought up one of the major hurdles they had to overcome. "Honey, how do we figure out the way these killers are choosing their victims? We know the victims are country people, but how are they chosen in the first place? What do we know about them that we haven't noticed before?"

She leaned back, her hands together with fingertips touching. "I can remember one psychic snapshot that might be some help. I saw this guy watching a crowd of people, looking at everyone passing around him. It looked like an event of some kind."

Bert thought about that for the next five minutes. Finally, an idea came to him. "Do you remember how many people we've talked with and where several said they last saw the victims?"

She thought about that a minute or two. "I think several saw our victims last at a ball game of some kind. In fact, nearly every case was like that. In one vision, I saw a baseball bat, too. Sports are somehow a part of this, Bert."

"Exactly!" he said. "It's occurring to me just now, also. A sporting event has a big crowd of people milling around and interested in the game and the concession stand. Very few would pay any attention to one or two guys who are dressed like everyone else. They'd just think they were fans of the other team. Our killers could wander freely through the crowd, choosing their victims. Later, they could follow them home and see where they live, then return a day or two later to abduct them. Even at night, they could just pin the victim's driveway on their GPS map as they passed. They could scout out the location more in daylight the next day or two and finalize their plans. If there are two killers with two vehicles, they could each follow someone and pick the better of the two."

"Oh my God, Bert, that has to be how they're doing this," she exclaimed. "I was just thinking of something else, too. Do you realize that almost all the disappearances and killings seem to have occurred early in the week?"

He replied quickly. "Oh, you're right, hon. If our scenario's correct, that means they're probably targeting a sporting event late in the week or on Saturday, Friday probably, and spending the weekend scouting and making plans. So, what's going on tonight in Lusk?"

The gravity of that question, and the time on the clock, hit them both. She was first to speak. "The high school football season is kicking off tonight across the state. I heard it on the radio yesterday."

"Shit!" he blurted out. "We can't get to Lusk in time. Any game will be almost over by the time we get there. All we can do is hurry like hell and hope there's some amount of the game left and that we can miraculously figure out who is killing and who might die." With that, he kicked up his speed to 15 over the speed limit. This wasn't unusual for Wyoming drivers. However, as all Wyoming drivers knew, there are two kinds of Wyoming drivers. There are those who've hit deer, and those who are going to hit deer.

Three hours later, in the dark and with knuckles still white from a couple of close calls with deer, they almost skidded up to a gas station in Lusk. Bert nearly ran inside to ask the attendant about any high school football game tonight. Then he slid back in the seat and closed the door as he started the car. That's when he heard Missy whining. "Good grief", he said to Norah, "I didn't stop to let her out even once. She must be about to bust."

As he followed the attendant's directions to the football stadium, he promised Missy she would be first out to pee as soon as they got there. Then he turned to Norah. "Lusk is playing Torrington at home tonight. The game kicked off at six, so is either over or about over. We'll just have to see what we can do. This is probably going to fall on you again, Norah."

They found the stadium quickly, but the crowd was leaving as they drove up. Bert didn't pull into parking but stopped just off the road and gave Missy a brief walk. She needed it. Then he grabbed the piece of handkerchief, pushed it under her nose, and ordered her to search. With her on the leash, he guided her as they pushed their way the opposite direction through the crowd of people exiting the stadium. As they were about to hit the entry point, Missy seemed to pick up the scent she was after and she tugged at the leash back to the right side of the throng of people. Bert trotted to follow her, but after she had gone a couple of hundred feet into the parking area, she seemed to lose the scent in the crowd. "Damn", he thought, "the son-of-a-bitch must've left."

Back at the car, his voice showed his frustration as he asked Norah if she was coming up with anything.

She was reluctant to answer him. "I hate to say it, but my sense of optimism has been replaced by one of dread and one of glee. The glee I sense from the killer. He's found his next victims and he's happy about it."

In near silence, they sat near the gate, watching for anything resembling a grey pickup with tinted windows. They saw none. With mutual sighs of resignation, Bert drove to a nearby motel. Norah's brain was exhausted from her efforts to connect with a stone-cold killer. It was time to call it a day and hope tomorrow brought new light.

CHAPTER TWELVE: THE COLD LIGHT OF DAY

Saturday dawned with a beautiful red sunrise, 48-degree temperature, and a brisk wind. It was Wyoming after all. Bert wore his heavier coat and cap as he took Missy out for the sunrise strolls that she really loved. Morning was her best time of day, as it was his. They had a great half hour walk at the edge of town, returned to another cooler breakfast in the room with Norah, and with coffee in hand, Bert leaned back in his chair.

"Well, babe, with a night's sleep and another day at hand, have you gotten any more insights into the guy?" Bert knew that their success or failure in saving someone's life fell upon his fragile wife. He knew just how important it was for him to continue to shield her from outside pressures and influences. He truly could not do this without her.

She leaned back against the headboard. "That coffee sure smells good this morning. I hope this day is as good as the coffee. Hon, I'm not getting anything new right now. I just keep seeing glimpses of that dang cow sign, and I still can't make out the writing below the cow. It really disturbs me that I continue to see brief spots of those two little kids playing. Such a contradiction to watch children at play, while knowing they're in grave danger. And, that damn number 42 flits by several times a day, but it doesn't feel like a road sign. I don't know what it means, but I have the strong sense that it means something critical."

Bert sipped his coffee for several minutes as he stared out the window, watching the sun slide above the horizon. He noticed a red-tailed hawk perched high in a tree a block away. "Gotta love Wyoming," he thought. "Norah," he said, "somehow we have to get a better idea of the potential victims. Let's see if we can narrow it down. Maybe we can find the killers by finding the victims, before they're dead."

She considered his thoughts for several minutes. "Well, besides what we discussed yesterday and have already concluded, the victims are getting younger, aren't they?"

Bert dug into his case notes, looking for ages. "You're right about that, Norah; I guess I was aware of it without really focusing on it. The first victims in Kansas were in their 70's. In Colorado they were sixty-something. Fifties in South Dakota; and essentially forties in Montana. If this holds true, then we're looking for a rural couple in their thirties. Or at least they look like they're thirty-ish. If they have kids, those are probably in their teens. Those kids are possibly in high school. That is, unless they got a late start, in which case they might have young children. Maybe there's a correlation with the rapes?"

It was Norah's observation which now took the conversation. "I know you would never notice a pretty woman, dear," she smiled at him. "However, I have noticed that the last two women who were raped were quite attractive and looked fit for their ages. This seems consistent with the desire to rape, I would think. So, we're looking for nice looking thirty-something couples, who might have young kids, boy and girl, and live in the country. And, they were at the game last night."

They both leaned back and thought about all this for a bit. Finally, Bert broke the silence. "Then we have to look immediately for couples who meet these criteria. The question is, how can we best do that in the least amount of time?"

Bert sat forward and pondered his own question. Norah watched him as she grappled with her own thoughts. Then she came up with an idea. "We both know that I'm most helpful when I can stay inside my head without distractions. Why don't I stay around the motel, while you ask around the town and see if you can come up with candidates? Missy can either stay with me or go with you. If you can get any pictures for me, that would probably help."

"It's a good thing I've only had one cup of coffee, because I think I'm going to be drinking several more. I'm thinking that a few coffee shops are a good place to start. There's often a table or two with old-timers telling stories and lying to each other. They will likely know everyone in the area." With that, Bert picked up his coat and a notebook, decided that Missy might be a conversation starter if with him, and blew a kiss to Norah as he walked out the door of their room.

The coffee shop of choice turned out to be in the front of a local gas station. A wooden table and chairs were the chatroom for a group of six, middle to old-age, guys, wearing everything from ball caps to felt hats, boots to mud-covered overshoes, and suit or blue jeans to bib-overalls. Bert was the instant conversation stopper, as he walked in with his Coywolf female on her leash. One of them couldn't resist the temptation to ask about her. That was the invitation he knew he'd get.

An hour later, with a bladder full of coffee, several stories told about Missy, and his table full of new friends, Bert saw the opportunity to direct the conversation. "Gents, if you don't mind, I would like to ask for your help. I'm here as a private investigator. My hairy companion and I are trying to find a young farm or ranch couple, around the ages of 35 or so, with a couple of kids. They are probably sports fans and were at the game last night. I know this may sound strange to you, but I work with a psychic who has had a vision of such a couple. She believes they are in grave danger from someone who means to harm them. I believe this lady. She is a great person and she's as honest and sincere as the day is long. For her to feel this strongly there must be something to it. If I can locate this couple, I want to warn them of what to look out for and to be very careful of the next week or two. It might save their lives, guys. Can you think of anyone like this around here?"

One older fellow dressed like a city dweller spoke up first. "Why not take this to the police?"

Bert calmly looked him in the eye. "If you were the Sheriff or police chief here, and a stranger leading a coyote walked in and told you a psychic had this vision, would you believe him?"

The old man leaned back and chuckled. "Well, you have a point there. No, I'd probably arrest you for jaywalking or something until I could check you out."

"Exactly," Bert replied, "that's my concern also, guys. And, if my psychic lady is right, this young couple might not have the day it would likely take for me to prove that I'm a legitimate investigator on a legitimate quest. My great fear is that in a day or two you'll hear of this couple, whoever they are, being either missing or murdered. If they have children, those kids are also in danger. You don't have to believe me, gents, but I hope you believe that I'm not nuts, and I am sincere in what I'm telling you. If I'm right and a couple dies, you can tell the Sheriff about me and what I told you. He might believe you then." With that, Bert sat back and rested his hands on the table, looking these men straight in the eyes. Missy continued to lie at his feet. Her eyes were closed as her head lay on her paws, but her erect and occasionally moving ears told Bert she was aware of everything being said.

An hour later, Bert thanked these men for their help and said his good-byes. He and Missy headed back toward the motel, by way of the town library. He wanted to see if he could check out the current school guides and yearbooks. Maybe Norah would recognize at least the older of the two children she was seeing.

Back at the motel, with a freshly made up room by the motel staff, Bert and Missy sat down near Norah. He filled her in on the things he had found out. They were scrolling through the most recent yearbooks of the elementary and high schools as he reported on his coffee talk.

"These fellas apparently felt they could trust me, because they came up with three couples who seem to meet our criteria, sweetheart. They were sure that all three were at the game last night. One couple has a ranch about twenty miles to the south off highway 85. They have a sixteen-year-old daughter and a ten-year-old boy, so don't fit your vision in that regard. Probably not them. The second couple has a small farm around ten miles west and a mile south of highways 18 and 20. They have a twelve-year-old son and a girl who's two. This might be our couple that you see. The third live only two miles out of town to the east but are off the road a couple hundred feet. While not what I would consider rural, they do have an eight-year-old boy and four-year-old daughter. There were three other families that came close, but for one reason or another I felt they weren't the ones we're looking for."

Norah was taking this all in and thinking as she continued to slowly view the yearbook pages. "So far, I'm not seeing those children in any of the elementary pages for those approximate ages. I can't help but feel that we're missing something, Bert. And, that's no bull."

Bert was a little surprised but tickled by her bull comment. "Hon, I don't remember you ever saying that bull phrase. I find it a little funny coming from you, being a proper woman and all." He laughed at that.

She didn't have a good answer for that. "You know, I don't know if I've ever said that before and I'm not sure why I said it now. It doesn't really make much sense. What's with that?"

They looked at each other, and both started laughing. He was glad she said it, because they needed a good laugh. Now back to business.

He spoke up first. "As I see it, we have three possible candidates, living in three different directions from town. Do we go to each and warn them? Take the risk of them calling the cops on us. We can't watch all three at the same time. We could stake out and watch for a grey truck with tinted windows; but what if there's another vehicle. We don't have any idea what it could be."

Norah could see their dilemma. "It still depends a lot upon me, I think. Somehow, I must channel this guy and get him to send me some clues about either their victims or themselves. If they're smart, as we know they are, they are probably staying at some other town miles from here. They'll do as little driving as possible; just enough to scope out their prey. They will strike within the next one or two days. Bert, Honey, I must tell you that I'm having a very bad feeling about this. I'm afraid we're not going to save this couple. I'm sensing fear and death."

Bert was stunned by her sudden fear. He knew he was feeling very stressed by the massive responsibility, but he hadn't perceived how it was affecting her so much. Maybe it just now showed up? He picked up his phone and dialed Bob Madison in Montana.

After the usual greetings and small talk, Bert got to his point. "Bob, you said you'd help me in any way you could, right? So, I need your help here in eastern Wyoming and we don't have much time. Is there any way you can come down here virtually right now, and help us try to save at least two lives here?"

Bob answered immediately. "Bert, it will take me one or two hours to line up what I need to do here, and about a six-hour drive to get to Lusk. That puts me there around seven or eight tonight. Will that help?"

"If you have a firearm and a concealed carry permit, bring both. This could be a dangerous thing we're doing." Bert was dead serious, and Bob knew it. "Do you think we should tell Sheriff Jim? He offered to help, too. Maybe he could get hold of the local law here in Lusk and get them on our side?"

Bob thought for a couple of seconds before answering. "Yes, I don't think it will hurt to tell Jim. My opinion of him is considerably higher than it was a couple weeks ago. He's on your side. He might be able to convince the local sheriff there to trust you. If he can't do that, though, I'm sure you know that they'll think you're a suspect if someone turns up dead!"

Bert was acutely aware of that possibility. "Let's let Jim make that decision and do what he thinks is best. Call me when you're an hour or so away and we'll arrange to meet somewhere. I'll make you a reservation at the motel we're in."

Even though it was a long shot, Bert decided that he and Missy would do some legwork for the afternoon, leaving Norah at their room to do what she could do from there. First, he scouted out the three main ranches of their most likely victims and pinned all three locations on his phone's mapping application. He was very tempted to stop but didn't. Who would believe a story like his?

Several times he let Missy out to do her search, but each came up negative. If those guys were by there, they evidently didn't leave their vehicle. Always he kept his eyes on other vehicles around him, looking for a grey truck. He didn't see any with tinted windows. As the afternoon wore on, the situation looked grimmer all the time.

At 8:30 that night, Bob finally arrived at the motel and checked in. Bert joined him for a beer in Bob's room. It took nearly an hour to go over all the nuances of the case and situation and to discuss the pool of potential victims. Bob finally asked, "How do you want to do this, then?"

Bert had been pondering that question all day long. "I wish I had the perfect plan," he told Bob, "But I just don't know what that would be. I think the two couples, to the west and east, ironically, are the most likely victims. They seem to fit all that we think we know. The family to the south doesn't fit Norah's vision. Their kids are too old. So, it makes sense to me that you take one to the west and I'll take the closer one to the east. I'll be closer to Norah, since she's going to stay in our room and focus on being a psychic. There are places we can park which will allow us to mostly hide in plain sight, so we don't alarm anyone while we watch those homes and driveways. If we see anything suspicious, we can either move in or try to deflate it; or call the Sheriff's office and call each other. If it becomes appropriate, we can get the law involved then."

"'We're unpaid and unappreciated angels of mercy, in other words." Bob laughed nervously. Okay, boss, I work for you this time. Let's do it. When do you want to start?'"

Bert checked his phone for the time, though he didn't need to have it right then. "Let's meet at that gas station three blocks south of here for coffee about eight. I'll introduce you quickly to my new buds at the coffee round table. That's if they're there? Being a Sunday, there might not be anyone up for a talk then."

With the next day planned out, they said good night and Bert headed toward his room. He barely took three steps before his phone rang. It was the local sheriff. He said he'd just spoken with the sheriff in Circle, Montana. Can you come down to our station and talk about what you're doing here, please?" Bert knew this was not a question. He didn't want to alarm Norah or Missy, so he continued past his room to the parking lot.

After more than an hour of explaining his reasons for being in Lusk, his relationship to Sheriff Jim, and providing his personal contact information, Bert was finally allowed to leave the Sheriff's office. Sheriff Roger Clemens didn't totally believe him, but he wasn't completely disagreeable, either. The Sheriff wanted one of his deputies to always accompany him and Bob when they were surveilling the two properties. This was as much to intimidate them as to help, Bert knew. However, he wasn't opposed to it, because the deputies were now witnessing whatever happened.

The next day, after coffee and introductions at the gas station coffee shop, which was surprisingly active, Bert, Bob, and their new shadow deputies left about nine-o-clock for their respective surveillance positions. Bert had gladly introduced Bob to five of his new coffee buddies, knowing that they might become character witnesses, if needed.

It was an understatement to say that this Sunday was boring. The four of them spent the day parked and milling around their vehicles, chatting among themselves. While their eyes were seldom off the road, they didn't see anything suspicious at either location. It was helpful to have the sheriff vehicles with them. Not only did they draw less attention from the public which could have compromised surveillance, but extra eyes were always a plus. There was very little traffic in the morning, and only light traffic in the afternoon. By dark, they all agreed to call it quits and resume the next morning, Monday, at seven. By now, the two deputies seemed increasingly friendly and convinced in the legitimacy of what they were doing.

Back in his room, Bert inquired of his wife if she had connected at all? He knew from her expression that she had.

"I don't like this," she said right away. "I'm having almost panic attacks, because every fiber of feeling is telling me we're overlooking something. I have the growing fear that death is going to win this one, again. I feel it. Something is wrong, Bert. I see several things over and over, not all the time but just in fleeting snippets. That damned cow won't go away; neither will 42. Those kids are starting to haunt me. Their faces aren't clear, but I can still make out their smiles. There's a new figure now, a man who looks like a cowboy. I can only see his figure, kinda fuzzy. He's wearing a cowboy hat. Damn, Bert, we're in the Cowboy state. What's special about another cowboy?"

Bert could tell the gravity of her feelings, and he knew to respect them. This was her territory, not his. He had to go with her perceptions and insights. He called one of the deputies, who was with him today. He was a nice younger guy, about 30, and he seemed to be very interested in what they were doing. "John, this is Bert again. I know you've probably had a fill of me after today, but I need to tell you that we may have a problem. My psychic is very afraid that we're missing something here. She has the strong sensation that we're on the wrong trail. I've learned to respect those feelings from her. She's usually right."

There was a long pause. "Hmmm, so what do you think we need to do? If we're on the wrong trail, how do we get on the right one?"

"If we're right, John, these guys are not far from Lusk. This is the place. The psychic clues pointed us here. I don't think our surveillance today is the answer, though. Tomorrow let's all meet about 6:30 at the same coffee shop and go as teams on the road in every direction. You and I can go east and then north; Bob and your other cohort can cover west and south. I'd suggest about twenty miles in each direction. I'll let my coyote tracker out whenever it seems logical. After that, maybe we can all meet in town at the closest intersection of our two roads and watch for the grey pickup. By then, we might find another farm couple meeting our description closer. By the way, John, does the number 42 mean anything to you? Or, the picture of a cow, maybe on a sign?"

Deputy John replied, "Bert, those two things don't mean anything to me. That number could be about anything from birds in a flock to a basketball score. This is ranch and cattle country so you can see cows all around us. I can't think of a picture or a sign with one, though."

They hung up. It was getting late and he had to get up early. Bert said good night to his sleeping wife and whispered his love for her.

* * *

Monday morning was cold and windy as Bert walked and then loaded up Missy and started the car. The red glow in the eastern sky promised sunrise soon over the brown fall grassland of this high-plains prairie. It would be chilly for a while, but the sky looked to be severe clear, and all in all it should be a pretty decent fall day.

He pulled up to the gas station and was leaving his car as Deputy John pulled up. Bob and the other deputy soon followed. The four of them huddled around their coffee cups, warming their hands, as they sat at the coffee club table.

They chatted about the weather and news of the day for about five minutes, and then Bert said, "Well, gentlemen, unless someone has a better idea, I suggest that we follow the plan from last night and let's get going. Someone in your jurisdiction is in grave danger, I believe, and we must do our best to find out who they are. Any ideas other than that?"

Nobody had anything better to offer, so they headed their respective ways. Bert and Deputy John headed east on highway 20, while Bob and the other deputy, Hector, went west.

Bert and John completed their trek about twenty miles to the east and were on the way back, when John suddenly pulled his sheriff's car to the side and waved for Bert to get beside him. He was talking intently on the phone as Bert pulled beside the deputy's car door and rolled down his window. After a couple of minutes, the Deputy turned to Bert. "Follow me and keep up. We've got a problem. Call the others and tell them to meet us on highway 85 going south at the edge of town." With that, he spun out of parking, and Bert had to lay rubber just to keep him in sight. Missy was bracing herself in the back, looking a little bewildered.

The four vehicles formed up at the last business just south of Lusk. Then the two squad cars led the way with lights flashing as they all sped south on highway 85.

Fifteen minutes later, the convoy turned west on a short driveway which led to a secluded ranch and house. As they drove up, a young boy came running out to Deputy John. It was obvious that he'd been crying. Bert felt his heart fall into the pit of his stomach. This was the third family, Zach and Sierra Hutchinson. They were the ones considered the least likely of the three couples to be victims.

"We did miss something," Bert sadly admitted to himself.

By noon, the worst was realized. The sixteen-year-old girl and her ten-year-old brother had gone on a Sunday school field trip to Cheyenne to tour the Air Base.   The girl had gone on home with a girlfriend when they returned, dropping off her brother at the driveway. He found the house empty, but wasn't initially too concerned, thinking his folks, Zach and Sierra, would be back soon. So, he went to bed. When he woke up this morning, an hour ago, he became very alarmed and called 911. Normally he wouldn't have slept that late, but nobody was there to wake him.

While waiting for John, he became very scared. The parents were missing and so was their Dodge Ram pickup. It didn't take long for Bert to find the lone nickel on the center island of the kitchen table.

It was a tearful hour as he sat in the motel room after saying good-bye to Bob, who felt he was no longer needed and had work to do back in Montana. Bert and Norah were about as heartbroken as professional investigators dare to become. It was no surprise to her. She knew the outcome before he told her.

Norah looked him in the eye. "I knew we missed something, Bert. I just knew it. Tell the Sheriff to look north of the ranch near highway 85. I've seen that road sign clearly and I've felt them both dies. She was raped. It was horrible. I can still taste blood in my mouth and feel their fear. That isn't all, Bert. This isn't done. I'm still seeing a sign with the same cow, numbers 35 and 42, and prairie grassland and big hills. This piece of cloth is showing me the future, too, Bert, not just the present. That's part of what I missed. I think Terry's trying to help me, too."

He nodded at her and knew before he asked. "Is there anything else, dear?"

She looked back with resolve glistening in her eyes. "Yes, I still see two little children, and I haven't seen any more nickels or dimes."

* * *

The Sheriff and his deputies did search the area to the north of the victims' home. It took a few hours with Missy's help to finally locate the two deceased ranchers. Like Norah had said, the woman appeared to have been raped before she was killed. Her husband was located a mile closer to their home than his wife. As Bert was preparing to put Missy back in their vehicle, one of the deputies came over to ask him a question.

"Mister Lynnes, didn't you mention that your psychic had seen visions of a prostitute, or something like that?"

Bert answered quickly, "Yes, Deputy, she was seeing that word in a number of her visions. Why do you ask?"

Well, Sir, I thought you should know that we are standing only a couple miles from the burial site of Ole' Mother Featherlegs, the most famous prostitute in Wyoming; and maybe in the entire US. Your psychic is the real deal, Mister Lynnes. Stay the course, Sir."

CHAPTER THIRTEEN: THE SANDHILLS;
THE END OF THE TRAIL

It was Tuesday, August 22nd, another typical fall day in the upper mid-west. A cool morning followed by clear blue skies and a warm afternoon. The sunrise had been spectacular with the beautiful red glow across the eastern horizon. Bert had pulled into the small park on the west edge of Lusk. He wanted to get some fresh air, give Norah a chance to sit outside at the distant picnic table, and give Missy time to meander around in the prairie grass which surrounded the little park. They enjoyed the warm sun and the scenery of the rolling hills, plains, and tall brown native grasses, waving in the breeze.

They were alone there, and it would give them time to talk about what to do next. "Let's take a look at what we know at this point, Norah," Bert said, "Your visions have not stopped. They obviously plan to kill one more time, it seems. The countdown is to zero."

"Yes, they will kill again unless we can stop them, Bert." She was resolute. "The spirits are telling me that those men will kill the parents of the little children, maybe even the children. These victims live not far from us, somewhere in the hills, valleys, and prairie of this upper Midwest area. That cow sign is a key to knowing where. The numbers will help us find the families. I wish I could sense how to tie it all together. However, the future is rarely clear, is usually fuzzy, and is always subject to being changed by action or inaction. The snippets that I see today can be changed tomorrow by the actions taken by those involved, today. Today, those children are in peril. Our actions, though, can save them. Then the future I see will be different for them. My visions work the same as life, itself, works, Bert. We can alter the outcome by doing something to affect it."

They became aware of Missy's barking a few hundred feet from them, on a shallow sloping hillside. A small group of cattle was passing down out of the hill, heading for the windmill and water a short distance in front of them. She had singled out one large animal and was having fun pestering it. "Oh look, Bert, Missy is letting off steam by picking a fight with that big bull." Norah was laughing at their canine's coyote-like antics.

Bert was watching with interest and amusement, also. He laughed out loud. "Sweetheart, that's no bull, that's just a big cow."

He and Norah watched this standoff for a few more minutes, until both Missy and the cow tired of each other and went their separate directions.

"Okay, dear, let's figure something out," he said. "It's obvious that we're still on the clock and this continues to be a pro bono case. Our only payment will be saving the lives of those children and their mother and father."

Norah sat quietly for a while, thinking about all that and gazing across the Wyoming scenery. "I'm continuing to see grassland and prairie scenery drifting through my mind, Bert. Big hills and valleys, cattle, fences; you know, ranchland. The other things, too. Still can't figure out the two numbers. They could mean anything, I guess, but I see them so often that they must be something important. I either see them both, together or I just see 42, sometimes. I do feel that they are in the future."

"Well, I think we need to figure out where these butchers have gone and where they intend to strike next, or last." Bert was very introspective in his reply. "It seems that this is the crime they've been building up to, sweetheart. They've already raped the last three women before killing them, so what can be worse than that?"

She thought about that for a minute. "For me, I think, if they either took or killed my children. That would make it more terrible. Also, if they take me and make me their sex slave for a long time before they kill me. Even worse if they take my little girl, too, and raise her to be the same. That would make me feel so hopeless. Months or years of insults; before the final injury."

Bert's face changed from an expression of concern to a look of horror and shock. "Oh my God, Norah, I bet that's it. That's what they've been aiming toward as the final event. All the others have literally been practices. That's why the couples and especially the women have been getting younger with each killing. You keep seeing those kids, too, and one is a little girl. This is it. We must find a way to stop them, even if we go to jail."

"I agree and I have the strong feeling that this will all happen very soon, dear." Norah seemed to be praying with her eyes open and hands pressed together before her chin. "I sense that this begins this weekend, somehow. We don't have much time, darling. So, we have to figure out where they will be."

Bert whistled for Missy, since she was wandering a little too far afield for comfort. He didn't want someone to shoot her thinking she was a wild coyote. Since she was almost a coyote and looked like it, anyone could mistake her for the animal that they thought killed a calf or chicken. He had to protect her from her own curiosity and instincts.

He came back to the big question. Where? "Well, we had some help getting us into Wyoming, but not so, now. So, let's look at this logically. The killing spree started in Kansas, went to Colorado, then South Dakota, Montana, and now Wyoming. These are Heartland states, big sky agricultural kind of states, with low populations, small towns, and small-town lawmen. This is where farmers and ranchers reside. If they hold true to form, then either Nebraska or Iowa are next. Both states are on or near several major routes, mainly Interstate 80, which lead back to the east coast, where these killers are apparently from. Nebraska has a population of less than two million along with big hills and valleys and is part of the Great Plains. Iowa has a population of over three million, half again more. Nebraska has tall-grass prairies, lots of corn, but also lots of cattle. The kind of things you're seeing in your vision. Nebraska is just a couple of hours drive from here, while Iowa is about eight hours away. Nebraska is right in the middle. If we look at this logically, Norah, then this killing spree has moved to Nebraska!"

"I feel that's it, dear," she answered. "Nebraska fits into everything I'm seeing and sensing. We have very little time, so I think we should try to confirm Nebraska. If we get there and drive a while, hopefully the spirits will tell me."

They gathered up Missy, very happily panting after having a good run and nearly getting run over by a thousand-pound cow. The cow apparently didn't have many good experiences with native coyotes and didn't care much about Missy's superior genetics. Missy didn't seem to care all that much about the cow's ancestry, either. The match appeared to end in a draw. They piled back into the doghouse.

From the front passenger seat, Norah looked over her shoulder at Missy. "Did you have a good play, sweetie? You need to pick your associates a little more carefully. Wrong ones can get you in trouble." She turned back to the front, laughing.

On the road again, armed with a plan and a renewed sense of urgency and optimism, B & N Investigations headed east on US highway 20. Next stop was the site of the murder of Lakota Chief Crazy Horse at the hands of the US cavalry in September of 1877. Besides also being the historic headquarters for General George Armstrong Custer, Fort Robinson State Park, near Crawford, Nebraska, was a logical bathroom, picnic, and rest stop as one entered the Cornhusker State from the northwest corner.

The drive to Fort Robinson was one of Nebraska's numerous scenic wonders. Besides the many curious sandstone formations, there were tall ridges, and sandstone cliffs. Trees, shaped by the harsh winters and winds, lined the many draws and pockets as one entered the northern Sandhills region. This was a part of the Pine Ridge area. Here, you had the chance to see groups of elk, an occasional bighorn sheep, bands of wild turkeys, and even buffalo, as you wandered in and out of pine dotted hillsides and shallow canyons. At one of the scenic overlooks, they stopped to drink in the undulating panorama of the tallgrass prairie beauty. Scenic beauty was a refreshing and pleasant distraction from the dark side of humanity, which Bert and Norah pursued.

They sat at a picnic area inside the Fort Robinson Park, just a brief detour from highway 20. It was noon and time to break out the cooler. There were few visitors to be seen, so Bert let Missy again smell the valuable piece of handkerchief and commanded her to find. She did her usual search pattern, but after about five minutes it became obvious that she wasn't hitting on anything.

After a hasty lunch break, their SUV, the doghouse, was once again on the road going east toward Chadron. As they passed through Harrison, Missy again did another unsuccessful search at a likely stopping point. Meanwhile, Norah continued to look to the cloth as a stimulant for her psychic powers, but she could not pick up anything new.

They continued east on highway 20, to the small but progressive tourist and cow town of Valentine, Nebraska. This small but entertaining little city of just under 3000 was a combination of cowboy, ranch supply, and hunting and fishing stores, along with saloons and restaurants and several good motels. It thrived in part on the base of tourists and outdoor enthusiasts, attracted to the area's lakes and streams. It was late afternoon now, and a good place to spend the night. They would retire early and get a sunrise start in the morning.

Before bed, Bert said they should review what they are hoping to find tomorrow, since it would be Wednesday, and Norah felt the killers were going to strike this weekend.

Norah spoke first about this. "I feel we're in the ballpark, Bert. This is going to happen in this region, but we don't know exactly where. I feel a pull from a southerly direction from here, maybe the southwest. I can't pinpoint it. I think we should maybe go a little farther east, but if I don't feel right about it, then go back south and west. I think I'm picking up a combination of signals from Terry Williams and maybe those children. Their spirits must be sensing their danger from me. I feel they are trying to pull us to them."

"Okay, sweetheart," he chimed in, "you're the boss at this point; you and Missy. I must rely upon you two to get us where we need to be. I know it's a big responsibility to have the lives of four strangers in an unknown location on your shoulders. We're on the northern side of a region called the Sandhills. This is an area of big hills, big valleys, many small lakes, small ranch communities, low human population, and many cattle. There aren't many people. This area was formed, according to some experts, when ice age glaciers pulverized the rock into sand, and it was deposited here in ripples which we now see as hills. It's a tallgrass prairie ecosystem, great for raising cattle, but generally not good for farming. It fits the description from some of your visions. The problem is that this encompasses almost the northern half of the state, which is 500 miles long. It would take us days to cover the main roads. We don't have days."

Norah had another concern. "Hon, the cow vision is a key to locating where this family is living. Somehow, we must figure that sign out or we'll be stymied. This is a land of large distances. Today has proven that. As you've said, we could run out of time just driving around looking for it. I have to read your tea leaves, as you love to say, to get us closer, soon."

"Let's get some sleep, then, and get an early start tomorrow." He knew they had much to do. "We'll be driving into the sun for an hour or two, but I don't see another option. We've got to locate the area and then find the event which the family will attend. I'm struggling with whether to start calling sheriffs or not. There aren't many who would give us much credibility, and most would think we're asking them to believe in ghosts or goblins. They would be as reluctant as Patrick Swayze's character in that movie to buy into it. I'm afraid it would cost us time rather than save it. We can't take that chance if we're to save this family."

It was a partly cloudy morning, chilly with a brisk wind, as Bert, Norah, and Missy proceeded east on highway 20. It was slow going, as they decided to pause to let Missy do her search for the killer's scent at every rest stop, they came to. Norah, also, continued to seek a connection from the handkerchief, but it seemed reluctant to let go of any secrets today. Darkness started to overtake them. They finally got to O'Neill and put into a motel for another night. The sense of urgency and a growing frustration made it hard to sleep.

The next morning, Thursday, Norah was feeling a westerly pull. Since they had been down US 20 with no sign of the killers, they decided to go south and take up another route back to the west. They headed south from O'Neill on US 281, stopping at fewer places to see if Missy's nose could pick up anything. It didn't! Finally, at another small farm town of Saint Paul, they turned west.

Nebraska highway 92 ran east and west pretty much into the heart of the Sandhills, so it seemed a good pick. A side benefit was that the prairie scenery became increasingly spectacular as they went westward. Three more stops to let Missy search proved fruitless. At a town of Ansley, highway 92 blended into State Highway 2, nicknamed the Sandhills Journey Scenic Byway. They continued deeper into the Sandhills ranchland scenery as they continued in a westerly direction.

Bert was craving a coffee and another chance to stretch his legs, so they stopped at one of the larger small towns along Highway 2, Broken Bow, apparently named by an early pioneer settler who found a broken bow at one of the Indian camps. He found a neat looking little coffee and gift shop, appropriately named "Prairie Grounds," along Main Street, and grabbed a quick cup of elixir. "Neat place, friendly people, good coffee," he said to Norah as he got back in the car.

By the time they reached another ranch town named Thedford, the sun was beginning its plunge toward the southwest horizon. Bert and Norah were becoming increasingly anxious about the time and lack of visions or signs to tell them they were on the right track. At this point, they only had Norah's feeling that they needed to continue going west. So, they continued west.

With the sinking sun in his eyes, Bert had sunglasses on and visor down as he passed another small spot-in-the-Road Town of Mullen. The road leveled somewhat from the hills he had been traversing to predominantly long lake valley geography. One of his favorite songs was on the local radio station he had just tuned in. The Righteous Brothers were singing "Unchained Melody."

He glanced at Norah and thought to himself, "I need your love. I hunger for your touch." He almost didn't notice one of the very few signs at the side of the road near the barbed wire fence, the standard fencing of this ranch country. Norah almost didn't see it, either.

"Bert, stop and back up," she cried out. "Did I see what I think I saw? Was that a cow on that sign?"

They backed up until they had a clear view of the sign. A big red cow with a white face adorned the center of the sign. Above the cow, it said they were "entering Grant County", and read something about a best community and the good life. Their eyes were drawn to the words below, though. "This is no Bull".

Bert looked at Norah with the look of someone who just got a winning lottery ticket. Amazement and disbelief wrapped in elation. A chill went up his spine with the realization of what he was seeing. "Oh my God, Norah, you've done it again, darling! Thanks to your visions, we have the chance to find this family and save them. Sweetheart, this is no bull."

Fifteen more minutes brought them to the small town of Hyannis, which they found out later had a population of about 350. It wasn't the smallest, though. The only other two towns in the county according to the motel clerk, had about 50 people each. The entire county had less than 1000 and was among the top ten least populated counties in the US. "So, this is where we have been brought to finish this," Bert stated matter-of-factly. "Who would've thought that?"

Just as soon as they were settled into their small room and Missy had done her spin into her usual spot in front of the window, Bert wasted no time in making a phone call.

He didn't give Bob Madison time to much more than say his name. "Bob, Bert Lynnes here to ask for help again. I'm very sorry but I can use you and I don't dare wait to ask."

"Say no more, Bert," Bob literally commanded. "I told you I'd help get those bastards and I meant it. Where do I need to get to and by when?"

"Bob, I need you tomorrow and probably through the weekend, in a tiny little town of Hyannis, Nebraska. We just got here so I don't know what's going on to bring people into town. Probably a football game, but I'll find out and let you know. If it's that, it could even be in the late afternoon."

Bob was stern now. "Bert, buddy, I'll get up early as hell and I'll try to be there by three in the afternoon. However, you need to pay me 50 per cent of that pro bono pay you're getting."

Bert said just as sincerely, "Bob, buddy, I'm gonna give you the whole damn bit. I hope you can bring your truck to haul it all back."

"I'll bring a tractor trailer," Bob retorted. "Anything else?"

Bert was somber as he added the last requirement. "Bob, bring at least two pistols if you can, and don't forget bullets and a couple extra clips. This is likely to get ugly, my friend. I don't see those guys giving up."

They hung up and Bert called Sheriff Jim Darling. "Sheriff Jim, and no I am not using your last name. This is Bert Lynnes. You said to call if I needed help. I need help. The problem is that we think it's going down possibly tomorrow but certainly by the end of the weekend."

The Sheriff sounded remorseful. "Damn Bert, before I even ask what planet you were sending me to, I have to say with hat in hand that I'm tied up with a case and hearing here tomorrow and it will probably drag into the weekend. I can't get out of it. Can I help in some other way?"

"Maybe," Bert answered. "Some advice, please. I have about as much tangible evidence to go on as I did in Wyoming, and this is a very small community of about 350 people. A thousand in the entire county. They've probably never heard of psychic evidence. I'm almost afraid to ask for help, because I just don't know how it would be perceived. I don't know the sheriff, of course, so don't know if I could trust him with what I'm sure we're going to have to do. I may end up in jail, Sheriff, because someone is going to die here, and I hope it's the killers. I don't want it to be this young family. Should I tell the local law or do what Bob and I think is right and go with the consequences. I'll trust in you to vouch for me however you can."

Sheriff Jim came back to him. "Bert, I can testify for you as a Sheriff and a friend, if it comes to that. Same for Bob. I know where your hearts are. One more bit of advice and make sure you understand me, Bert."

"Yes, Sir, I'm listening," Bert replied.

Sheriff Jim was very serious. "If you must shoot, shoot to kill. Aim for the center of the chest and don't stop shooting until you know he's dead. You got that?"

"Sheriff, friend, I've got it and I won't forget it. I'll keep you updated. Thank you, my friend!"

Then Bert called Deputy Sheriff Bill Haskins and updated him on the case. He didn't ask Bill for help as he knew his job would preclude him from being involved down here. Like Sheriff Jim, Bill promised to vouch for him and Bob, should the need arise.

With that, Bert was satisfied that they were not in this alone. He would probably need help, and help was on the way. Somewhere around here, there is a couple with two small children who are counting on this team to save their lives, but they don't yet know it.

He had one more thing to do before joining Norah in the bed. He excused himself and went down to the local Hyannis Hotel, which is on the historical record, so he was told. He wanted to drink a beer, but he was after information. He ordered a beer and asked the waitress if there were any ball games or other events going on in town.

"Why sure, the high school football game is tomorrow evening. It starts at 7 PM. We're playing Hemingford. Where are you from? Are you going to the game?" She was a friendly gal, happy to answer his questions and ask her own.

Bert was happy to have a conversation. "I'm from Wyoming. I have an investigation company in Cody. Yes, I'm going to be here for a few days it looks like and I'm going to the game. Ought to be fun. Where do they play?"

"That's great," she said. "The ball field is down the road to the east, on the left just after you pass the school and as you're leaving town. You can't miss it." She was attracted to this man.

He needed to know something critical. "How's the parking? Is there a problem getting in and out?"

She was happy to reply. "Oh no, parking is usually plentiful, and you just flow around counter-clockwise. Visitors go all the way around the field and park on the north side, while the home team generally parks on the south side. Keeps the fights down." She laughed at that.

"I suppose you can get a ten-dollar hot dog there, too?" he asked.

The little gal laughed again. "Oh, you bet, but you'll be disappointed that it'll only cost you four bucks instead of ten.

There's a pretty good concession stand at the west end of the field."

Considering the remote area, he needed to know about the other team. "Where is Hemingford, my dear?"

"Oh, it's a bit of a ways from here. About 70 miles to the west."

Bert thanked her and drank his beer. It was a welcome chance to relax as he watched a couple of the local guys flirting with the cute bartender. He also was quite interested in the hundreds of pictures on the walls. Most were autographed with everyone from football and rodeo stars to rodeo queens and an occasional movie star. One guy played on a national championship football team in the 1990's. A few pictures down was another of a professional rodeo champion saddle bronc rider, another of a calf roper. Bert could have spent an hour just looking at all the pictures. However, he knew he needed to get back to Norah and get some sleep. Tomorrow looked to be a very busy and critical day. It might be one of the most critical days of his life. It might even be the last day of his life.

* * *

Friday was another cool day with light winds and partly cloudy skies. He decided to drive a couple miles east of town and give Missy a walk around the rodeo grounds, which were presently empty. The waitress and pictures last night had made him aware of another interesting footnote about Hyannis. It was the home of the nationally famous Old-Timers Rodeo. After the short drive and a good walk with Missy, this was a planning day. First, he and Norah needed to be crystal clear on who they were looking for at the game tonight.

From Norah's visions, they knew that a young couple with two small children, a boy about 5 and a girl around 3, are the intended victims. They must be able to find and identify this couple tonight. This needed to be done as early as possible so the investigator team could identify where they lived.

At the same time, they needed to try to identify the killers, if possible. If the grey pickup with tinted windows was there, that could be done relatively early on. If the grey pickup was not found, then they had to search the crowd to find a pair of white guys matching the little bit of description they had for them. This could be quite difficult if those guys are as cunning as they seem to be. They might disguise themselves in some way, and they will probably dress to blend into the crowd.

If it all comes together, and Bert's team can identify both the expected victims and the killers, then they should have at least a day, based upon past M.O., to decide how to proceed from there. The killers have always taken at least a couple of days to scout out their victims and prepare for their attack.

His last act before noon was to drive around the area and become familiar with the lay of the land and check out the football stadium. Since anything could happen that night, they needed to have a feel for the locale and terrain, as well as the people. There were potentially at least 70 miles of possibilities between them and the people they hoped to protect.

The town of Hyannis sat in a pass between the hills, and it literally crawled up both sides of this natural bowl. The pass, and town, was a natural separation between two large valleys, one to the west of town and the other to the east. The two valleys proceeded for at least five miles in each direction. The hotel side of the main road was a steep incline up the two blocks to the top, where a community center overlooked the entire town. Hyannis sat on a busy coal-driven railroad system, and the east-west track divided the north third of the town from the south two-thirds. The only railroad crossing and protected light guarded the entrance to highway 61, which wound its way north for many miles until connecting to highway 20 at Merriman, about an hour-and-a-half west of Valentine.

He found a road just before a small town of Ashby and turned south for a mile or so. It was so desolate that he figured it was a good place to test fire his 40-caliber Ruger pistol. He wanted to make sure it was in firing order, and make sure the laser dot sight was still accurate. He quickly obliterated a gopher mound about fifty feet away. When he got back to the room, he would clean and oil the gun, reload the clip, and load the gun with a round in the chamber. He decided to replace his Sneaky Pete holster with a latch-controlled belt holster which activated the laser upon drawing the weapon. A concealed carry vest would keep the weapon discreetly out of sight.

* * *

Bob Madison called about 2:30 that afternoon. He was about an hour away and wanted to know where to meet up. They arranged to meet at the Hyannis Hotel, discuss the plan over a sandwich, and then go check out the area and the ball stadium. Norah was going to stay in the room and periodically see if the piece of handkerchief inspired other visions or feelings. Bert could tell that she was under a great deal of pressure and stress. He frequently noticed her on the verge of crying. He comforted her and tried to reassure her, but the visions in her head were the dominating force.

Missy rode around with Bert so he could give her an outing now and then. She seemed to love this wide open and sparse land. He wondered if she knew it was full of her coyote cousins.

After a quick sandwich at the hotel, Bob and Bert arrived at the football stadium. Stadium was a pretty big word for this small-town football field surrounded by three or four wooden and metal bleachers on both sides. The parking area consisted of a dirt road around the entire field, with grassy to sandy parking areas beginning about forty feet back from the field. It could probably hold a hundred vehicles; maybe more. The small concession stand on the west end looked well maintained and appeared to be a popular half-time spot. The railroad track passed just north of the field in an east-west direction. There appeared to be a lot of train traffic.

"Bob, I think we should get here a little early and split up with both our vehicles." Bert was planning it out in his head. "I'll park near the entrance on the home field, south, side and you can park around the field on the visiting team side. We're looking for the killers' grey extended cab pickup with tinted windows. Don't be surprised if they've changed to a Nebraska license plate. We're ninety-nine per cent sure these are two guys, good sized and in good shape. All our information about them is entirely circumstantial, but we suspect they are two white guys. They seem to be masters of disguise, so expect the unexpected. They will likely blend right in with the local crowd."

Bert discussed the cellular service with Bob. Bob brought up that they'd need to be able to talk during the game. Bert and he both knew they would need to know what the other was doing.

"So far, I've had decent phone service," said Bert. "Let's just plan to do a quick call every fifteen minutes for quick updates. That shouldn't be too suspicious. We don't want these guys to get wind of us and leave. This is our best chance to get to them. I'm wearing a pair of my round toe western boots, blue jeans, flannel shirt, jacket, and a winter weight ball cap. That should look normal for around here this time of year. I'm carrying my Ruger semi-auto on my belt under my coat. I have a second clip with me. What are you packing?"

Bert watched with satisfaction as Bob opened his thigh-length jacket slightly enough to show a full-size revolver on his belt. "I have a small semi-auto on my ankle, but this 44-mag will damn sure put a stop to those dudes."

He nodded to Bob and continued. "We're looking for a family of four. The couple will look to be in their twenties, and the woman will probably be attractive. Norah is certain that they will have two kids; a girl about three years-old and a boy around five."

"Where will Norah and the wolf be," Bob asked.

Bert ignored the wolf comment. Bob knew what she was. "They will be in our SUV during the game. Norah doesn't like crowds and tries to stay alone during these cases, as you know. Her mind is her main asset, and we must keep it uncluttered. If this gets messed up, Bob, then her mind is all we've got. That, and Missy's nose."

"If you can engage the victim couple, do so very casually. See if you can find out anything about them without alarming them. I hate to say this, Bob, but we have no choice but to let them be decoys for these killers. If we save this couple by tipping them off, we're probably just dooming another family to death. These

218

guys aren't going to quit. We must end this here. We'll figure out tomorrow how to save them. Tonight, we need to know who they are and where they live." With this plan in place, Bob and Bert agreed to go back to their rooms and relax for the remaining two hours before show time back at the field. They needed to be in place well ahead of the 7:00 PM kickoff. For this case, it was now show time.

CHAPTER FOURTEEN: THE BEST MADE PLANS

Six-o-clock seemed to come far too soon this Friday evening. Despite their planning, Bert and Bob both felt uneasy about the task ahead. Just as they discussed, they paid for parking ahead of much of the crowd and were in position on opposite sides of the field, near the main entrance and exit road. At first, Bert took up a seat near the top row on the home side, and Bob did similarly on the visiting team bleachers.

Norah and Missy were resting uneasily in the B & N Investigations vehicle, hidden in plain sight behind the tinted windows. Norah periodically stared at the handkerchief remnant on the dash and cleared her mind for any connection it might make to a murderer. Missy alternated between dozing and watching out the windows, sniffing the small amount of air that passed through the one back window which was slightly lowered.

Cars and pickups streamed intermittently into the little football field over the next hour, slowing to a trickle only ten minutes before kickoff. Bert called Bob. "I haven't seen any sign of the grey pickup, Bob. I don't see it anywhere over by you, either. It isn't here, at least not yet. There are seven grey vehicles, but none are the one we're looking for. There must be two hundred or more people here, and probably about seventy-five vehicles. I'm trying to pick out the killers. Do you have any candidates over there?"

Bob's voice came back over the phone. "Pretty much the same here, Bert. I do have a young couple here on the visiting, Hemingford, side, who match our victim profile almost exactly, though. They came in a green Dodge four-door pickup and are sitting in the middle bleacher, about in the middle. Any chance that the victims could be on the visiting side?"

"Anything is possible, I think, Bob. If your Hemingford family fits the profile as well or better than anyone over here, then we have the challenge of following them over 70 miles back to that town. I have two young couples over on the home side. Both mothers are attractive, and both have a boy and girl about the ages we're looking for. Somehow, we need to try to eliminate at least one of these families. We can't be in three places at once. If nothing else, let's see if we can rub elbows with them at halftime and try to strike up a conversation or eliminate at least one of them. I talked with Norah a few minutes ago at the car. She feels the presence of the kids she's been seeing in her visions. She thinks they're here, but she doesn't know what they look like in the face. Says she's feeling a sense of dread, too. The killers are somewhere near here. She says the entire football field feels like it's pulling on her. It's kind of overwhelming her, I think. The anxiety may be muddling with her mind and interrupting her ability to channel anyone."

"I can only imagine what's she's going through," Bob replied. "I'm watching several pairs of guys over here. All seem to be locals. Dressed like cowboys, ranchers, and the like. Nobody out of the ordinary. Hell, these guys might not be sitting together. They might have come in different vehicles for all we know. We might need to be looking for individuals rather than a pair. They might be on both sides of the field."

Bert replied. "I have the same problem here. Nobody is standing out as a possible out-of-towner or murderer. I knew it might be tough to pick them out, but, damn, this is looking impossible. Unless we can overhear an eastern accent maybe at halftime, we'll just have to try to pick the best candidates for cold-hearted murderers and go from there. Norah's mind is just exploding, she says, with more feeling than vision. She's having a hard time."

Throughout the kickoff and the entire first half, both Bob and Bert were engaged in surveying the crowd. They tried to discern any slightest nuance that might identify a killer from a cowboy, or a victim from a fan. The first half seemed to pass far too quickly. Neither of them could narrow the field from the three potential victim families they'd identified earlier. Neither could they identify any good suspects for the killers.

The halftime score was 28 for Hemingford and 20 for Hyannis. It was a surprisingly good game, thought Bert, who was a fan of the sport. It seems to be true that Nebraskans love their football. Even in a little community like this, the crowd was really into it. As the high school bands took the field for their part of the festivities, Bert and Bob headed for the concession stand, along with about half the crowd.

Both men moved methodically through the small throng of people crowding the window for something to take the chill off on this 38-degree night. Bob found his way close to the couple he was watching and managed a short conversation in line with the father. Bert was doing the same with one of the other two on his side. The other family was still sitting in the stands after a trip to the little porta pots at the edge of the parking area.

Bert was keeping an eye on two individual men for no particular reason. Maybe it was just a feeling he had. The one guy seemed to be alone and just a fan of the game. He was a strong looking, solidly built man looking to be around forty years old. With a lined denim coat and a red winter cap, he looked like he just arrived on a horse. Bert managed to bump him "accidentally", just so he could say something. The big fellow didn't bat an eye in telling him not to worry about it. His country accent seemed genuine.

A second man, about thirty, also waited in the line for a coffee. He was about six feet tall and built like a linebacker. Not a guy you'd want to wrestle with, Bert figured. The man's brown Carhart work coat was slightly worn but looked well cared for. His dark brown felt hat had a turned down brim in front, a common style among the men here. Bert worked his way in the crowd to get close to this guy. When the man had his coffee in hand and was turning back toward the stand, Bert managed to bump his coffee hand, spilling a good bit of it. He apologized profusely to the fellow and offered to buy him another one. The man just brushed it off with a "No problem, Bud. It happens." He continued back toward the home side of the field.

"Damn," thought Bert to himself, "he sounds about like everyone else around here. I hoped to pick up on a different accent. No such luck."

The second half of the game continued to be a good one. Bert and Bob, though, were increasingly less interested in the game and were beginning to feel the panic one feels when your plan doesn't seem to be working as well as hoped. All three young couples lived in the country and worked on ranches around the region, from what the investigators could discern. The two families on the home side lived within about a half hour of Hyannis. Bob's Hemingford couple was indeed over an hour-and-a-half from here.

Bert looked at the scoreboard. There were less than seven minutes to play, and Hemingford was leading 35 to 31. Bert felt a growing anxiety and fear in the pit of his stomach. Even though he knew it would be hard to determine with certainty whom they were seeking, it was gut-wrenching to have this much confusion. The passing of the third train since the game began did not help his anxiety.

His introspection was suddenly interrupted by the roar of the crowd. Hyannis had just scored a touchdown on a 45-yard run. It looked like they were going for a two-point conversion. With a minute-and-a-half left in the game, the conversion was successful on a short pass in the right corner of the end zone.

Bob and Bert moved to the outside of both sets of bleachers so they could talk more freely on the phone. He asked Bob if he had anything more there?

Bob was almost apologetic. He said that the guys he'd been checking out just didn't stand out as killers. He told Bert they were probably going to have to follow the Hemingford couple and pin where they live on their phone map. He was hopeful that they could figure out more tomorrow.

Another roar from the crowd made them both look back to the game. Hyannis had recovered a fumble with just over a minute to go. They were near mid-field. Two running plays and an incomplete pass, each followed by Hemingford timeouts, left the Hyannis team on fourth down at the Hemingford twenty-five-yard line. There were thirty-two seconds left to play.

Bert told Bob that he would follow the couple that Norah feels best about over on the home side. He told Bob that if the one on his side seemed to be a genuine possibility, then to find out where they live. They would compare notes after that and see where to go next.

A huge cheer went up from the home crowd again. The Hyannis team had just kicked a field goal to increase their lead to seven points. Hemingford would get the ball with about twenty seconds to play, and no timeouts. The game would go down to one or two more plays. It was a nail-biter, as Bert often said of close games. He made his way toward the exit, so he could scan the crowd more closely as they began to leave. He wanted to get behind the two families he'd been watching and make sure he knew their vehicles. Norah was going to have to tell him which of the two to follow. It always seemed to fall on her shoulders.

A final big cheer erupted from the home team, followed by clapping from all around the field. Bert looked at the scoreboard. The clock read all zeros. His first thought was "No nickels or dimes this time, only zero." The game was over. He fixated on the final score. Hyannis had won, 42 to 35. Were these the numbers which Norah had been seeing since the beginning of this serial killing spree? Was she seeing months into the future to this one moment in time? Was this the final confirmation that they were on the right trail?

He had to decide and fast. Bert called Bob as he walked briskly to his SUV and entered. He looked at Norah. Their minds connected. She nodded in agreement. "Bob, forget about the couple from Hemingford, let's put our faith in the number 42. I need you to follow the other couple over here. They're driving a black SUV and just about to leave the parking spot now."

Despite the darkness and the homebound traffic, Bert and Bob were able to follow their respective targets to their driveways. They set a pin at the driveway on their map programs so they could find them tomorrow. Both families did live in a country setting, apparently working for area ranches. Bob followed his family nearly ten miles west on highway 2 to a one lane road on the south. Another eight miles or so down this winding, hilly road, led to their driveway exit on the west side of the road.

Bert's couple went east from Hyannis about seven or eight miles, then turned north toward a ranch headquarters which appeared in the darkness to sit a quarter mile across the valley. Bert set the pin on his map for the turnoff and turned around at the next opportunity. They drove back to Hyannis.

"Norah, are you getting any more definite feelings about our choices?" Bert wanted to know what she was sensing.

In the dark interior of the car, he could hear the strain in her voice. "Sweetheart, I'm so full of feelings, sensations, and cascading visions, that I can't tell anything definite yet. All I can say for sure, Honey, is that this is it. We've been brought to this time and it's going to end here in this small country community. I only wish I knew for sure how it will end."

He could sense her fear and trepidation, and knew she was probably crying silently as she looked out the window into the darkness passing beside them. What other visions are haunting her, he wondered? Hopefully a decent night sleep at the hotel would help bring a more relaxed pace tomorrow morning and she could see more clearly the road they must take.

* * *

A night of fitful sleep did help some, but not a lot. Saturday morning was mostly clear, breezy, and cold. Bert and Bob put their heads together over a coffee at the hotel. Bob would go south and see if he could get a clear look at the home of the couple he had followed and develop a plan for keeping them under surveillance. Bert was going to do the same east of Hyannis. Norah and Missy would go with him, hopefully to provide more psychic insight into the overall situation.

Norah was still obviously very uptight and filled with anxiety. Bert had never seen her so full of self-doubt and fear during a case. She just sat quietly, living inside her head as they drove east. He noticed a few tears trickle down her cheeks. He knew she was consumed by some aspects of this case.

It was about ten in the morning. They didn't pass a single vehicle by the time they arrived at the pinned location and slowed to look down the long gravel driveway to the two-story ranch home, nestled at the base of a large looming hill with a handful of trees around the yard and other outbuildings. He saw the young couple's vehicle sitting in front of the house.

Bert drove on past the turn, looking for a place where he might keep the house under surveillance for a while. He was a couple hundred yards past the turn when a white pickup passed him from the opposite direction. There appeared to be two men in it, and it was slowing down at the young family's driveway. He watched in the rear-view mirror as it turned down the driveway and proceeded slowly toward the house. "Is that the killers?" he thought aloud. "Or just ranch workers or a couple of friends coming for a visit? We've never seen that truck before."

Norah sat forward and looked at him. "Bert, something's wrong. I just had a huge feeling hit me. It's a feeling of fear and dread. Those are our guys, I think. I'm scared, Bert. This is happening too fast."

He wasn't ready for this so suddenly, either. Based upon their history, he had expected these guys to scope out their victims for a day or two. This was far too fast and not expected at all. "I have to get inside that house, Norah. There's no other option at this point." He called Bob as he turned around.

"Dammit," Bert blurted out. "I can't reach Bob. I'll have to leave a voicemail and hope he gets it soon."

They waited for about ten minutes at the turn-around point, barely able to see the house and vehicles. Bob still was not returning his call. Bert knew he could not wait any longer. He shifted into gear and headed back toward the driveway, checking his pistol as he drove. The lump in his throat and tightness in his gut made it difficult to say anything more. A chill started at his neck and arms and proceeded down his spine, causing him to shiver. He would have to wing it and hope for the best. He flicked the safety on his gun from safe to fire.

Norah looked at him with fear and tears in her eyes. Her voice quivered as she spoke to him, "Be careful, my darling. You're in danger, too." She placed her hand on his.

He pulled up perpendicular to the pickup, which was parked near the front yard fence, partially blocking it in with the rear of his SUV. He noted that the trees and shrubs probably made it hard for them to see him drive up. His heart was racing as he walked to the sidewalk. He noticed Missy out of the corner of his eye. She had evidently jumped out his door right after he exited without him even realizing it. She was investigating the white pickup.

Bert summoned his courage, grasped the right zipper of his unzipped coat so he was ready to pull the coat open and reach for his pistol in virtually one motion. He knocked on the door with his left hand, loudly, and took a step back.

He knocked twice more before the door cautiously opened. Framing the opening was a familiar man, one who could have been a college linebacker, judging by his build. Bert had seen him at the game last night. He'd spilled his coffee. The guy didn't look so friendly now. His grey eyes stared into Bert's with an icy coldness that gave Bert another chill up his spine.

"What do you want, bud," the big man asked, in a voice that would make most guys shy away.

Bert had to keep his cool. "I told these folks I would stop by and pick up their kids this morning. Are they here?"

The steel-eyed stranger paused a few seconds, as if contemplating his next move. He looked Bert in the eyes for several long seconds, reading him. Reading his resolve. Then, he stepped back a few steps into what looked like the main living room. "Come on in, bud, they're right over there." He motioned over his right shoulder with a nod of his head.

As Bert stepped forward into the living room's dimmer light, it took just a couple seconds to see a young man and woman and two small children on the couch at the end of the room, to his left. In an instant, Bert realized they were bound and gagged with duct tape over their mouths, and the children were sobbing. At the same instant, he saw the gun coming out from behind this killer. He knew he was already in trouble; the guy had his gun up toward Bert before his own weapon could be drawn. Bert instinctively spun to his right and ducked down, trying to buy a second before the inevitable bullet reached him. As he turned, he caught a flash of movement coming through the open doorway.

As Bert ducked and did a complete turn, pulling his Ruger from its holster, he heard the first gunshot. A bullet zinged past him into the far wall. This was followed instantly by a yell from the big man. A forty-pound bundle of primordial fury had launched through the door and a mouthful of sharp teeth were latched into his gun arm at the wrist. The force of this now wild animal, driven by the instincts of her wolf DNA, turned him nearly halfway around until Missy lost her grip and her teeth slid down his hand. Somehow, he managed to keep hold of his pistol, though, and he swung it back toward Bert.

Bert had a half second advantage now, though, and his shot exploded in the thickening air of the room. The assailant yelled again, stumbled back, and almost went to his knees. Bert knew he hit him, but he didn't know where or how hard. He didn't have time to find out.

A movement from the stairs behind him caught his eye. Another equally well-built man was sprinting down the stairs, a gun in his hand. It was coming up toward Bert, who was now in complete autopilot, just reacting without thinking, trying to stay alive; trying to kill.

As his own Ruger was turning toward this second killer in what felt like slow motion, another flash of fur passed in front of him. Missy launched her second attack toward this new threat to her alpha male. In mid-air, the stairway assailant's gunshot split the air. Missy let out a loud yelp and landed on the stairs next to him. The distraction was just long enough for Bert's green laser to land on the man's chest. He fired three shots in rapid succession from his semi-auto Ruger. His ears were ringing from the detonations of gunpowder in the small living room. The second assailant bellowed and fell back against the stairs. Blood instantly stained the front of his shirt. His lifeless body slid down toward the floor and against Missy.

"You son-of-a-bitch!" It was the first man. He had regained his feet and his gun was pointed squarely at Bert's torso. The bloodstain on his lower left side gave away the non-fatal wound.

Bert instinctively knew it was futile to try to complete the half turn required to draw down on this man for the second time. It would be less than a second before the killer's shot would send a 22-magnum bullet directly into his chest, but he had to try. The sixth shot in the last ten seconds would probably kill him.

Instinct had taken over. Bert began to turn toward his assailant, seemingly in slow motion as before, bringing his Ruger toward the first man. He heard the shot, a blast which shook the house. He grimaced, expecting the bullet to tear into his body. Instead, he saw the hatred on the killer's face turn to shock and pain. The assailant's body pitched forward violently to the floor. Bert's surprised look was the last thing his lifeless eyes would see.

In the doorway; framed against the outside light; stood Bob Madison. Smoke billowed from the barrel of his 44-magnum revolver which was clutched in both hands.

It took a couple of seconds for these two men to come to grips with the suddenness and totality of what had just taken place. Fifteen seconds of their lives had been stretched into what seemed like fifteen minutes. They stared at the fallen murderers, lying silently where they'd fallen, not moving. A pool of blood was forming around the torso of both men. Then they looked at the four captives, huddled together in terror in front of the couch where they'd all fallen.

Bert holstered his gun and ran to the frightened boy; scooping him up in his arms and holding him close. He helped the mother up with his other hand. He began to peel the tape from her mouth. Bob was holding the tiny, screaming girl and helping her father. It warmed their frantically beating hearts to hand both children to their grateful parents.

Bert looked both the young man and woman in their eyes. "You're safe now. We're the good guys. We've been on the trail of these two men for several months and finally caught up to them right here, right now. My name is Bert Lynnes of B and N Investigations. My partner there is Mr. Bob Madison, a citizen and friend who felt it his duty to help me and to save your family. These men would have killed your entire family. They have murdered ten other innocent men and women, those whom we know of. Let's get your family outside and away from this scene. Please don't touch anything. Leave everything just as it is for the police. Once we have you out of here, I'll come back inside to check on my animal. She helped to save your lives and mine." Bert's emotions were running high, fearing for his beloved Missy.

After helping the family get outside of their blood-soaked home, Bert asked Bob to call 911, while he went back in the house to check on his faithful furry companion. He knew she had been shot by the second assailant but was still alive. He didn't know how badly she was hurt and whether she would survive. He could hear her whimpers and whines of pain. She was on her belly on the floor, slowly trying to crawl toward the front door.

Bob and the young man spoke with the dispatcher and then they all huddled into Bob's pickup to wait for the sheriff's black pickup, ambulance, and veterinarian's mobile truck to arrive.

When the veterinarian arrived, Bert helped them evaluate Missy's injury where she lay between the front door and the dead man on the bottom stairs. Her blood stained the floor where she had crawled, trying to reach her master. When satisfied that she could be moved, he helped carry his canine partner to the vet's truck, exchanged phone, name, and address information, and watched with a mix of relief, anxiety, and fear as they pulled away. He had to believe that she was in good hands. He had to believe she would survive. He almost couldn't dare to hope she would recover fully.

He checked repeatedly on Norah. She was emotionally distraught and just wanted to stay in their SUV. The events of the previous hour had taken all her strength just to deal with the wild, runaway emotions she was feeling. Being a psychic was not easy. She had to deal with more feelings than just her own. The dead were also talking to her. Two angry and recently dead spirits were talking very loudly.

After the Sheriff, a man they called Shawn, had surveyed the scene around and inside the house, he approached Bert and Bob.

"Who can tell me what this was all about?" he asked.

Bert proceeded to recap the entire case, from Kansas to Nebraska. "Since Montana, Sheriff, we've been trying to catch up to and get ahead of these men. We're a different kind of investigative company, with a heavy reliance on psychic inputs and the nose of a coyote-wolf hybrid. We were concerned that you wouldn't believe us, if we went to you before about this situation. We had very little concrete evidence about the killers, mostly circumstantial and psychic. That evidence brought us to this house this morning. Fortunately, we got here in time to save this family from the same fate as the previous five. These two men have killed at least ten people, five men and five women. Those are the ones that we know of."

The Sheriff's head was spinning at the magnitude of what he was hearing and seeing. Multi-state serial killers had just been killed in his jurisdiction. News media and probably the FBI were going to be all over this, and soon. "Okay, Mister Lynnes, I'll need you to stop in town at my office and fill out a statement. At the hotel, go one block up the hill and to the left and you'll see the Courthouse. My office is inside on the right. Just state what you told me now. Mister Madison, I'll want you to do the same. Gentlemen, from what this young couple have told me in their sworn statements, you saved their lives from those murdering thugs."

It was two hours later before the Sheriff and ambulance were ready to seal up the scene. Bob and Bert were waiting outside their respective vehicles, waiting for the Sheriff to clear them to leave. Norah remained inside their SUV. She was mentally drained, and Bert wanted to leave her to herself to work out the many emotions she was feeling. Missy had long since arrived with the veterinarian in Hyannis for surgery. The initial report about her was encouraging. They thought she would survive her wound.

They all drove into Hyannis, made their statements, and Bert and Bob agreed to meet at the veterinarian's office to check on Missy. Satisfied that she was in stable condition and well cared for, they rendezvoused at the old Hyannis Hotel for a couple of beers and a good talk. Bert left Norah at the hotel they had stayed in near the east edge of town. That location was most favorable for Missy, though she was going to stay at the vet's overnight.

These two men, now bonded friends, enjoyed good conversation over a couple of cold beers. They chatted about the old Hotel and its history, displayed in pictures on every wall and almost floor to ceiling. When they knew it was time to say good-by, they shook hands warmly.

"Bob, I have never been so glad to see someone, as I was you in that doorway." Bert's moist eyes spoke volumes about his sincerity. He had been grappling with his own emotions.

"I know, Bert," Bob replied. "I'm glad that I got there in time. I drove like hell and wasn't sure I could make it."

Bert's brow furrowed and he felt confused. "Bob, when we left this morning, you were going to check out the family south and west of here, probably at least a half hour drive away. What made you come back here?"

Bob seemed a little confused too. "Well, my friend, I don't think I'm psychic, but before I got very far down highway 2, I heard a woman's voice tell me to turn around and come back to help you. I think it was your wife, Bert. It wasn't a phone call; she was talking inside my mind. She said you had to have my help, right now. If I didn't believe in her psychic powers before, I do now."

"She doesn't have or use a cell phone; hates the electronic clutter. So, she really must have summoned you with her mind. Wow,

I've never known her to do anything like that before." Bert was noticeably stunned.

With Bert's pat on the back, Bob headed upstairs to his tiny room. He was comforted and amused by the knowledge that his room was over the hotel bar. He was going to leave early in the morning for his drive back home to Montana.

Late the next morning, after Missy was cleared for travel by the veterinarian, and getting her settled into the back of the vehicle, they headed out of Hyannis, going west on highway 2. Bert glanced at Norah as he drove. He had a nagging question that had been weighing on his mind. "Hon, how did Bob know to come back to help me yesterday?"

She answered softly. "I told him with my mind to turn around and help you, Bert. I knew you needed him."

"You must have summoned him at least a few minutes before we passed the turnoff and saw those guys. How could you have known that I would need his help?"

She looked at him with tears glistening in her eyes. "Bert, I have seen you die in my visions for the past two days. You were not going to survive in that house, and neither was that young family. I had to find a way to change the future."

CHAPTER FIFTEEN: BACK HOME

The SUV was unpacked, and the equipment cleaned and put away, waiting for the next case. Bert was physically and emotionally drained from the stress of the Nickel/Dime case, as he had named it. He talked about it with Norah the first day home as they sat in the den. He could tell she was emotionally wrung out, as well. Missy was sore and recovering from a wound which narrowly avoided being fatal. It would take weeks of recovery, but she was expected to eventually return to near normal activity. The rest of the day, they just tried to relax, rest, and enjoy the scenic beauty of their Wyoming surroundings.

The next day, Bert donned his backpack and hiked all day into the mountains to the north of his home. He needed some time alone just to enjoy the beauty and serenity of the backcountry and to give his mind time to relax. Norah chose to relax at home for the same reasons. He stopped frequently to sit on rocks and bathe in the warmth of the fall sun, listen to the birds of prey as they soared and screeched high overhead, and drink in the visual gifts provided free by Mother Nature.

The following morning, after a breakfast of coffee, biscuits, and steak, which he shared with Missy, Bert called the prior clients of the Nickel/Dime murders.

First, he called Myrtle Kennedy, in St. Joseph, Missouri. "Myrtle, this is Bert Lynnes, calling to update you. I hope you're doing well. Is your family coping okay with the loss of your parents?"

"Hi, Bert. Thank you," she replied. "Yes, we're doing as okay as one can do following such a tragic loss. I was wondering how this was going. I've tried to follow your other cases on the little bit of news I could find. They weren't generating much more than local coverage, it seems."

"Well, I do have generally good news for you. It's over, Myrtle! I've provided the various law agencies with the best updated information I have about the entire string of cases. They're putting the pieces together to confirm that the same killers were involved in all six cases. I'm sure this will be confirmed by all the evidence. You will undoubtedly be contacted by the law involved with your parents, if you haven't been already. The other good news is that these two men met with justice and they are both dead, Myrtle. They will never kill anyone again."

She began sobbing uncontrollably for a couple of minutes. When she regained her composure, she managed to answer him. "Oh, thank God for that, and for you and your wife and animal, Bert. You have brought justice for my Dad and Mom and ended this nightmare for my family. Now we can begin to heal. What happened to those men?

He wasn't sure how much detail to give her. "They were in the process of abducting a young couple and their two small children near a small town in west Nebraska. A good friend and I were able to intercede, and they attacked us. We shot and killed them, Myrtle. I owe my own life to my wife, this friend, and our canine, Missy. I would be dead without their help." Bert almost choked up with that and had to struggle to keep his own composure.

She asked for the name and address of his friend, Bob Madison. She wanted to contact him and thank him personally. With that information, they said good-bye. He could feel her tears through the phone as they hung up.

The following calls to Tom Davenport, and Troy and Toni

Lamont, went the same way. Like Myrtle, they were very thankful for the update and wanted Bob's information. Bob was a hero, and everyone could see it. When Bert explained how Norah's psychic intervention had brought Bob to his rescue, they wanted him to hug her and thank her from their families. They vowed to keep in touch with him and recommend his company at every opportunity. Each call had its share of tears.

He had found the names and phone number of Zach Hutchinson's parents, who lived in Cheyenne. He had not met them, they were never clients, but after the death of their son and his wife near Lusk, he wanted to provide some closure for them. They had a good talk, discussing the case and finding out about their son and his wife and children. When they prepared to say good-bye, these heartbroken parents were nevertheless very thankful for the role his investigative team played in finding their son and daughter-in-law. The orphaned children, now living with their grandparents, also got on the phone and thanked him in their own ways. It saddened and warmed his heart at the same time.

Bert also set up a conference call and updated Sheriff Jim Darling in Montana and Deputy Bill Haskins in South Dakota. They were both thrilled to learn of the killers' fate and offered to buy a steak and beer anytime Bert and company might be in their area. He agreed and offered the same to them, saying that they needed to have a reunion sometime soon. Bert's innate distrust of lawmen was seriously degraded after his talk with both men. Bill promised to see what he could find out from the ongoing investigations into the two killers' past.

For the next two weeks, Bert and Norah just chilled out at home. They took lazy walks into the surrounding countryside, sat and read on their front porch, and he answered a few inquiries from various media and law enforcement about their role in the Nickel/Dime Murders.

Then Bill Haskins called early one afternoon. He had been checking into the various investigations seeking to uncover details about the killers' background. "You need to sit down," he said, "This will blow your socks off!"

"I've been hoping you would call and update us on what may have driven them to such a vicious path," Bert anxiously replied.

Bill launched into the revelations being discovered about the two men. "One guy, 26 years old, is of Turkish descent. His parents migrated here legally before he was born, so he is a natural citizen of the US. He goes by Jack Burakgazi. Interestingly, the last name in Arabic means 'warrior'. He was a problem teenager, and his parents eventually sent him to a boys' ranch near you, outside of Cody, Wyoming. There, he was quickly put in his place by ranch boys who didn't play his game. He seemed to straighten out after six months there and getting his butt kicked regularly, so he returned home. His attitude didn't last long, and he again became a problem, even smacking his mother around at one point. He had low regard for women. The father then sent him to live with a brother, the boy's uncle, on a working cattle ranch in north central Nebraska. That uncle was a no-nonsense kind of man, and he didn't hesitate to put on boxing gloves as needed to keep the nephew in line. Although the three summers spent with the uncle seemed to be having a positive effect; inwardly, the results must have been negative. This now twenty-something young man had apparently developed an intense hatred toward country people."

"Yeah, I can see where this may be going," Bert noted.

"His hatred toward country people spilled over to the US, and his own father and mother," Bill continued, "led him to look online for support. It didn't take long for him to become enthralled with the ISIS ideology. As he gravitated into this community, he met another similarly disenfranchised guy about his age, named Malcomb McKearney. Malcomb was a student at the University of Pennsylvania, on the verge of failing and getting kicked out. His only successful pursuit was in acting. He thought he wanted to become an actor and he was taking classes in makeup, among other things. He quit halfway through his junior year when his father, a successful businessman, gave him an ultimatum to shape up or he would no longer pay for his education. Ironically, both parents died of natural causes, as far as we know, around this same time. The inheritance received by both these sons left them very well off; rich by some standards."

"So, we have a perfect storm of disenfranchised young men, with major chips on their shoulders, and money enough to go on a well-funded killing spree in the name of a religious ideology, and fueled by a personal vendetta," Bert reflected.

"And the training in weapons, received during trips to several US camps operated by these fundamentalist organizations, right here on American soil," Bill said angrily. "Combine this with training in makeup and rudimentary acting skills, and you have two guys capable of using deception to fool both their victims and the law. Guys who might show up at your door looking and sounding like a Mormon missionary or a cop; or asking you for a can of gasoline because their car is nearly empty. You have guys smart enough to use or not use technology to stay off the grid and out of sight; smart enough to hide victims and their vehicles in ways to delay the law from getting on their trail. Guys who had high IQs and high opinions of themselves and devised a unique way of taunting and testing the cops, using calling cards and countdowns consisting of nickels and dimes."

"Thus, is born the Nickel/Dime killers," Bert proclaimed. "Two guys who looked and sounded like average Americans, yet had the intense desire, and the means, to go on a multi-state killing spree aimed at rural farmers, ranchers, and women in the region which held embarrassing memories for them. The perfect combination of hatred, time, money, radical ideology, intelligence, training, and a like-minded accomplice. A recipe for cold-blooded serial killers."

Bert remembered their white vehicle. "I guess they must have traded off the grey extended cab pickup for the white one, before they hit Nebraska?"

"No," replied Bill. "They both had trucks and drove them separately from the east coast. The grey extended cab belonged to this Jack character. The white one to McKearney. This was apparently one more way they sought to confuse any cops trying to investigate them. They were very cunning. The grey truck was finally located and identified a week later in a truck stop parking area in Ogallala, Nebraska, almost an hour's drive to the south. It contained five different caliber handguns, three with silencers. Also, seven different large blade knives, rope, and even a garrote. And, a fully loaded makeup case and disguises! They were prepared to deceive and kill in a variety of ways, Bert."

Bert was shocked. "Oh my God, that's frightening, Bill."

"Those killers would have taken that mother from Nebraska, and maybe her little girl, as sex slaves and who knows what else,"

Bill said. "Considering their disdain for the women in their lives and their lackluster social skills with girls in their schools, these two seemed bent on taking that mother hostage. You and Bob saved her and probably her daughter from humiliation, torture, and eventual death at the hands of those two, Bert. You, Norah, Bob, and Missy are the heroes in this story. Society owes you for removing those two from the gene pool. Gotta go now, my friend, but know that you're always welcome at my door. Please tell Norah the same."

"I will tell her that, Bill, and thank you." His glance at Norah told him she had heard and nodded in approval and thanks.

After this call, Bert quietly fed and treated his injured Coywolf companion. She was progressing and healing well and could get around on her own, although slowly. He then went back outside to the garage. He pulled up his coat collar against the Wyoming breeze, which had just arrived in advance of an approaching cold front. In the garage, he turned on the local radio station as a favorite song was just starting. The melancholy strains of "Answer" by Sarah McLachlan began to play. Standing in silence until the end of the song, Bert turned off the radio. He felt an urge that he had not acknowledged in many months. He knew he needed to do something he had been putting off for a long time. He said aloud, "If it takes my whole life, I won't break, I won't bend. The star may have gone out, but you continue to burn so bright."

* * *

Bert guided his vehicle east on the Yellowstone Highway to Cody. The high craggy peaks on the north gave way to a mix of rugged river valley and high-country plateaus around this bustling little cow town and tourist Mecca, now calm after the busy summer season. He turned north on Gulch Street. In a few hundred yards, he pulled into parking at the Riverside Cemetery, turned off the SUV, and began a slow, deliberate walk that would take him toward the north area of the cemetery. This was a place he remembered all too well. It held his heart.

Before he could leave the parking area, though, a young boy, about twelve years old, paused to look at him, laid his bicycle down, and then trotted quickly to him. Bert stopped and waited for the approaching lad.

"Mister Lynnes; are you Mister Lynnes," the youngster asked.

Bert smiled at him. "Yes, son, what can I do for you?"

The boy was all serious. "Sir, I'm Tommie. I met you about a year ago when you were talking with my Dad in their gift shop, the Curious Horse, down on Main Street. His name is Edward. You and he had a long talk that day about supernatural stuff. He's interested in that stuff, too. I sat at the end of the counter and listened to both of you go on and on."

That day slowly came back to Bert. "Why, yes, Tommie, I remember you and having a good talk with your Dad. How are your parents doing? I think your Mom was around there, too."

"Sir, my Mom died a couple of months ago. It was real sudden like." Tears welled up in the boy's eyes.

Bert was touched. "Son, I am very sorry to hear about your mother. I know how difficult and painful it is to lose someone you love." He felt his own eyes starting to tear up.

244

"Sir, when you were talking with my Dad, you said you were thinking about writing a book. I think you called it a psychological thriller. Did you ever write that book?"

"Yes, I remember telling your Dad about that. At the time, I really didn't know where the inspiration came from to think about doing that. I couldn't explain it to your Dad, either. It just felt like something in my future. I never wrote it, Tommie. I got busy with my work and just didn't have time. Why are you asking about that?"

The boy faced Bert squarely. "Sir, when you left that day, my Dad told me he thinks you're a psychic or medium. I had to look that up. It says you can see things that aren't there and even talk with dead people. Sir, I miss my mother so much since she died." Tears streamed down his face. "If you really are a medium, Mister Lynnes, do you think you could help me talk with my mother?"

Bert was stunned and totally unprepared for that question. "Son, Tommie, there is something very private that I need to do in here. If you want to wait a bit and meet me out here shortly, maybe we can talk more about that?"

Tommie's tears slowed as he seemed to gain his composure. "Yes Sir, Mister Lynnes, I'll visit my mother's grave, then wait for you right here. Thank you, Sir."

With that, Bert walked resolutely into the right side of the cemetery. He arrived at a gravesite and stood reflectively in front of the clean and newer looking granite stone. His hands were clasped in front of him as he looked down at the resting place of a loved one. After a few minutes, he closed his eyes, and quietly whispered, "I've really missed you! It seems like only yesterday when we last talked. Though your body is gone, I feel your presence and talk with your spirit every day. You're my guide and I could not do what I do without your inspiration and help. I see you everywhere I look. 1 ache to hold your hands and feel your warmth. I am truly nothing without you."

Bert knelt, placed his hands on the cold stone, and silently read the words placed there so lovingly, "Here, my partner for life waits for me."

He said aloud as tears flowed down his face, "I talk with you every day. I miss you so much. I am nothing without you. I wait for you here, until we meet again there."

His gaze shifted to the bottom line.

Born October 25, 1965, loving wife Norah departed this life September 5, 2016

* * *

He could see Norah standing about ten yards beyond the grave, her flowing red hair shimmering, and looking at him with her sweet smile. He heard her say, "I'm nothing without you, Bert Lynnes. You're the reason I stay."

ABOUT THE AUTHOR

I grew up on a west Nebraska cattle ranch, the oldest of four children. Hills and valleys were my playground; cats, dogs, and a raccoon were my playmates until younger brothers took their places; windmills, BB-guns, and haystacks were among my playthings; horses and cattle were my workmates. Like the hardy people I grew up among, I have many hours working cattle on horses, using heavy machinery, and learning about the flora, fauna, and geography of the region. My early education came by way of one-room country schools. I often rode horses the three-plus miles each way to school or drove myself in a little Jeep. Two-hole outdoor toilets, coal stoves, and kerosene lanterns are among my childhood memories. Because of Nebraska weather, no phones, and no drivers' license, I boarded out most of my first two years of high school. I was athletic, loved sports, and participated in all available sports throughout high school.

Growing up without a neighbor in sight or other kids of my age to play with, I learned to live in my head and developed a vivid imagination. That imagination serves me well in creating fictional mysteries. Work ethic came from being the oldest son and starting to work full-time, outside of school, at the age of eight.

I have a degree in Animal Science from the University of Nebraska, and I've loved nature and animals all my life. Coyotes were part of the ecosystem, though largely unseen. Their howls welcomed most sunsets. The coyote-wolf hybrid was a natural character for this story, and I wanted to introduce it to the reader.

I first learned of the coywolf hybrid from an Animal Planet documentary, "Meet the Coywolf." I felt I knew coyotes well and had almost no fear of them, only respect. Then, I happened to see another documentary named "Killed by Coyotes." This caught my interest immediately, because I knew of no adult human deaths by coyotes. However, an aspiring folksinger, Canadian, Taylor Mitchell, aged nineteen, was killed in 2009 in Novia Scotia by coyotes while hiking in a national park.

I feel that wolf DNA may have played a role in this tragic attack. Such behavior is not typical of the coyotes that I know. For this reason, I decided to introduce the coywolf to readers. While my female hybrid is a well-trained and domesticated fictional animal, the real hybrids are a blend of wolf and coyote and reflect the characteristics of both. The real animals are not necessarily pure coyote-wolf but may have varying degrees of DNA, to include dog.

Readers should understand that this hybrid is spreading across the United States as well as Canada, because of its resilient coyote blood. The wolf DNA makes it a larger, more aggressive, pack hunter, and therefore more dangerous than a coyote. The coywolf, like the coyote, can live and thrive in urban environments. It may be living and thriving in your city. With a typical weight of around forty-five pounds, it's large enough to be considered an apex predator.

I'm a retired Air Force officer and pilot, and I have traveled extensively across the United States, lived in three foreign countries, and have flown in about 40 different nations. I owned and operated a bed and breakfast in Cody, Wyoming for five years, during which time I was a freelance writer for the Wyoming Livestock Roundup newspaper. That experience developed my interest and love for writing.

I worked as a private investigator for two years, in Arkansas, conducting surveillance investigations in a variety of locales and situations. That experience is part of the background for the Bert and Norah stories. I've also had a lifelong fascination with psychic phenomenon.

I have published a second book in "The Bert and Norah Mysteries" series. This second book is called "The Missing." At the time of this writing, I am publishing book three: "Into the Light."

Read on for a sneak peek at the next book in the Bert and Norah series.

"The Missing."

Sneak Peek: The Missing

My second book in the "Bert and Norah Mysteries" series is "The Missing." "The Nickel Dime Murders" introduces the characters and lays the groundwork for the following books. I like to provide real insights into the area and history within my stories. The following sneak peek will give you a taste.

Bert & Norah

The Missing

CHAPTER ONE: THE MYSTERY MAN

"Albert Lynnes, Bert, as he was usually known, relaxed and sipped his coffee on the front porch of his Cody, Wyoming, log home, situated west of town in the North Fork valley. It was a beautiful fall morning in October 2017. The reds and yellows of the shrubs and sparse deciduous trees accented the beauty of this North Fork of the Shoshone River. Nestled between the mountains and ridges, the Shoshone River followed this valley as it snaked westward toward the east entrance of the Nation's first national park. President Teddy Roosevelt referred to this drive up the Yellowstone Highway as "the most scenic 52 miles in America."

Just west of Cody, the greys, yellows, and browns of the often-sheer cliff facings plummeted down to enclose three tunnels totaling almost a mile in length. They connected Cody to the Buffalo Bill Dam and Reservoir. This reservoir accented the east end of the North Fork valley like a crown jewel, atop the throne at the west end, Yellowstone National Park."

Bert fit well into this western setting and lifestyle. A retired Army officer, he had always stayed in good shape and worked out regularly. He was only about five feet eight inches tall, but he had the strength, stamina, and work ethic of men half his age. His dark brown hair was only slightly giving away his age with a little bit of greying around the edges. He was a gun owner, outdoorsman, and hunter, and had always loved the natural world. His skills and interests were well served in his private investigation business, B & N Investigations.

The ringing cell phone interrupted his quiet reflection on nature's beauty and the peacefulness of the surroundings. "May I help you?" Bert asked.

"Is this B & N Investigations?" The man on the line asked.

Bert instantly felt uneasy with this call. "Yes, this is Bert Lynnes of B & N investigations. How may I help you, sir?"

"I want to meet with you in town in an hour to discuss a possible case. Can you be at the Irma Hotel then?" The man spoke in a hushed tone.

Bert checked the time on his phone, looked at his coywolf companion and tracking animal, Missy, lying under his cedar coffee table, and answered back, "Yes, I can meet you at the Irma at nine. Let's grab a coffee and sit outside on the east side porch area. It's usually quiet there this time of year. What's your name, sir?"

"My name isn't important right now, Mr. Lynnes, for reasons that will be obvious later if we decide to work together." There was an air of superiority in the way this mystery man presented himself.

"Okay, sir, but we won't be doing business unless you're willing to be honest and forthcoming after we meet. I want you to know that before you spend your time going to the Irma. I'm willing to hear what your situation is about, and we can go from there, if you're okay with that?" Bert wanted to be clear that he wasn't playing this game.

"Fair enough," the voice on the phone replied, "I will see you at the Irma at nine, but I prefer to meet inside toward the back corner if that's okay with you. I don't want to be on the street."

Bert knew he could find this fellow, but wanted to know anyway, "How will I know you sir? What are you wearing?"

"I'm wearing a leather jacket, no tie, and a brown felt hat with the front brim turned down, Outback style." The man hung up without another word.

Bert walked into the house, with Missy on his heels. He looked toward the kitchen. "A rather strange phone call. I have to meet this guy at the Irma at nine and see what's going on with him. Wouldn't even tell me his name now. Not sure about this one, Sweetheart."

There was no reply, and he didn't expect one after he remembered that Norah, in spirit, was with her mother who was terminally ill in a Minnesota hospital. He had grown accustomed to this relationship; a joining of their two realities. The trauma of her unexpected and devastating death in September of 2016, had triggered a dormant "gift" in Bert. It awakened an ability to see and communicate with the spirit of his departed loved one. It was a bond formed by undying love. It held the spirit to the living.

He walked out to the garage and instructed Missy to stay home. Her nearly imperceptible limp was the only reminder of her injury five weeks earlier and her rapid recovery. He got into his dark blue Dodge SUV. He had recently started to jokingly refer to it as the doghouse, because he and Missy spent so much time in it. It was only a 15-minute drive to the Irma Hotel, but he preferred to be early and scope out the situation he was getting into on this Wednesday morning, October 4th. He guided his vehicle down to the Yellowstone Highway and east toward Cody.

As he signaled his left turn onto the highway, his eyes fell upon a man standing near the stop sign. This fellow stood silently, looking straight at Bert, and then he raised his right hand and slowly waved. As he did so, a Siberian Husky with dark grey and white markings, lying next to him, raised up to sit on its haunches. This canine also looked at Bert, as he proceeded to turn left onto the road toward Cody. Bert returned a quick wave to them as he made the turn.

Bert guided his vehicle into the right-hand lane to allow an overtaking vehicle to pass and then he looked in his rear-view mirror back to the stop sign, now a quarter of a mile behind him. The man and dog were not in view. "Damn, that's unusual," he said aloud to himself. "I've never seen anyone on foot at that intersection before, much less with a dog. That's a beautiful Husky!" He turned his attention back to driving.

The highway turned into Main Street as it entered Cody, passing by the world-renowned Buffalo Bill Historical Center. Visitors from all over the globe could and did spend hours going through the many halls and exhibits. It was a visual and audible celebration of the Wild West days, made famous by William F. Cody, Buffalo Bill, as he was popularly known. The firearms exhibit was one of the most extensive in the world. It and the western art and plains Indians exhibits were Bert's favorites.

A few blocks later, he arrived at the Irma Hotel and parked along the street. This hotel was among the town of Cody's most recognizable and desired destinations for locals and visitors alike. It was built in 1902, with a couple of later additions, and was considered by Bill Cody to be "just the sweetest hotel that ever was." He named it after Irma, his youngest daughter.

Once inside the Irma, Bert exchanged a few pleasantries with the waitress, Mary, a cute woman in her early forties, with whom he'd chatted a few times before. She said she would bring his usual coffee with cream and Honey. He was impressed that she remembered how he liked it. As he walked to the back, his eyes once again scanned the stunningly beautiful Cherrywood bar given to Bill Cody by Queen Victoria. It is one of the most sought out and photographed features in the town of Cody. Once he chose a table in the back corner, he leaned back and collected his thoughts about how to deal with this mystery man.

Something told Bert to expect him to be fashionably late. It was about ten after nine when the man walked in and went straight to Bert's table. He was a good-looking fella, about six feet tall, trim and well built, dark hair, and roughly in his fifties. He sat down without a word and without removing his hat, as was customary for most ranchers and cowboys. He looked intently at Bert, then Bert stuck his hand out and broke the ice, "Hello, I'm Bert Lynnes."

"Right now, Bert, just call me Sam if you don't mind," he responded in a strong and clear voice as he shook Bert's hand. "I want to talk a bit with you before we go beyond that. He turned to Mary, who had approached the table, "Honey, if you would, please, a coffee with cream. That's all I want right now. Thanks."

Bert knew there was something familiar about this guy, but he couldn't quite place it. He had seen him before, he was sure of it; but where? "So, Sam, what brings you to town; I don't think you're from here?" He noticed that Sam seemed to make eye contact for just a second with another rancher looking fella sitting in the middle of the dining room.

Sometime later:

"Norah closed her eyes and looked internally for a good while, before answering him. "Bert, I sense that this is a dangerous case. And something bothers me, dear. I'm seeing a vision of a fox pursuing a cottontail rabbit. As the fox gets closer the rabbit panics and ducks into a thicket. The fox goes in after it and they disappear for a minute. Then the fox runs out of the thicket at full speed, frightened. A big wolf leaps over the thicket in hot pursuit of the fox. The fox runs for its life and they disappear over the hill. Sweetheart, this is telling me that you, the fox, may be the hunter now, but you are going to become the hunted at some point, by a big adversary. Be very careful, Honey; you're treading on dangerous ground in this case."

Then there's Missy:

"Missy trotted down the road a hundred yards in front of him, barely visible in the still dim light of approaching sunrise. She was ever attentive to her surroundings, stopping frequently to cock her head and listen to sounds of gathering morning. In the distance, one of her wild cousins was initiating what would become a yapping chorus for twenty or thirty seconds. Missy raised her muzzle to the dark sky and returned their greeting. In the darkness, her first two yaps evolved into a long, soulful, and melancholy howl. Then another and another. The cacophony would end just as abruptly as it began, as if on some kind of instinctive cue. After that, silence.

A sadness came over Bert, as he couldn't help but wonder if she missed her kind. Was her vocalization a token of a primitive longing for canine companionship? If so, he understood, because he too, sometimes felt the urge to cry to the darkness for those things lost and so unattainable. He wiped tears from his cheeks before they froze.

Check out the rest at
www.amazon.com/Bert-Norah-Missing-Bernard-Burgess/dp/0960006907/

Available in paperback or Kindle

Made in the USA
Monee, IL
21 August 2020

38899179R00152